Dale Mayer

A Psychic Visions Novel

Coveted

COVETED
Beverly Dale Mayer
Valley Publishing Ltd.

Copyright © 2024

ISBN-13: 978-1-778865-91-6
Print Edition

Books in This Series:

Tuesday's Child
Hide 'n Go Seek
Maddy's Floor
Garden of Sorrow
Knock Knock…
Rare Find
Eyes to the Soul
Now You See Her
Shattered
Into the Abyss
Seeds of Malice
Eye of the Falcon
Itsy-Bitsy Spider
Unmasked
Deep Beneath
From the Ashes
Stroke of Death
Ice Maiden
Snap, Crackle…
What If…
Talking Bones
String of Tears
Inked Forever

Insanity

Soul Legacy

Coveted

Endgame

Boxed Sets and Bundles

https://geni.us/Bundlepage

About This Book

So, what happens when one desperately wants something but can't have it? And what happens if that person puts plans into motion to get all that is coveted? And... what happens to the innocent victims along the way?

Kylie Oakwood is a new police sketch artist with an amazing talent but also a very secretive past. She's desperate to make a good life for herself and to forget all about the tragedy in her life. Not that it's easy being in the one field she should most likely avoid.

Detective Porter Hanson takes note of the nightmares in the back of this young woman's eyes, but it's so easy to forget when he sees her artwork and how well she handles the witnesses. She's a unique personality, and that rubs others in the department the wrong way. But, for him, something about her brings out his protective instincts.

The trouble is, he cannot figure out why he is supposed to be protecting her—or maybe that should be more about *who,* or better yet, *what?* Especially when weird things start happening around her …

Sign up to be notified of all Dale's releases here!
https://geni.us/DaleNews

CHAPTER 1

"HEY, KYLIE. ARE you ready for this?"

Kylie Okovi turned to look at Detective Porter Hanson. Kind compassionate eyes searched hers, and she realized that he must have noted her clenched fist and her white-knuckled grip on her sketch pad. She took a deep breath and said, "I will be, but I don't think any of us will walk away from this unscathed."

"We're not supposed to," he said, "from any crime scene."

"But this one"—she motioned at the evidence of the mass shooting all around her—"this, ... this," And she stopped, the words dying in her throat.

He nodded. "I understand," he said. "Nobody should ever have to go through something like this and certainly never twice."

"And this is your second, isn't it?" she asked, turning to face him.

He winced and nodded. "Not as if we're counting or anything, because I don't want to keep track of it in that way."

"No, I'm sorry," she whispered.

"I wasn't expecting to come to work today and to deal with twenty-two deaths." He hesitated, then added, "Twenty-three now. The latest victim ... died in the hospital."

Kylie took a deep breath and slowly nodded. "And the killer?"

"We have no idea at the moment. They're running through videos, looking for him. There were eyewitnesses, but they're all fairly contradictory."

"How is that possible?" she asked, staring at him. "I know I'm fairly new to the detective side of this, just being a sketch artist, but … is that normal?"

He smiled, nodded. "Particularly under stress, people think what they see is what they're seeing, but often it isn't. Their minds try to make logical sense of the jumble of events in their memories, when really it doesn't work because this can never make sense. It's not intended to make sense. It's supposed to be horrific. The people doing this want it to be horrific. They're after a big show, some final ending to whatever it is that they have planned."

"How could anybody have planned this?" she whispered, her gaze going to the chaos of the masses in the casino all around her. It's just too unbelievable.

"That's why we're here, to make sense of the chaos," he said. "If it's too much for you …"

She held up a hand and said, "Don't."

"I'm just letting you know this will affect all of us."

"And I'll turn your words back on you and say it's supposed to," she replied ever-so-simply.

He patted her on the back and suggested, "If you need some downtime, let us know. In the meantime, I don't even know if you can do anything here."

"I was called in," she stated, turning to look around. "I'm not sure why. I think they just want sketches of the scene and more photographs."

He waved a hand at that. "You and I both know how the

boss feels about that."

"I do. I'm here to put some personality into it," she confirmed. "That also makes it something we can use on the stand."

"But it's never been about the trial with you, has it?"

She winced and then shook her head. "No, I'm not so much about making them pay as making sure that they're caught," she whispered.

"So you do you, whatever that means in this instance, and I'll check in with you in a little bit." And, with that, Porter disappeared.

Kylie adjusted the cap on her head—to keep her hair from contaminating the crime scene—took a deep breath, and slowly walked forward. It was all about impressions, all about sights and sounds and scenes. Yet everything was running through her brain at top speed, and something inside her screamed that this crime wasn't something anybody could make sense of.

Kylie stood inside one of the largest casinos in Vegas. Somebody had decided to walk through with heavy artillery and had gunned down their victims in what appeared to be random shootings. Twenty-three at last count. Yet in the chaos, random people, EMTs, rescue workers, volunteers had moved the dead, had picked up the wounded, had quickly raced away with survivors and everyone else who was looking for medical assistance. Some were families and friends, who had grabbed their loved ones, some dead, some alive, and had moved them.

Yet Kylie also knew instinctively that, once the shooting began, people scattered, as self-preservation kicked in. Yet, had she been here during this mass shooting, she's not sure how she would have handled it.

To even think about leaving a loved one behind, for more bullets to be riddled into their prone body, seemed so completely wrong, and yet most people would instinctively run. In this case, at least three families had grabbed their loved ones, trying to save them, and had booked it to the other side, where they had all been attacked instead of saved. Several were still alive and now in the hospital, and several others hadn't made it that far.

Kylie was here with her sketchbook to try and sort out some of this evil, at least as much of it as she could.

It was an odd case for her, and she was here more at the request of the detective than anything else. She still didn't quite understand why. She was a police sketch artist, but occasionally she had also worked crime scenes. This type of crime scene was one she never ever wanted to get called in on again.

With a deep breath, she pulled out her sketch pencil, walked to one corner, figuring that that might be the easiest place to start, and turned to a clean page on her sketchbook and started drawing.

CHAPTER 2

KYLIE WORKED FOR several hours, finding a spot a little bit away from the craziness all around her. Clean-up was happening. Photos were taken. Bodies were moved. Several times people asked Kylie to move out of their way, and she did so willingly. Then she had to regroup and finish the drawings still in her head, before she could move on to the next section. She sketched as fast as she could, hampered by something that others wouldn't recognize, but she did— her need to get this down, to document this scene, to have every ounce of data available so the cops could solve who had done this and why.

She knew there would be a why, even if nobody cared about it. Motives were always important. She'd somehow found herself in this very strange field after going to art school, against her aunt's wishes, when she had literally written Kylie off. She apparently didn't have the brains to be anything important, but she should have done something a whole lot better than becoming an artist, at least according to her aunt. Maybe Kylie had done it on purpose to get back at the aunt.

Kylie felt such a sense of relief at having her aunt out of her life. If ever Kylie should have cut out someone from her life, it was her aunt. Yet it had been a long time coming. It took time to get here, but Kylie finally managed it and ended up at art school, following one of her passions. If she could follow at least one, she figured that could be something important later on in life. Something she could be proud of, but how the hell did she end up doing this work for the local authorities?

She stopped drawing, as tears rolled down her face. People looked at her strangely. Yet nobody mentioned anything because, in this situation, she was not the only one crying over the devastation laid before them. Nearby three family members had huddled together—at least seemingly related from their similar features—all three shot, as if one bullet had taken them all down. Kylie's breath caught in the back of her throat, and a sob threatened to escape.

She quickly moved outside into the back alley, where she took several long, slow, deep breaths, trying to regain control. Of course Porter found her not very long afterward.

"Are you okay?" he asked, his tone sharp.

She turned and glared at him. "As well as anybody else in there is."

"Good point," he replied, his tone a little gentler. "Just so, it's hitting all of us pretty hard."

"I'm fine," she said, with a wave of her hand. "Go on back in there, where you can deal with more of it. I'll be inside in a minute." His gaze searched hers, and she shrugged, then gave him half a smile. "I just saw the family where the bullet went through the father and right into the child."

Porter's face turned grim, and he nodded. "An extra victim for the shooter, and one he didn't even have to work for," he noted, his voice tired. "We'll be here all day and all night, so pace yourself." And, with that, he turned and went back inside.

"All day and all night," she repeated to herself, staring off into the distance. She wasn't sure that she could do this. It wasn't quite how she thought her career would go. And then a reminder slipped through that she wasn't doing this for herself but for them, for all the victims. She had to remember that. Looking around, she was thankful to be alone. She knew the crowds were out front of the casino, with all the TV reporters, their artificial lighting, the cameras, working in the garish morning light. It was all so surreal. She'd come up against it a couple times in other cases, but nothing to the extent of this one. This surpassed everything she had ever seen so far.

Gearing up, she took several more bracing breaths and gave herself some harsh truths, then pushed herself back into the room of death. She had only taken a few steps, when somebody stopped to talk to her. She looked him over and noted he didn't have a badge. She pointed outside and declared, "Get out now. Move it."

He held up a recorder, the microphone in her face, and asked, "Could you give us a statement?"

The man was quickly picked up by the scruff of his neck and hauled to the nearest exit. Security was being slammed for letting anybody in, and yet, in this blurred sea of pain and the shocking reality of what was going on, the guards were as overwhelmed as anyone else.

Even as she had that thought, she felt *it* coming over her. She didn't want it and desperately needed it to go away, but it wasn't listening. It was coming in harder and faster than ever before, and all too soon the room had morphed into something completely different, and she grabbed onto the nearest wall.

The transition would be hard and fast, though usually

she could keep that private, while Kylie tried to not let others watch when she went into these trances. She could only hope that, with all the chaos going on around her, nobody else would notice. By the time the transition was completed, she stood in what appeared to be a matrix-like room. She understood that her role in this would be larger and more in-depth than any other time she had been involved—up until now.

It was one thing to stay professional and to just do the artwork as needed. It was another thing to realize that, in this crime, the killer could go free. And, God help her, she couldn't afford to let that happen. Before she realized it, her pencil moved at lightning speed across her page, and she filled page by page by page, as she sketched out the scene before her.

PORTER PIVOTED AND caught a quick glance of Kylie, just to confirm she was doing okay. In fact, she seemed to be really focused on her work now and, with a nod of satisfaction, he returned to the body in front of him.

His partner, Neil, looked over at him. "She's one weird chick."

Porter smiled. "Maybe, but this is pretty traumatic for anybody."

"It sure is," Neil muttered, as he looked around, slowly rotating his shoulders and neck. "What a completely fucked-up mess this is."

"I'm not sure those are quite the right words."

"I'm sure we'll find out the killer's had all kinds of social issues, yet he managed to buy a gun without any problems," his partner hypothesized in a sardonic tone. "Plus unemployed, so living in the basement of his mother's home. He's probably been stocking up ammo for a while to avoid raising any alarms."

"Which is very typical of any mass shooter," Porter pointed out. "They want to take out their rage on the world, making sure everybody suffers, before disappearing. They all go out via suicide-by-cop, so why did this one not go out in the line of fire too?"

"I don't know," Neil replied.

Porter stared down at the elderly man on the ground in front of him. "It makes no sense in some ways, but we also know that, if the shooters can get away, they do. It's not as if they always walk through a police barricade, just waiting to be gunned down. Suicide-by-cop is not everybody's choice, particularly when these shooters feel all-powerful and can make this happen."

"Yet," Neil noted, "all I'm seeing so far is carnage, as if he didn't have a specific target. He just hit randomly, without discrimination. If someone was available to shoot down, he shot them down."

"Also fairly typical of mass murderers," Porter pointed out.

Neil glanced back to where Kylie was working. "I don't even know what she does."

"She's doing crime-scene sketches."

"That would make sense," Neil replied, "but what can she see from over there?"

Porter rolled his eyes, knowing what was coming.

Neil began his usual spiel, "We are in the modern technology age. Starting with a photographer. And then a step up from that is called security cameras. Why do we need somebody out here hand-sketching the crime scenes?"

Porter didn't say anything, yet he understood very well why Kylie was here. Most common were artist sketches done in courtrooms, but the captain had specifically requested that Kylie come here to the casino. Porter guessed that people on the federal end were making suggestions too. Certainly an unlimited budget would be set aside for this case because all kinds of government money and federal agencies would flood in to help solve it. It would entail a massive manhunt, and the local officials would need all the help they could get. So, if Kylie could provide something in the line of help, Porter was good with it.

"What a fucking waste of time. She's such a …" Neil groaned. "I don't know why I'm picking on her today, but you've got to admit that she's pretty weird."

"She's definitely her own person," Porter noted in a noncommittal tone.

Neil snorted. "It's almost as if you're sweet on her."

With a shake of his head, Porter groaned. "Why don't we just do our work and forget about any of that BS?"

"I would love to," Neil said, "but it's not exactly an easy thing."

"No, it's not an easy thing, and, if you need to take five, there's no shame. Go out, grab some fresh air, and then come back in." Just as Neil went to do that, Porter added, "After all, that's what Kylie just did." Neil glared at him, so Porter gave him a wry smile. "See? You're not so different from her after all."

"That's a low blow," Neil muttered, as he now rejoined Porter, where he was crouched beside an old guy.

Porter shook his head and muttered, "It makes no sense. You come to a casino, spend a few hours of fun, probably to just get away from the wife for a little bit of a break, and you get shot down, doing a hobby you enjoy."

"You don't know that," Neil pointed out.

Porter gave him a one-arm shrug. He'd already searched the man for an ID—Richard Norman, a local who lived not very far away.

"Shit," Neil muttered. "I hope we don't have to do all these death notifications. That would really suck."

"I imagine in this case we'll spread it out, but I'm okay to do a few of them."

"I'm not," Neil declared, swearing under his breath. "Don't you go volunteering my ass for this."

"Wouldn't think of it," Porter replied cheerfully, as he straightened and glanced around. So many bodies, so much chaos, and so many crime scenes. People were trying to do their best, but, with so many victims, it would be hard. Then again, it's not as if this shooter had hidden what he was doing. He had stormed into the casino, where tons of cameras caught an abundance of evidence against him. The problem was, the good guys didn't have an ID on the shooter and still hadn't found him.

Porter heard someone calling out to him and turned to see his captain, talking with the mayor.

With a wave for the mayor to follow him, the captain walked over and announced, "We have an ID on the guy, a local."

"Name?" Porter asked.

"John Smith."

With a groan and one eyebrow raised, Porter snorted.

The captain laughed. "No, really. That's his name. Not a fake. The tech guys triple-checked his image against facial recognition and online driver's license photo, yada, yada."

"Good enough," Porter replied. "Have you sent a team

to his house?"

"SWAT is en route as we speak."

Porter frowned at him. "Wouldn't it have been better to check if he was there first?"

"He was seen heading in that direction on the road. His vehicle was spotted. And, yes, he was driving his own car."

Porter whistled. "Do we know if anybody else is in that house? That's who is most likely to get the brunt of the shooter's next move."

"He lives with his mother." The captain grimaced.

"Of course he does," Porter muttered, hating the fact that this scenario so often was the case. "And we don't know if she's alive or dead at this point, do we?"

"No, but we're also getting reports of another shooting at a school, where a teacher was shot, currently alive."

"Oh, that's interesting. And we're thinking it's the same guy?"

"Don't know. I want you to go there and find out."

Porter nodded. "Good, I'll take my partner with me."

"Why? Is Neil having trouble handling this casino scene?"

"Everybody is having trouble handling this," Porter stated, turning to look at the captain, "as expected."

The captain nodded. "I didn't mean it in a bad way."

"I know," Porter conceded, "but today is not the day for everybody getting on each other's case."

"Which just means it'll happen more and more because we're all so edgy," the captain pointed out.

Porter winced. "I'll head to the school. Let me know when all the forensics stuff here is done. I want to have a walk-through, after I see the camera footage."

The captain nodded. "What about the shooter's house?

Don't you want to go there?"

Hesitating, Porter sighed. "I don't think he'll be there. I would hazard a guess that he's got a hit list of who else he wants to take out while he's still free and clear. Now that he's been this successful, I wouldn't be shocked if he isn't currently adjusting that mental list of who he wants to take down, and he'll get there pretty damn fast at this rate. Then he'll book it someplace, where he'll be ready to hole up. But this teacher could be connected, so I'll check it out."

His voice shaking, the mayor interjected, "We don't know much about this shooter."

"Within the next ten minutes, we should know everything there is to know," the captain claimed, his features hard, his tone flat. "We know that he doesn't currently have a job and that he got fired from his last one."

"Was that the inciting incident, do you think?" Porter asked, turning to look at him.

"It's quite possible, but we haven't confirmed that yet. We need to talk to his mother and see what's going on."

"You're hoping his mother is still alive?" Porter asked.

"Yeah, I am at that."

Tilting his head, Porter thought about it and nodded. "Look. I could go to the mother's place first. I still don't think our shooter will be there. However, if you've already got SWAT there …"

"Right. SWAT's already there and handling this, so don't worry about that. You go find out if the teacher was involved in any way with the casino murders."

"Great." Porter nodded and called out to his partner, "We're heading out, Neil."

Neil raced to his side, as they walked out the back and got into their vehicle. "Thank God we're getting out of there," Neil muttered. "You can get only so angry and not do anything with it before it all starts to churn in your gut, and you gotta explode. I was about ready to clock somebody."

"I know," Porter murmured, "but you won't like the next stop any better. Looks as if he may—and I say may because we don't have any proof it was our casino shooter— but there was a school shooting, so we have a suspicion that it may have been our guy."

"Great. So, what then? Is he on some binge spree now?"

"Looks as if he might be, and we've sure seen that before."

"That sucks. They take out anybody, everybody, whether they deserve it or not. It's a hell of a way to go, facing somebody with a private vendetta against you."

"I know, but we don't know if the shooter's mother is alive either. The captain already has SWAT on their way to the house."

Neil looked over at him and snorted. "Yeah, I wonder why he sent SWAT, not you?"

Porter shrugged. "Look. The captain and I have our issues. As far as I'm concerned, we're dealing with them."

"Whatever you say, man." Neil shook his head.

Porter snorted at that, as he pulled into traffic, which was completely snarled for blocks.

"Jesus, we'll be lucky if we get the hell out of here in time to even get to the school before dark," Neil complained, as he turned around and stared at the traffic. "Head over in this direction." Neil pointed off to the right. "The traffic is much better over there."

Following his partner's directions, Porter managed to get them out of the congestion around the mass shooting locale. Both of them breathed a sigh of relief, as they got farther away from the casino.

"That'll be a fucked-up mess for days."

"It is until we find him."

"That's exactly what we should be doing, not going to a school."

"Maybe so, but this is what I was told to do, and orders are orders."

"It's bullshit," Neil stated. "As much as I didn't want to stay at the casino, I didn't want to be sent on a wild goose chase either."

"We don't know if it's a wild goose chase, and somebody has to find out what happened at the school. So, if we get that done, we can head over to the mother's house afterward."

"I can't believe they sent SWAT in, especially if they didn't know for sure our mass shooter was there. The poor mother is liable to have a heart attack."

"Let's hope not," Porter noted, "because we both know how hard this stuff is on the families."

"Christ, what a mess."

They drove in silence for the next ten minutes. As they pulled into the high school parking lot, they found several other cops there. Hopping out, Porter and Neil quickly walked up to the front door, flashed their IDs, and headed inside.

As soon as they strode down the main hallway, Neil looked around and whispered, "It feels different."

"Yeah," Porter murmured, "but that's not the issue."

"Are you sure?" Neil asked. "This doesn't feel right."

They walked through the high school to the rear of the building. They got to the back exit, where the ambulance was being loaded. Porter stopped at the side of the gurney, where the injured teacher was in pain but conscious. "Do you know who did this?" he asked.

The older woman nodded. "A former student." She gasped for breath. "Tom Leroy."

He frowned at that, and she nodded. "Do you know where he went?"

She nodded again. "Told me that he would go out back and blow off his head, but he wanted to confirm I paid first."

"Personal grudge?"

"Apparently I was a shitty teacher," she shared bitterly. "Nobody ever tells you of the dangers of being a teacher in this world."

"I'm sorry," Porter replied. "Hopefully your injuries aren't too bad."

"They're not life-threatening, that's for sure. Honestly, I don't think Tom planned them to be. I think he was looking for a chance to be heard and for somebody to listen."

"And did you?"

"I tried. God knows I tried. I tried all throughout his school years too, but he wasn't very happy to be listened to back then. He was angry and wanted people to pay."

"The paying part worries me," Porter noted. "I don't know if you heard, but we had a mass shooting at the casino, with the shooter ID'd as John Smith, also a local."

She stared up at Porter in fear. "Do you think that was related to Tom's shooting too?"

"I don't know, and that's what we need to figure out. When did Tom leave?"

She blinked several times and then whispered, "I've lost track of time, but I think it was maybe twenty-five minutes ago."

Porter considered that. "I suppose it's possible that Tom

could have been at the casino earlier, before he came here. Yet our tech guys followed John Smith on the casino's camera feeds. They didn't mention a second shooter."

She nodded in relief. "That would be good. … I would hate to think Tom would put such a stain on his soul." Porter stared at her, and she nodded. "I don't think Tom planned on surviving this, just like his best friend. Now that's a different story."

That piqued Porter's interest. "Who is this best friend?"

The teacher took several deep breaths, as she tried to regain her composure and to breathe through the pain. "The name he went by was Devil, David the Devil, and he was a devil. I couldn't wait to get him out of my class. His grades were terrible, and he finally dropped out in grade eleven, or maybe twelve, but he was heading for trouble. His father was convicted of a murder-for-hire apparently, but I don't know if that was just a story or the God's honest truth. His mother abandoned him to the system years ago, so I doubt he ever knew her. So Tom and David bonded real fast. I tried hard to get Tom away from him, but it wasn't easy to do. Tom was pretty hooked on having this guy as his friend. It wasn't good for Tom at all. My God. David was such a terrible influence. All he could talk about was taking the world by storm and forcing people to stand up and to listen."

"Could you see Tom's friend, David the Devil, being part of a mass shooting?"

"Oh God, yes," she declared.

"Do you know any more about David?"

"Only that he lived in a foster home, but he spent most of his nights on the streets. If there was ever a definition of evil, I would have said David was it. Honest to God, at one point in time, I was convinced that this kid was completely possessed by something beyond evil."

Just hearing that made Porter's skin crawl. "Did you ever see anything like that?" he asked.

"Like what?" she asked, frowning at him.

He shrugged, not knowing how to ask the question delicately. "Just wondering if there was any sense of this evil coming off him. Like, do you think it was medications, or do you think it was an evil soul? I don't really even know what I'm asking here, but you brought it up, and I wondered what you might have seen, heard, …" She silently stared at him for a long moment, and he saw the fear in her eyes. "You're wondering the same thing."

"Wondering and putting it into words are two different things," she whispered in such a low tone that Porter could barely hear her. "Let me tell you this much. If there is such a thing as an evil spirit, David was one of them."

"How so?"

"He was a character beyond anything I have ever seen in all my years. God placed him on this Earth to torment us all, and I don't know why God would do that. Yet, if God cared for us, God would have raptured up this David asshole a long time ago."

When the paramedics started to move her toward the door, she called out, "Wait, wait, wait," and the paramedics stopped. She twisted slightly, so she could look over at Porter. "Detective, David's not your man, if that's what you're thinking."

Porter walked closer and asked, "Why not?"

She gave a wave of her hand. "David the Devil died last year, so he's definitely not involved." And, with that, the paramedics wheeled her out to the ambulance, leaving Porter staring after her.

CHAPTER 3

KYLIE FELT THE sweat running down her spine, a part of the cold clamminess that had taken over her system as she sketched to the best of her ability for as long as she could. Even then she had to collapse. She sank down against one of the walls, tears streaming down her face, as she stared at the frozen remnants of the carnage around her.

An absolutely horrific day, and a horrific thing to even contemplate happening, and yet it had happened. It was a done deal. A crazy mess. So many dead, and for what? She didn't know, but she knew a story was here. Something was here. She just didn't know what it was, and a part of her didn't really want to find out.

She sensed so much sadness, so much pain, so much fear, and all she could do was sit here and put a pencil to paper. Yet that made it easier, much easier. It was that one step removed, that one step away from being directly connected to it all.

A kindly paramedic stopped in front of her and crouched to ask her in a low voice, "Are you okay?"

She gave herself a firm shake then mustered up a smile and whispered, "I don't think any of us will be okay after this."

The older woman nodded. "I'll go home and hug every person I know and love because we never have any guarantee that tomorrow will ever come."

And, with those fated words, the woman stood and headed to where her partner was waiting. It wasn't long before the older woman left. Kylie watched the EMT go, wondering at the compassion in her tone, and realizing this was a classic case of somebody who was in the right place, doing the right job, for the right reasons. Kylie could hope for that for herself. All she wanted was peace, and yet peace ended up being the one thing she never seemed to find. How terrible was that?

Kylie wanted to do so much in her life. She thought she could do so much, and yet here she was, once again, not cowering in a corner, yet almost. She still sat against the wall, trying to ease the energy flowing through her. She shook her hand out several times and then noted she had attracted the captain's attention, as he strode toward her.

He crouched in front of her, an odd look on his face.

She waved him off. "I'm fine. My hand is just cramping."

He nodded. "Not to mention all the chaos around us."

"That … hurts everyone here."

"It does, indeed, which is why we need your help."

Something odd was in his tone, and she just raised her eyebrows and eyed him. "I'm pretty sure your detectives are all over it."

"They absolutely are," he confirmed with a nod, then looked at her quizzically. "Are you picking up anything unusual here?"

She stiffened ever-so-slightly, not sure what he meant. Surely not the way she interpreted it. Shaking her head, she replied, "Outside of the carnage, outside of the complete lack of care, the shooter was happy to have victims, any victims, preferably as many as possible. He took great delight in having shot two people with one bullet. … Other than all that," she said, trying to clear her throat, "no."

His gaze narrowed and then intensified with a shimmer.

She raised an eyebrow back at him. "Is that not what you were expecting?"

He gave half a snort. "That's kind of what I was expecting." He stood, looked around. "I'm heading back to the station. As soon as you're finished, send the sketches to me." He didn't say anything else and walked away.

She stared after him, wondering just what he expected. What was anybody expecting from her? She didn't know. God knows she tried to stay out of any conflict.

Her aunt had taught her well. Conflict didn't do any good for anybody, and it usually ended up with one person getting hurt, and that was usually Kylie. Her aunt had been a very domineering and uncompromising woman, and you did as she said or else. And always the *or else* got Kylie. There hadn't been a whole lot of love in her life, and there certainly hadn't been any joy. She'd been shoved out into the world as soon as the aunt feared anything would make Kylie happy. That was just one of those extra memories in life that she chose not to dwell on. She was long rid of her aunt, and yet she still didn't know even the beginnings of why she'd ended up there, with her, in the first place.

Her aunt told Kylie that she'd been dumped on her doorstep, and any decent person would have taken her in, but that was the extent of what her aunt's kindness would allow her to do. And yet, for the same reason, Kylie had been brought up with Aunt Agatha. Kylie had had a roof over her head and food on the table, and she did get through school. So, she could hardly blame the woman, as Agatha had at least done that much, and Kylie would be forever grateful—but not grateful enough to maintain contact with such a negative and toxic influence. Not that Agatha wanted it anyway. Agatha didn't like so much or couldn't handle so much about Kylie that her aunt tossed Kylie out into the world when she was about eighteen, including final instructions.

"Now, don't come back."

Of course Kylie didn't return. What would she come back to? It's not as if Agatha wanted Kylie. Her aunt had never married and sure, it was easy to say, *No wonder*, since she was such a miserable old woman. Yet something was also very sad and lonely about her aunt. Not that Agatha wanted anybody's pity or, indeed, anybody's friendship from all Kylie could see.

Out on her own had been a really hard awakening in life, but Kylie had already been well tuned into her aunt's proclivities for not so much the constant nastiness, but more of a general distancing. As far as Kylie knew, her aunt had moved, as she was wont to do often. Even if she still lived in the same place that Kylie had shared with her, it wasn't a place that Kylie could call home. She'd never been welcome to call it home. It had been the place where she had been allowed to sleep and eat, but that was it.

She shook her head as she slowly made her way to her feet, still shaking out her hand as she realized just how sore she would be later today. She glanced down at her sketchbook and froze, after basically filling it. As far as her hand was concerned, it was beat, but she was only stopping because she had no more paper to draw on. That was something completely bizarre in her world. She didn't remember having completed this many sketches at one time before, and certainly never this quickly.

She wandered around the now nearly quiet space, as forensics continued to collect as much evidence as they could. There would be mountains and mountains of it here. She kept looking to see if she had missed anything else, anything that she still needed to sketch, and yet all she felt was that sense from before that she was good. She had done what she could do, and she could leave now. She wanted to leave. God, she wanted to leave. A part of her was desperate to just get out the front door and to run as hard and as far away as she could. Yet she wasn't sure that would be allowed in this case.

Finally, with a sense of completeness, something she always had to wait for, she walked out the front into the reporters and journalists, the blast of cameras flashing in her face. She quickly made her way to her vehicle, got into her car, and left. She wasn't even sure where to go, and so she drove around for at least a good twenty minutes, while she tried to reorient herself to the world, dragging herself away from the carnage she'd left behind.

She ended up heading back to her office. She had a small single room in the basement of the police department. Even there it was hard to work sometimes, but she preferred it over being with people who would constantly stop to look at what she was doing. Art was not necessarily private when you worked for the police force, but it sure as hell was something that Kylie didn't want people questioning her about, at least not until she was done evaluating it, not until she had absolutely every bit and piece in place.

Nobody ever commented to her about her loneliness down here, or about her need for privacy. The captain had given her the room, had asked her if it would work, and had left her to it. It was really just part of a storeroom. Nobody came down here but her. The hardest thing was the lack of natural light, and she admitted that she often took her drawings home to finish them, where she could step out into the sunlight and see them. Sometimes they revealed things she didn't really want to see either. Maybe it was better that she stayed down in the bowels of the earth, where even fewer people had a chance to view her sketches, especially those that she didn't want viewed.

If anybody would have grabbed her sketchbook right now, they would see horrors that she hadn't intended on unveiling, yet sketches her soul needed, sketches her soul craved, all as a way to process everything that had just happened. However, they weren't necessarily anything anybody else would understand, and Kylie had met more than a few people who were completely turned off by the weird art that she did for a living. Rarely did she find anybody who even considered these police sketches as art, and even more rare was anyone who could simply accept them for what they were, crime-scene drawings.

Back in her office, she sat down with a hard *thump*, absolutely hating how dark and dingy her world looked at the moment. When her phone rang, she glared at it and shook her head, sending out a mental message. *No.*

And a mental message came back. *You can't keep hiding.*

"Oh, hell yes, I can," she muttered into the air.

A half laugh came back. *No, you can't.*

She groaned, picked up the phone, and hit Redial. "What do you want?" she asked, her voice exhausted and barely able to get the words out.

"You need to rest and recuperate."

"I was trying to do that when somebody interrupted

me."

"No, you weren't. You were trying to shove it all underneath, to ignore it, as if you could walk away from this completely unscathed."

Tears clogged her throat, as she whispered, "If that's what I was just doing, you would know that absolutely no way can anybody walk away from that unscathed."

Stefan's tone was filled with compassion as he whispered, "I know, and that's why I'm calling. I'm worried about you, Kylie."

She shook her head. "I don't even know why you bother."

"Because I care, and you know that."

The smile in his tone was evident. "Sure, I know that." She wiped away her tears. "But is this what you do with failed psychics?"

"How are you a failure?" he asked. "More about milestones than hurdles to me. You're just struggling to accept what you can do."

"Of course I am," she stated. "I don't want to deal with dead people."

He laughed. "A lot of us deal with dead people. They're not scarier than live people."

"And I'll go right back to the conversation we just had," she snapped. "Have you seen how bad real people are?"

"Yet you can't just hate them en masse," he noted, "because they're not all the same."

Kylie sighed, shaking her head. "Right, … but it doesn't take long for one nasty asshole to ruin it for everybody else."

"You've had that one nasty asshole experience, and you're ready to throw in the towel and not have anything to do with anybody," he pointed out. "And I get that. But now, as long as you keep protecting yourself, I'll leave you to do your thing, but you were leaving yourself wide open there today."

"No, I wasn't. Not deliberately at least," she muttered, as she tried to collect herself. "But sometimes I don't have the same control as you do. Just because you can walk among the dead and not have them completely turn your life upside down doesn't mean all of us can."

"I understand that, but I also know …" He hesitated.

That silence struck her just as badly as his words. "You know what?" she growled, ready to drop into that mood again.

And again she heard the smile in his tone as he replied, "I also know that resisting doesn't make a damn bit of difference." And, with that, he disconnected.

She glared down at the phone, knowing what he meant, but also not willing to take that step. The fact that she'd even been sent out there today was enough to drive her crazy. She didn't need that; her soul didn't need it. Hell, nobody needed that. Nobody needed to see the carnage of what one person could do to others. There had to be some law against it.

At that, she broke into hysterical laughter because, of course, there were laws against it. Plenty of them. There were a lot of laws against killing people, but the persons committing the crimes didn't give a shit. They were either in so much pain or were so twisted up inside that all they wanted to do was hurt others. Therefore, that, of course, is what ended up happening. People wanted to hurt others, and then just lashed out and took down as many as they could in the hopes that it would ease their pain inside. If it didn't, good riddance to the world. It was almost always followed by good riddance to the perpetrators too, also not something Kylie particularly wanted to dwell on.

She got up, and with her small coffeemaker, made herself a small pot and stared out her small window. At ground level, all she could do was stare out at the feet of the people walking past. She was even with the back alley, staring at the parking lot and delivery vehicles. Most of the time that was exactly where she wanted to be. Except right now, all she could see were the same images at the casino that had twisted and whirled through her mind as she had sketched, as if a madwoman. And now, the last thing she wanted was to check out her drawings because they would show things that nobody else would see, just her, and that was a nightmare she wasn't ready to open.

Even as she stared outside, her energy started to calm. It should have calmed a lot earlier than this, but she was grateful to see the shift finally happen. She could almost hear Stefan's voice in the back of her head, saying, *I told you it would.*

She groaned. "Do you always have to be such a know-it-all?"

Then came a shout of laughter that echoed around her room, and, of course, that was the other advantage of being here, alone in her dark little dingy corner. This way nobody else would think her crazy for talking to herself. She knew she wasn't talking to empty space, but that didn't mean anybody else did.

She sure as hell didn't want anybody to understand who she was talking to either. Stefan liked his privacy just as much as she did. Or she thought so, but he kept poking his nose in her business, so maybe not. Again his gentle laughter rolled through her room, and she groaned, scrubbed her eyes, and sank down to the floor, seated against the wall. She slowly put herself into a meditative state, where she worked at cleansing away all the images that she knew would haunt her forever. But no way she could work and do what she needed to do with all that chaotic energy still clinging to her.

It took several long minutes before she got into the right space, and then a good thirty minutes later before she could get the whiff of blood and gore out of her mind. Just as she stood back up again and gave herself a mental shake to get back to her drawings, a knock came on her door, and it opened. She looked up to see Porter walking toward her.

She stared at him. "What the devil are you doing down here?" she asked him.

He looked around and frowned. "What the devil are you doing down here?" he asked in the same blunt tone. "This isn't an office for an artist."

"No, but it's the office I have, so don't mind me." She gave a wave of her hand, as she sat in her desk chair. "What are you doing here?"

"I came to check on you," he replied briskly, his gaze narrowing.

When she looked up at him, she asked, "So, you do know this is my office?" He blushed a bit, and that brought a smile to her face. "I'm fine."

He nodded. "You're always fine," he said casually, but no bite was in his tone.

She frowned at him and asked, "Any particular reason why you're worried?"

"No, I just saw you there."

"Ah." She nodded. "I'm pretty sure you could have asked any one of us who were there the same question, and you would have had the same sense of something wrong."

"I know that," he said, as he looked around. "You don't even have a visitor's chair."

"That's because I never get any visitors," she quipped, with a note of humor.

His gaze flipped her way and then back around, before he took a position leaning against the wall.

"Did you guys catch the shooter?"

He shook his head. "No, SWAT went through his mother's house, where he lived, only to find that his mother is dead as well."

Kylie slowly lifted her gaze to his and frowned. "He killed his mother?" she asked, shocked.

His gaze narrowed. "We don't know that for sure. All we can say is that his mother was also deceased, shot while in her home, in her own bed."

"Was she ill by any chance?" she asked.

He raised an eyebrow and asked in a cutting tone, "Does it matter?"

"No, but, if she was still in bed, I just wondered if he considered it a good thing to put her out of her misery."

"Potentially," Porter conceded, "but that still doesn't make it right."

"Of course it doesn't make it right," she agreed. "I'm just trying to find a reason for what he did."

"Sometimes there is no rhyme or reason," he replied, his gaze still intense as he stared at her.

She nodded. "I'm not looking for an excuse," she murmured. "I guess I just want to try to understand."

"Sometimes there is no understanding it either," Porter noted.

"I know," she whispered. She pulled her sketchbook toward her, looked over at him, and stated, "I do have work to do, so is there anything else you need?"

He frowned at her and then at the sketchbook in her hand. "I really want to see those."

"No, you don't," she declared, "and nobody sees them until I'm ready."

"Oh, I get it," he said. "You're always very closed off around your work."

"Of course I am," she stated sharply. "As far as I can tell, so are you. You share information when you need to share information, but you certainly don't volunteer it."

His eyebrows shot up, and then his gaze narrowed, as he studied her face. "That's quite a judgment, considering you don't know me."

It was quite a judgment, and, if she were smart, she would have kept her mouth shut. "I suspect it's very typical of all detectives," she added in an effort to cover her tracks and to get out of a big gaffe. She didn't know him very well at all, so making that statement would cause all kinds of speculation on his part.

He nodded slowly. "And that is true, but it's an interesting thing for you to say."

"Not really," she replied, with a headshake. "Ignore it. I'm not myself."

"The fact that you aren't yourself and yet said that makes me wonder if finally some of your defenses are down and if maybe some of us can get in behind them." When she stiffened and glared at him, he went on. "And I can see how that comment really disturbs you."

"How would you feel if somebody made a similar comment to you? Would it not put you on the defensive?" she asked, stone-faced.

He considered the point, while she stared at him.

"You're right," he admitted, a bit placated. "I guess that's probably guaranteed to get anybody's back up, isn't it?" He laughed. "It's amazing just how much communication matters when it comes to this stuff because it seems too easy to put people on the wrong footing, even if it's not intended."

"That's true," she murmured. "On the other hand, sometimes what we think *isn't* intended really *is* intended, and we'll have to sort it out ourselves."

He frowned at that. "Okay, that's getting even more discombobulated."

"Why don't we just agree we both said something we shouldn't have and be fine with it?"

"Okay."

"Good," she replied, with a note of humor and a hint of sarcasm. "Now that we have sorted that, did you have a particular reason for being here?"

"Nope, other than checking in to confirm you're okay," he stated, with a smile. "The answer to your particular question is … no. I don't have any reason for being here. On the other hand, it does seem as if you were pretty knocked for a loop today."

"I was," she acknowledged, "and I would think my humanity is what kept me going in this case."

"Of course it is," he agreed. "Enough things happen in our world that can send us flying, but a mass shooting where you watch such heartache …"

"I think it was the callousness," she pointed out, cutting him off, "that really threw me. The fact that he didn't care if that old man had an old woman at home, a wife who now gets to spend her last few days, weeks, maybe months of her life, mourning somebody taken so quickly—or the family with the child killed by the same bullet as the father. ... It's almost as if the shooter took joy in it, a wildness, a carefree I-don't-give-a-shit attitude."

He studied her for a moment. "That's an interesting take."

"I don't know if it is valid or not with this shooter," she declared. "I just know it wasn't as random as I expected."

He frowned at her and asked, "In what way was it not random?"

She sighed and shook her head. "Other than my gut feeling, I can't really explain that right now. I would have to go through my drawings first and see."

"Your drawings?"

Her gaze flashed to his face, him eyeing her, a quizzical look in his gaze. "Yes," she repeated, peeling her gaze off his. "My drawings."

"I really want to see those drawings," he stated, his gaze dropping to the sketch pad in front of her.

"So do I. However, I'm not ready to share them yet. I have to be a little more centered before I review these initial sketches, in order to not prejudicially judge what I see on the page."

"Oh, that's interesting," Porter murmured. "Now I'm even more fascinated by what's on the page."

"A lot of it may not make any sense to you yet," she noted, "and that is something I have to sort out."

"When will you have that sorted?" he asked. "Because I really want to see them."

"I don't know. The captain asked for them quickly, but ..."

"But you have to sort through them yet."

"Yes," she replied, not sure that she should give away as

much as she had. "I know I'm peculiar. After all, I'm an artist."

"But this is hardly a work of art." Porter stared at her, confused, as if he wasn't getting the point of it.

"Yet it is a work of art. I think that's the point people are missing. You may not see it that way, but it is a work of art." He stared at her, confused. She added, "I'm not talking about my viewpoint, but his. To him, to the killer, this was his work of art. And just as my art is important to me, his art is important to him."

"And yet"—Porter slowly straightened and neared her desk—"you just stated it wasn't random."

She frowned, then nodded. "I did say that."

"And now you're saying it was the shooter's work of art."

"Yes, it was a work of art from his viewpoint," she agreed, yet shaking her head. "And, no, I don't know how to express that any better at the moment, so give me a little bit of time. I'll go through what I have, what I've done, what I've created, and I'll see if I can come up with a better explanation."

"I know you have to show this to the captain," Porter stated, "but I want to see it too."

"And you will," she promised, "but …" She left it at that.

He sighed. "You have to go through it first."

She gave him half a smile. "Yes, I do."

"Fine," he muttered, his tone back to business. "Just let me know when you're done because I want to be here."

"For what, the unveiling? It's hardly that kind of art."

"No, but it feels as if, to you, something really important is in it, and, if there is, I really want to see that." And then he quickly disappeared through her doorway, and she heard his footsteps receding down the hallway. Somehow he'd left her with an added sense of disquiet, as she stared at the sketchbook that even she didn't want to open.

NEIL WAITED FOR Porter at the end of the hallway. "She's weird, isn't she?"

He shot him a hard glance. "Just different."

"Oh no, no, no, don't say different. Different always means you're interested."

"I didn't say that." Porter gave his partner a stern look. "Come on. We have one hell of a case to work on."

"Not really. An APB is out on our casino killer, so cops everywhere are looking for him. The guy shot his mother for Christ's sake, and, if you ask me, he's probably been a fuckup from the beginning. For me, it's a pretty open-and-shut deal. Even for the unrelated school shooting, … the cops are out looking for that kid too. Both shooters caught on video. However, forensics are spread thin, so there won't be other answers for a while."

"Maybe," Porter muttered, as he thought back to what Kylie had told him.

Neil shook his head. "Don't make it more complicated than it is. It's bad enough already. We don't need any theatrics to go with it."

"Not planning on theatrics," Porter stated.

"Yes, you are. I can see it all over you."

Porter snorted at that. "You can't see shit, and we both know it. You're due for your eye test anyway. We'll go get that done, if need be, since clearly you need new glasses."

"Don't change the subject on me. My eyesight has nothing to do with it," he argued. "I can see your face just fine.

She'll mess you up bad, so just don't go there."

"And who said I was going anywhere?" Porter asked in exasperation, but in truth he found something very fascinating about Kylie. He didn't understand what, how, or why, but no doubt something was unique about that woman. Even as he thought about it, and the comments she had made about her drawings and the artwork and the artistry behind the shooting, he had to wonder. "Do you think the casino shooting was random, or was it just somebody out there creating, I don't know, a piece of art?"

Neil looked at him in shock and then snorted. "Jesus, I don't know what the hell she told you, but there is no art in this fucked-up murder mess."

"Maybe not, but … our shooter created a hell of a masterpiece, didn't he?"

"That was not a masterpiece. That was just one major fucked-up mess, so don't put any good or beautiful connotation to it."

"I wasn't, … but I have to wonder what was in his mind when he went on that rampage."

"It sure as hell wasn't anything nice."

They strolled back to their desks, which faced each other in the main bullpen area. As Porter walked over to his desk, he threw himself into his chair and stared at his computer, his mind still consumed with the concept of this mass murder being a work of art somehow, at least from the shooter's point of view.

"Don't go there," Neil reminded Porter, his tone sharp.

One of the other guys looked over and snorted. "*Uh-oh,* trouble in paradise with you two?"

Neil shook his head. "Hell no, the two of us are absolutely wonderful. Aren't we, darling?" he teased.

The other detectives laughed. "You two act just like an old married couple. All you do is bitch and complain."

"Ha. If that's all me and my wives did," Neil shared, "I would still be married to my first one."

That set off a round of jokes and laughter from everybody. Neil was on his third marriage, but that one was just about over as well. He never seemed to understand why he kept finding women who didn't appreciate anything about him. Yet it seemed he was always choosing women who were there for a good time but not for the long haul. All he really wanted was to settle down and to have a family and seemed to think that's what he was doing with each and every marriage. Still, somehow he ended up with women who had completely different ideas on what their relationships would look like.

Porter studied his friend and partner, Neil. Porter had been with Neil for all three marriages—or rather all three divorces—with the third strike coming on fast. Each time Porter kept telling Neil to not go in that direction, to not marry this one, and that it wouldn't be what Neil wanted, and each time he had forged ahead with each marriage, so sure he had found true love this time, and the woman in question would be there for him. Sadly true love hadn't lasted for Neil, not even close, and Neil had been heartbroken each and every time.

Porter had met each of Neil's wives and had to admit they were all beautiful, collected, powerful women. Yet somewhere along the line, this major disconnect happened over what Neil wanted and what each wife wanted.

Porter had even been best man for the last two weddings. And now all he saw was the shambles of Neil's personal life, and Porter couldn't understand how Neil kept coming back to the same nightmarish mess of marriages that were doomed to fail. Neil was a good man, but he was also judgmental in many ways. In his mind, one way was right, the other was wrong, and nothing in between was to be considered. For Porter, he always felt something resided in between. He just didn't ever tell his friend what that in-between compromise was.

CHAPTER 4

KYLIE WALKED TO the captain's office and knocked on the door. When no answer came, she hesitated and knocked again.

A woman behind her said, "He's having a nap."

She turned and nodded to one of the women who answered the phones. "Okay, I'll just leave him a message."

The woman eyed the sketchbook in Kylie's hand and suggested, "Unless you want to leave that behind."

"Nope, I sure don't," she replied cheerfully, as she turned and headed toward the elevators, leading back down to her little basement room. The last thing Kylie wanted to do was to leave any of her artwork behind. Just as she approached the elevator, a roar from behind her had her spinning around.

There was the captain, shoving his hair out of his eyes. "I told you to come in," he snapped.

She frowned, as she headed back toward him. "I didn't hear you. Plus, I was told you were having a nap."

He snorted. "Hardly a nap."

"You're entitled to catch a few minutes."

"Doesn't matter whether I'm entitled to or not," he muttered. "Get in here." He motioned for her to get inside his office. As soon as she stepped inside, he slammed the door shut. She winced at that, then he frowned.

"Sorry, not trying to upset everybody."

"It's an upsetting time," she murmured.

"Yeah, you're not kidding," he agreed. "Have you got anything for me?"

She studied him for a long moment and nodded. "I feel as if an undercurrent of something is here."

"Yeah? I don't really have time to waste," he noted. "So did you or did you not find anything?"

"I found all kinds of things," she replied cautiously.

He waved his arm in an irritable manner. "Stop with the constant prevaricating," he said. "Did you or did you not find anything?"

"What is it you expect me to find?" she asked, as she walked to his desk and dropped her sketchbook on it. She watched as he walked around the room.

"I don't know what I expect you to find, but I feel as if you'll find something."

"That's nice. Maybe you should tell me what I'm supposed to be looking for," she snapped, "before you start giving me orders that I don't even understand."

He stared at her for a long moment. "So, do you not understand, or don't you want to see it?"

She let out her breath slowly. "I think an explanation is in order."

"If I had an explanation, I would give you one," he growled. "At the moment I'm a little overwhelmed with all kinds of shit happening."

"Of course, but I feel as if you're looking for something from me that I don't necessarily have to give." He didn't seem to like hearing that.

"Look. I was told you could do more than just sketch."

She froze. "Do more than just sketch?" she repeated.

"What does that mean?"

He glared at her. "I don't know what it means. However, because I trust the person delivering that message to me, that is the only reason why I have you here at all."

She sank into the visitor's chair. "Meaning that I wouldn't have a job except for this person?"

He shrugged irritably. "To a certain extent, yes, though you do a great job when we have people who need something. However, I'm not sure we need a sketch artist in a full-time position."

"Maybe not," she agreed. "So, are you firing me?"

"No, I'm not firing you, damn it," he snapped. "You haven't answered my question."

"You didn't ask me a question," she stated in an equally forceful tone. "And who suggested I could do more than just draw?" The captain glared at her, not saying anything. She sighed. "His name is not Stefan, is it?"

His eyebrows shot up, and he shook his head. "Who is Stefan?"

She stared at him in confusion. "Look. Obviously we have different expectations of what's going on here," she began. "Could you please answer the question as to who suggested I might do more?"

The captain glanced at his shut door, as if seeing the bullpen on the other side, and shrugged. "It's probably not a good idea if I do that."

"Maybe not," she conceded, "but it might make my life a little easier."

"Sure, but it'll make mine worse," he admitted, with a wry look. "So can you or can you not?" When she just stared at him, he reached for the sketchbook, flipped it open, and sucked in his breath. "Christ." He pinched the bridge of his nose. "Your drawings pack a punch."

"Art is more personal than snapshots," she explained, as she stared at him and the sketchbook in his hands. "A photograph allows you to distance yourself, but hand-drawn pictures like these are pretty hard to separate yourself from the emotions tied to the scene."

"Yeah, you're not kidding," he declared, still a bit unnerved. "Why the hell do you want to do this work anyway?"

"At times I would have said, *Because I don't have a choice*, but I'm not even sure that is the truth."

"And that's what I'm talking about. Something's ... off about you. I'm sorry. That came out wrong. ... Something's different about you," he corrected, waving his hand. "I'm not explaining myself well, or maybe it's more like I can't explain it."

"If you told me who said something about me, then I could at least clarify expectations with them."

"Nope. I can't do it," the captain replied. "It was a recommmendation given to me in confidence. I started this journey on my own, and I won't involve them."

Frustrated, she could only groan at him. "If you won't tell me what you want or expect from me, how is it you expect me to do my job?"

"I was hoping for more, although this"—he stared at the gruesome scene on the page—"is fucking brilliant. Mind you, it's disgusting, nasty, and horrible, but it's also fucking brilliant. Christ." He closed the sketchbook, leaning back to compose himself for a moment.

"I'm sorry," she said. "Was I supposed to draw these in some way other than just as I see them?"

"No, no." He waved a hand at the sketchbook. "Obviously you're supposed to draw them just how you see them.

Yet there's sketching, and there is real life, and this is a whole lot closer to real life than any of us were expecting."

She nodded. "I'm a realistic artist. I'm sorry if that's not what you were expecting." Then she hesitated. "Though I have done drawings for you before."

"I know. I know," he snapped, covering his face with his hands.

"Maybe I should come back later."

He glared at her. "There won't be a later if we don't get this solved."

She stared at him for a long moment and nodded. "Do you think my drawings will highlight something that'll help you solve this casino case?"

He dropped his hands and asked her, "Can you?"

She was so surprised that she wasn't sure what to say to him.

"I mean, seriously, can you? Is there something you can find in any of your artwork that can help us? I'm grasping at straws here, but that's exactly what I need." He almost looked relieved that he'd finally gotten it out.

"I'm not sure. I just draw what I see."

"No," he countered, "you're drawing more than you see. That's obvious because we were all there, and we didn't all see this. Christ, you got the expressions nailed and even pearls on this woman's neck."

"Yes, and I am sure anyone else would have seen them too. She was wearing pearls after all," Kylie noted. "I got the impression they were a family heirloom, something passed down from generation to generation. This killer didn't just destroy one family. He destroyed multiple families."

He stared at her and added, "But I don't think anybody else would have noticed the pearls under all that gore and blood."

"Maybe not," she said, "but they would have eventually. I see the details."

"Yes, and I need those details," he declared, and then glared at her shrewdly. "Anything else that you might feel is important?"

Her lips twitched. "Sure, I would like to know who recommended me to you."

He sat back, obviously feeling as if he were on safer ground. "Yeah, I might have another talk with him about it later."

"Of course," she replied smoothly, then smiled at him. "Do you want to go through the sketches now?"

"No, Christ, no, I don't want to," the captain admitted, glaring down at them. "But apparently I have to." He opened her sketchbook again, took a deep breath, then slowly, wincing a couple times, went through the pages she had drawn. He stared at the sketchbook for a long moment. "I feel as if you almost did a time capsule of their individual lives."

"Maybe I did," she noted cautiously. "It's what I saw."

"An awful lot of detail is here, but that may not be all of it."

"Meaning?"

"I don't know," he said. "You tell me. A lot of pages were ripped out."

"Yes," she confirmed, taking a careful tone, "not all of them were ones I could show."

"How so?"

"Sometimes … I draw uncontrollably, things like the families crying," she explained. "I left a bunch in, but they're really not part of what I saw."

"Yet they're just as important perhaps."

"Some people were moving dead bodies," she shared. "Some people were covering them. Some people were lying on top of them because they couldn't stand to leave them."

"I know," the captain acknowledged, trying to calm down. However, his gaze still held a look of wildness. "I've looked at various scenes similar to this, and it's horrific."

Kylie nodded. "Everybody goes to pieces, and, therefore, some of the crime scene areas were changed."

"Yes." When he flipped through to the second-to-last drawing, she stiffened. He glanced up at her curiously. "What's important about this one?"

She shrugged. "I don't know. You tell me."

He flipped to the last one and stared, then flipped back through several others, and she slowly relaxed. He glanced at her and asked, "Okay, so what did you expect me to see?"

She shook her head. "One of them is different."

"They're all different," he snapped. "They're all horrific. Christ, I'll have nightmares forever after looking at this."

"And yet the real-life pictures, the photos, would do that to you as well. It's nothing you haven't seen already."

"Yes, they will affect me too," he conceded, "but the photographs allow me to step back a bit. These are just way too real." He closed the sketchbook, crossed his hands together on his desktop, and asked, "Which one is the one that you were expecting more of a reaction to?"

She suggested, "Go through them again, but look at them from more of a detective's point of view."

He rolled his eyes at that. "I'm always a detective."

"No," she replied, taking a deep breath, not sure if he would ever get it. "You're a father. You're a husband. You're a mother. You're a wife. You're all things to all people, and you're also trying to keep the department together on one of the most horrific incidents you have ever seen." He stared at her in surprise, and she could see the emotions working over his face, as she nodded. "I saw it, even if you didn't want anybody to."

"You can just un-see it, damn it." He started flipping through the pages, stopping to look at each one briefly. When he got back to the last one, he wanted to close the book, then backtracked to stare at this second-to-last drawing.

He looked from the page to her and then back at it again. "Jesus, did you actually see this one?"

She nodded. "I did."

He stared at it and shook his head. "And just like this?" She nodded. "I haven't got the crime scene photos yet to match up with your sketches," he muttered, staring off in the distance.

"No, they're not out yet, but you should get them soon."

"Yeah, but how the hell did you do all of these by hand so much faster than the photographers could develop their films or print their digital images or whatever the hell they do?"

She shrugged. "My sketches come from the heart, not from technology."

"I don't even know what that means, and I don't even think I want to." He went back to the same drawing and tapped it. "This one is staged."

"Yes," she confirmed, adding a long hiss.

He lifted his gaze, narrowed it, and asked, "What the fuck is going on?"

HEARING THE CAPTAIN shout for him, Porter stood up from his desk, turned, and watched as Kylie walked away, no sketchbook in sight. Porter immediately walked to the captain's office, who waved him inside and ordered him to shut the door. As he closed the door behind him and sat down, the captain glared at him.

"What did she say?" Porter asked.

"I don't know what the hell is going on with that one," the captain began, "but I need you to look at a few things." He pointed to the sketchbook.

Porter nodded and reached for the sketchbook.

The captain sat back and stared at him. "Why the hell did you tell me that I should bring her on board?"

"Because she sees things," he stated, "and you know that."

"I know you see things too," the captain pointed out, "and it's gotten us into trouble before."

"Yes, it has, but only generally on things like the budget," Porter clarified, as he flipped open the sketchbook. The first picture made him sit back, all the air squeezing out of his chest, as he stared down at the picture of the father holding the young child, the bullet having gone through both of them. She was a realist when it came to her drawings. Everything looked exactly as in real life, only more painfully emotional. She caught the victims' expressions. She caught the heart of each person on her page. Something just magical and devastating appeared each time. "Christ," he murmured.

"Right," the captain agreed. "I can hardly even look at this. Nobody does work like this."

"She does," Porter stated, "and obviously, as you can tell, she does a hell of a job at it."

"Yeah, I know. I see that, but holy shit."

Porter flipped through the pages one at a time, wincing at the clarity and the emotions, the pain, the loss, the suffering on each and every one of the victims and even the survivors. It was so evident that she had picked up on all the things that caused the emotions, and it was hard to forget. In a low voice, he murmured, "I keep wanting to tear away my gaze, but I find I'm fascinated and can't."

"Exactly," the captain muttered, as he leaned across his desk, his arms clasped in front of him. "I don't think I've ever seen anything like this."

As Porter made his way through the sketchbook, her images were impaled into his memory, and he knew he would never forget them. Even though he had seen many of these same things, he'd learned to distance himself from the crime scenes, taking a step back so he could sleep at night, but these? These were more haunting, were more personal in some way. They were shocking, and yet, at the same time, the artwork involved was absolutely incredible.

When he got to the last one, he wanted to close his eyes and bow his head in grief, when suddenly it hit him. His eyelids flew open, and he turned the page to the previous sketch, his gaze narrowing. He lifted his gaze to the captain and then looked back down at the second-to-last drawing.

The captain waited.

"She's fucking posed."

The captain nodded with satisfaction. "Right."

"Kylie told you that?" Porter asked.

"She waited to see if I caught it first, and I admit that I didn't see it the first time through. So, you caught it sooner than I did."

Porter stared at the woman, her thighs wide, her skirt ridden up high, her arms and legs outstretched, almost as if struck midflight, yet still landed gracefully. He leaned into the picture. "Is that a bullet wound in each hand?"

"Yes," the captain agreed. "That was my take on it and with her feet too."

Porter asked, "He crucified her to the floor? With bullets?"

"I think so. Did you notice that her clothing has been cut from top down? I won't know for sure until we get her into the morgue, and we have the autopsy results, but she was definitely treated differently."

"She was the target then," Porter declared, as he closed the book, then sat back and stared at the captain. "Who the fuck is she?"

"I don't know. At present, we know nothing, so I need you on it. This is your case. Thoughts?"

"We'll need to know everything about her life and everyone in her life because, whoever did this, isn't the same killer as the one who took out everybody else."

CHAPTER 5

KYLIE LET HERSELF into her small house, dropped her coat and her sketch pad, the one she kept as a spare in the office, and kicked off her shoes. Walking into the kitchen, she poured herself a glass of red wine, carried it outside to the deck, and collapsed onto the huge oversized deck chair she kept there. To say she was exhausted put it mildly. To say she was overwrought was just another way of saying the same damn thing. And yet none of the words conveyed the torment of her soul right now.

When her doorbell rang a few minutes later, she groaned, momentarily wondering if she should just not answer it. When it rang again and then again, quite insistently, she frowned, not sure she wanted to go at all now. She stood and headed to her front door. Peering through the peephole, she saw a very disturbed Porter staring back at her.

"Open the damn door," he snapped.

"And why the hell would I do that?" she asked, still eyeing him through her peephole, "especially given the mood you're in."

At that, his eyebrows shot up, and his hands fisted on his hips. She couldn't see below that as he was too close to the door. "Obviously I won't hurt you."

"Obviously I don't know that because of the mood you're in," she snapped right back. "I can't see anything about the way you're acting that makes me want to let you in."

He closed his eyes, took several deep breaths, then repeated, "Please just let me in."

"Oh, as if that'll work," she muttered, glaring at him. He just continued to glare at her. Deciding that he wouldn't go away, so she might as well deal with whatever the hell he was angling for, she opened the door. "Jesus Christ, what the hell are you even doing here?" she muttered. "My day is over."

"Yeah? My day is over too, but it's not as if anybody has that opportunity to stop working."

"I do," she argued. "I did what I was asked to do, and that was it."

He frowned at her and asked, "Can you really turn it off?"

"No, of course I can't turn it off," she snapped, "but that's hardly the point." She was fuming on the inside still.

"Maybe," he muttered, as he looked around her place, "Where were you sitting?"

"Outside on my deck," she replied, not sure what he was getting at.

"Good." Then he nudged her toward the deck. "I'll follow you out there."

"And why the hell would I want you out there?" she muttered, glaring at him.

"Because I'll pour myself a glass of wine too," he snapped. "It's not as if you'll be friendly enough to offer me one."

"No, I probably won't." She raised her hands but turned and headed back out to the deck. When he rejoined her, he did bring a glass of wine with him. She sighed. "So, did you just come here to mooch my wine?"

"This cheap shit?" he asked, holding it up. "Hell no."

"If you don't like it, you don't have to drink it," she retorted, shooting daggers. "It's not as if you were invited, after all."

"The chance of your inviting anybody is pretty-damn slim."

She stared at him, surprisingly hurt by that remark. "I'm not completely antisocial."

"Maybe not, but you're not in any way social either."

"I don't have to be social," she replied. "You guys are all work colleagues, but that doesn't mean you have to be my best friends."

He walked out farther onto the deck and turned to look at her. He had a sip of wine, while he assessed the seating.

She knew what was coming next. "Don't even think about it," she warned.

He shrugged. "Already thought about it. Only one place to sit, so I guess I'll join you." And, with that, he sat down in the oversized chair beside her.

She scrambled to her feet and glared at him. "You just take the cake," she snapped.

He smiled. "Sometimes, yes."

"What the hell are you being so obstreperous for?"

"Obstreperous?" he repeated slowly.

"Oh, don't give me that. You know what I mean."

"Difficult, cranky, miserable. Yeah, I've heard all those complaints before, but yours is not a common one."

"Doesn't matter if it's common or not." She glared at him. "Stop making fun of me."

"Now that … I would never do."

"So, what the hell are you doing here then?"

"I saw your sketchbook," he replied abruptly.

She winced. "Oh, great, just what I wanted to hear."

"You knew I would see it. I told you I wanted to see it, at least twice."

"I figured you would at some point in time. I didn't realize the captain would go running to you so quickly." His gaze narrowed at that, and she raised her hands, palms up. "So, what if you did see my sketchbook?"

"That's what I'm here about. You've seen crime-scene sketches before. I've seen crime-scene sketches before," he began. "I have never seen anything quite like yours."

She frowned at him. "What do you mean?"

He eyed her. "Surely you can't possibly misunderstand what I'm saying."

"I don't really know what you're saying," she declared, "so I guess I am. What are you talking about?"

"They're phenomenal," he said, pausing, as if trying to find the right words. "They're also painful."

"It's a painful subject," she stated, her tone deliberately short, wishing he would quickly move past this. And she was sorry for having asked.

"I just don't understand it, so help me out, okay?" Still, she frowned at him plainly. "I think you were more affected than all of us, yet you still managed to create those amazing sketches."

"It's what I do," she said, as she walked to the edge of the deck and sat down on the steps, turning to face him.

He smiled. "Nice chair you've got here."

"Yeah, it would have been," she replied, but she pivoted to stare out at her backyard, knowing that he was here and wouldn't leave until he got to the bottom of whatever. "So, what about my drawings?" she asked, with a wave of her hand. "You knew I was working on them."

"Yes, I did. I had no idea you would create something like that though."

Frowning, she turned to study him, but he appeared to be sincere. She shrugged and turned again to stare out at her backyard, but she was acutely aware of everything he did. When he got up and walked closer, sitting down on the steps beside her, she couldn't help herself and shifted away from him.

He nodded to himself. "That's what I thought."

"What is what you thought?" she asked, glaring at him.

"It's not just me," he replied. "It's everybody. When you get a chance to move away, you do."

She flushed. "So what? I don't like people in my personal space."

"If only that, it would be okay," he clarified, "but it's not only that."

"So what if it isn't only that?" she asked, staring at him. "Will you go dig up and pry into everybody else's business? How do you think that's okay?"

"No, most of the time I can't stand being in anybody else's business," he stated, "but this job doesn't really let me off the hook."

"So, go deal with your casino shooter."

"I would love to," he replied, shaking his head, "but apparently, not only has the shooter killed his mother and is on the run right now, with hundreds of cops out there after him, I'm also very concerned with that second-to-last drawing in your sketchbook."

She stiffened and then slowly relaxed, hoping he hadn't noticed, but of course he had. He was a fucking detective, and she never expected it to go unnoticed.

"Exactly. That one," he noted. "We're still waiting for

the crime-scene photos to come our way, but I did go down to forensics to see if they had any, and they did have one—one like that—and it was similar but not exactly the same."

She frowned at him in surprise. "What do you mean?"

"There were slight differences. Technically speaking the details were all there, but some things were different."

"What are you talking about?" she asked, staring at him. "I drew what I saw."

He nodded. "Except I suspect that, with this particular sketch, you drew what your third eye saw, not what you saw at the crime scene." She stared at him and blinked. He smiled. "Yes, I'm the one who told the captain about you. He told me that you were rather anxious to know who had asked him to have you brought on board."

"Why the devil would you tell him that?" she asked, staring at him in shock, still reeling from what he'd just said.

"Maybe I'll reconsider it at some point," he acknowledged, "but it was my professional opinion that you would be a huge asset to the department, and that second-to-last picture you drew just reinforced it."

"God no," she argued. "It's just a drawing from the crime scene."

"Not quite," he countered. "I compared the two renditions myself, your hand-drawn scene and the camera-generated picture. The two are very close, but yours is clearer, crisper, and far more detailed."

"Meaning that I filled in information that wasn't there?" she asked, abruptly affronted that he would accuse her of that.

"No, I'm not saying I think you made it up. Absolutely not. I'm thinking maybe somebody adjusted the body and changed something in the context of that woman's death between the time of your sketches, which happened first, and the time the photographs were taken. That is a consideration."

She pondered that, feeling some of the shock inside her easing back at his words. "I guess that's possible," she relented. "Such madness filled that casino. Everybody was busy doing their own thing, and it seemed as if one million people were running all over the place."

"And there probably were," he agreed. "However, that doesn't change the fact that whatever you drew is different from what the camera noted. Not all of it," he clarified, waving a hand, "just a little bit."

"So?" she asked, watching the tic in his jaw as he studied her.

"So, I want to know more about your sketch."

"Everything you want to know is on that sketch," she stated. "I just drew what I saw."

He nodded slowly. "Somebody posed the woman after death, even with everybody around, amid all the craziness, yet before the official photographs were taken," he suggested, "which is a little bit disconcerting, considering so many cops were around. Yet somehow you picked up a bit of extra information and put that into your picture."

"Could be a lot of things, and none of it is my concern."

"It is my concern. The question is, did you see anybody around the victims who wasn't supposed to be there?"

"How would I know that?" she asked, striving for calm, her mind racing as she wondered if she had come up against somebody who had posed the body differently. "I did have one reporter tossed out, but we were at the backside of the casino, not near the staged woman. Everybody else had jackets with some official emblem on them or ID tags around their necks, designating them as supposed to be there."

"That's very true too," he agreed.

"So, that woman, who was she?" Kylie asked.

He sighed. "She was a senator's daughter."

She stiffened, then turned and looked at him. "Seriously?"

He nodded. "Which is also why we're wondering what the hell is going on."

She shook her head. "And you're expecting me to tell you?"

"I'm not expecting anything." He waved his hand about. "Yet you did definitely bring up something that needs to be questioned."

She groaned. "It's what happens when I work," she muttered. "Everything goes to hell all the time."

He smiled. "So, you can see how we're wondering if we have a second shooter."

As she thought about it, she nodded. "That would make sense. And yet it's such a horrific act that it doesn't make sense, and who else was there who could have done this?" she asked. "And did one of the two shooters then kill the other shooter?"

"All very good questions," Porter noted, "and believe me that I'll get to the bottom of it."

"I'm glad to hear that … because, right now, it's all looking pretty confused."

"Yes, and no. We were happy to lump the senator's daughter into this mass shooting for the moment, but eventually we would have come to the same conclusion, once we compared your sketches to the crime scene photos."

"And yet you said those crime scene photos didn't show

that.”

“No, they didn’t.” Porter frowned as he took a sip of wine and stared out across her backyard.

“And if that’s the only reason you came to see me,” she pointed out, “I can’t help you.”

“Maybe, maybe not,” he mumbled, still staring off, as if processing information.

She groaned. “I won’t get rid of you very easily, will I?”

He laughed. “No, you sure won’t.”

“Damn,” she muttered.

“You could be easier to deal with.”

“I could be, but I won’t be.” She just shook her head and waited.

“So,” he began, “the next issue then is, … if, indeed, we have two shooters or two killers in this mess, did they work together?”

Immediately her mouth opened. “No.”

He studied her and nodded. “That would be my guess as well, but, in your case, you spoke as if maybe it wasn’t a guess.” She glared at him, and he nodded. “I think I would agree with it anyway. I can’t see them working together if the one guy’s only doing one killing.”

“No, but then the other guy, the mass shooter, he’s proud of his work,” she stated. “At least somebody is proud of their work. There was a sense of artistry to some of it.”

“Some of it, yes, but then the question is, who and what?”

“That is beyond me,” she declared. “I have no idea.”

“And, of course, that just brings up more interesting questions. If it wasn’t meant to be that way, who else would be targeted?”

“I don’t know what you mean,” she said.

"I'm just wondering if this young woman, the senator's daughter, was targeted, and the mass-murder shooter was set up to prime the pump so the second shooter could kill a single woman."

"And then what? Did both shooters leave together? I would think there would be videos of it," she guessed. "It's a casino, for Christ's sake. They have massive security systems in place to catch the card counters. Supposedly cameras would be everywhere."

"Yes," Porter agreed. "They do have cameras, and, of course, not all of them worked."

She stared at him, the color draining from her face as she whispered, "But that means …"

He nodded. "It means a couple things. It could mean that it was an inside job, but that would be way too easy to suggest," he noted in a laconic voice. "What do you think?"

"Or it could just mean that they knew some power outage had happened, or they created a power outage or something that would take down part of the security systems. Or maybe they paid somebody, or … I don't know," she said, raising her hands.

"Exactly. The casino hasn't reported any losses or sustained outages at the same time."

"Oh, good God," she muttered. "Are you saying that the shooter could have been camouflaged for something else completely?"

"When you think about it, while all that carnage was going on, consider how much damage could have been done to their security systems, and how much money could have been stolen."

"And the casino people are not speaking about it, I suppose?"

"I haven't really found the right person to loosen up about it," Porter clarified. "I was thinking that maybe you could help me there."

She shook her head. "Oh no, no, no, that's not happening."

He just smiled and waited, as he sipped his wine.

"What the hell are you even going on about?" she snapped, glaring at him. "That's not the shit I do."

"Oh, it's not the shit that you've agreed to do in the past. I can confirm that," he declared, "but that doesn't mean it's not something you might agree to do in the future."

She frowned. "I'm not saying what the future will bring, but I am saying that isn't the work I want to do."

"Of course not," he murmured. "Who the hell would?"

"You, apparently," she shot back. She hopped to her feet and paced the pathway in front of him. "That would be incredibly diabolical, to set up somebody who is primed and ready for a shooting like this, then take advantage of the chaos to go kill somebody he needed to take out for whatever reason," she noted. "But to do it in such a way that involved robbing the casino or something like that is just way too far out."

"Is it?" he asked. "I'm not saying that they were robbed. I'm just saying that potentially a window of opportunity existed that might have kept somebody else's mouth shut."

"Well, shit." She ran her fingers through her hair and then shook her head. "No, it doesn't feel right."

"What doesn't?" he asked, eyeing her intently.

"The whole crime scene thing, that doesn't feel right."

"Why do you think that?"

"It was a different killer for that poor woman," she stated, "and yet I agree it's possible that this mass murder could have been set up as a way to just target the senator's daughter. God help her and her family for that because that's one of those memories you'll never, ever get rid of."

"Of course," he said.

"And now you must catch two killers."

"We're on it," he replied, "the trouble is getting anybody convinced that there are two."

"But I took sketches of it."

"But the crime scene doesn't have any evidence of it."

She frowned at him. "You think that I staged that woman's death?" she cried out in shock. "Is that what you're suggesting? That I set up and changed things at a crime scene?" Shocked, stunned, and horrified, she could only stare at him in complete shock.

"No," he snapped. "That's not what I'm suggesting at all. But I am suggesting that maybe somebody saw you sketching the senator's daughter, and somebody decided it was a little too obvious or recognized what was happening or what all of that meant, then disturbed that particular death themselves. That would explain why your sketch is different from what the crime-scene photographer caught on film just half an hour or so later."

She sank back down onto her deck steps. "You mean, somebody who would be offended, somebody who would be angry?"

"Or somebody who thought the dead woman's pose was sacrilegious," he added. "A woman lost her life there, and I'm sure it would have upset a lot of people to think that she was intentionally posed in such a seductive way."

Kylie didn't know what to say to that. Just so much shock was involved that it made no sense to her, but since when did anything ever make sense in this stupid world? This world that she somehow got on the wrong side of. "I don't know. I don't even know exactly what it is you're suggesting."

"I'm not suggesting anything," he replied. "I'm working through a problem with your help."

She glared at him. "Then why do I feel, if I don't say the right thing, you'll lock me up?"

"I would never lock you up," he stated. "That happened to my sister, and it sure as hell is something I would never allow to happen to you."

She stared at him dumbly. "You want to explain that?"

"Nope, not right now at least."

"Do I know you, like from before?"

"No, you don't," he stated. "It would have been nice if we had known each other though," he noted, a smile playing at the corner of his lips. "It would have made some of this easier."

"Were you—" She stopped, then realized what he'd said. "Your sister, why was she locked up?"

"Because they considered her crazy, completely unstable, and not safe to be on her own."

"And was she?"

"She was certainly unstable, though she was doing much better on her medication. Now she's doing a whole lot better."

"And what do you mean by that?"

"She's working with somebody specifically to help her."

"That's good. That's what therapists are for."

He smiled. "In this case, it's hardly a therapist."

"Oh God." She stared at him, suddenly realizing something about his sister.

"Yes," he confirmed. "I know it's a word you don't like. A word you try hard to never voice apparently, but, yes, she is psychic and is working with a group trying hard to help her stabilize, and it's been amazing. She's done a complete 180 and is doing phenomenally."

"I'm really happy for her," Kylie whispered, "but that has nothing to do with me."

Porter smiled and nodded. "I know that's not how you want the world to think of you, but you've got to realize that sometimes people out there see things, and it's not just you."

PORTER WAS CERTAINLY dancing around the issue, unsure if Kylie would freak out if he shared that he'd seen her at the same hospital where his sister had been admitted. Kylie had been working the angles very hard to get herself out of there, and he sure as hell couldn't blame her. And Stefan had mentioned something about her too. Apparently she was incredibly strong, untrained, willful, and very locked down, after being raised by her aunt, where love and affection had no place, and having raised her to adulthood, then promptly kicked her out.

Porter never understood people like that, and where the hell did people ever end up raising a child who needed so much more? But Kylie had survived, and she had become incredibly strong. According to Stefan, Kylie's aunt had been 100 percent against Kylie having any abilities and had been extremely dominant in all aspects of her life in order to shut down Kylie's gifts. Kylie's aunt had been horrified to think that her young ward would have any abilities that would come in to question God's will. Therefore, her aunt had been inclined to shoot it down very early. Only after several incidents did Kylie end up exploring it at all, and, even then, she felt nothing but fear because her aunt had been extremely violent in an effort to discipline the child.

Porter studied the young woman beside him. Kylie had honey-gold hair that fell in large ringlets, pulled into a ruthless bun at the back of her head right now, as she struggled to comprehend the changes that had just happened in her world. He'd seen more of her gift when he'd seen her drawings, and her gift had been unmistakable. He just didn't realize that she had no clue about her gift, even as an adult. Stefan had been extremely vocal about Kylie's abilities as a child, to the extent that neither Kylie nor her aunt wanted to deal with Stefan. Kylie's aunt was afraid to even have Kylie around because Kylie's gifts must have appeared at a very early age.

Up to this point Kylie had been able to keep them somewhat under control. However, the casino crime scene and the violence there was enough to shake up any veteran, including himself. So Porter hated to shake her up as badly as he was. Yet it was important because now they had a second killer—and this second killer would get away scot-free if somebody didn't figure out who he was and what else he was up to.

And, yes, there was a chance that the first shooter had already taken down the second shooter, or vice versa, but Porter wasn't so sure that was the case. It felt as if something sly, something deep and dark was involved in this case. This was not just the random shooting by somebody who had gone off his meds and had decided to destroy the world just because he could.

There were people like that all over the world, and, yes, in many instances they could do exactly what they threatened to do, but this case? … It didn't feel that way. It didn't have that same sensation. Definitely something was off about the whole thing, not that it would help Porter right now. What he really needed rather desperately was for Kylie to acknowledge what she could do to help them. But, from the looks of it, all she wanted to do was kick his sorry ass out the door. "Stefan says hello, by the way," he added. She startled and frowned at him in shock. "He's helping my sister," Porter added.

"Good God," she muttered, staring at him. "I'll never be rid of that man, will I?"

He smiled. "Why would you want to be? He seems to add a bit of sanity in a world gone crazy."

She shook her head. "I don't know about that, but definitely nothing is easy about any of this."

"I'm sorry if I gave you the impression that I thought anything would be easy," he noted, "because I would agree with you that none of it is easy. Yet it doesn't have to be all chaos and confusion."

"It doesn't?" she asked, with a mock smile. "Because that's exactly what it feels like."

"I'm sure it does. In fact, I'm sure that all this together just makes you want to roll up in a ball and cry."

"I didn't want to until I went to the casino," she admitted, "and now I can't get anything but that in my head."

"I'm sorry, but it'll be the same for all of us for a very long time."

He saw the tears well up in her eyes, and he realized just how hard that would have been for a person as highly tuned and sensitive as she was. No way his sister could have gone into that casino. It would have torn her to shreds, and she would never have been able to stay calm or conscious through the entire assignment there. He loved her to bits, but she was so fragile in a world gone wrong, and she just didn't do well where other people thrived. She could never do his job in any way, and she kept telling him that he was losing his soul to his work and that he needed to get out while he still could.

He wasn't sure he even had an option to get out. It seemed as if that option was long gone, yet maybe it was just his own sadness and depression that brought it out.

"Why did the captain send you?" she asked abruptly.

"He didn't," he replied, Kylie just staring at him, trying to push back the tears still threatening to spill down her cheeks. "He didn't send me at all tonight. I mentioned you a while back." When she frowned at him, he shrugged. "There was just something very powerful about your artwork."

"No," she replied, "nothing is powerful about my art-work at all. It's just me, crazy, uncontrollable me." She stood and looked at him. "You need to leave now."

Surprised by her sudden about-face, he rose and added, "You don't have to keep hiding from your aunt anymore."

Shocked, she stared at him and asked, "You investigated me?"

"It wasn't hard," he noted, "and I'm sorry for what hap-pened to your family that put you in such a position, but again … that's not your world. That's not what you have to live in right now."

"Easy for you to say," she muttered, staring at him. "You think you know everything, but you don't know anything at all."

"Then tell me," he urged. "Let somebody inside your world."

"No. You're just somebody else who wants to take advantage, and I have to protect myself from that at all costs." She motioned him toward the front door.

He added, "It doesn't have to be this way."

"Yes, it absolutely does."

Frowning, he made his way to her front door, which she opened all too quickly. There he stopped and whispered, "If you ever need a friend …"

She gave a startled laugh. "You aren't a friend. At the moment, I don't want to know if you're an enemy either."

And, with that, she shut the door in his face. He stood there on the front step for a long moment, wondering what he could or should do before slowly walking down the steps to his vehicle. He got in and sat there for a long moment. He never wanted to move, considering the way he left things, and just then Stefan called him.

"Are you all right?"

"Yes, I'm all right, but I can't say I've ever had a meeting with somebody that went like that."

"You went to see her anyway, didn't you?" Stefan asked, with half a laugh.

"I'm not sure how to avoid it," Porter noted. "That's just too bizarre to walk away from."

"I'm sure she didn't appreciate it."

"No, she sure didn't, and basically ended up kicking me out," he shared, with a sigh.

"Did she say anything about her sketches?"

"No, not anything that was helpful, but I think I got her thinking about some things at least."

"Even that might help," Stefan noted, with a chuckle. "She's very powerful, but again she's untrained, and, because she's untrained, she also doesn't have the proper boundaries around her. Instead she's got the opposite, fears upon fears of what would happen if she crossed the line."

"I saw that," Porter shared, "and I saw her in the hospital, before she managed to get control and to present herself as someone the doctors were totally okay to release."

"I'm not at all surprised. She is good at it, a coping mechanism she's had to use her whole life."

"And yet my sister didn't know how to do that at all."

"Your sister is very sensitive, and for her to manipulate her own personality in the ways required to get out of there were far too hard for her. She wasn't nearly strong enough."

"And yet Kylie did just fine. She is okay, right?"

"What do you think?" Stefan asked.

"I think she's incredibly strong, but I think she's also terrified."

"And that is very true," Stefan agreed. "So, you might get some cooperation from her, and you might not."

"We need her," Porter stated forcibly. "She definitely saw something."

"Just because she saw something doesn't mean she knows what she saw," Stefan pointed out. "You're talking to her like she's a cop, and you can't force a memory like that. Maybe she saw the person who changed the crime scene. Maybe she didn't."

"What if she did it herself?" he asked.

Stefan was shocked for a minute. "Are you thinking she was involved?"

"No, no, and yes."

"That's as clear as day," Stefan replied thoughtfully.

"I know it'll sound very strange, but what if she was following somebody else's instructions?"

"That would be an interesting thing because you're assuming she did it without anybody knowing or without even knowing herself."

"Yes, that's what I was wondering, if it were possible."

"I suppose it's possible, and we've certainly seen a lot of things happen that caught even the best us by surprise, but I don't think Kylie would take kindly to such a suggestion."

"No, I don't imagine she would," Porter acknowledged, "and that in itself is hard too."

"Of course it is. But, all other topics aside, she's a good person, with a good heart. Give her a chance, and she will come to you."

"Yes, but will she come to me in time?" Porter asked.

"In time for what?" Stefan asked, his tone sharp. "You've already had the shooting. Aren't you all collecting evidence and doing whatever needs to be done?"

"Sure, but this shooter, whoever he is, whether it's one or both of them, … we both know he's not done."

CHAPTER 6

T HE NEXT MORNING Kylie woke to a gray sky, a gray
world, and a gray heart. She didn't even know what that
meant, but that's the way she felt. It was stupid really. She
had no reason to feel guilty or to feel as if she hadn't done
everything she could because she had. She had no reason to
feel like shit, the way she did currently. The question was,
could she have done anything else?

She didn't have an answer for that. The very thought
that she might have seen somebody changing a crime scene
while she had been there sketching nearby bothered her in
ways that she couldn't begin to explain.

Mostly she thought it bothered her because she was the
one in the trance at the time of her sketches, and, if somebody had seen her, what had they seen? She prided herself
most of the time on looking normal while she sketched, just
in her own world, her pencil moving quickly, and most of
the time people left her alone to do her job. She did have a
jacket as well as a badge that identified her as law enforce-
ment, so everybody generally just gave her space while she
went about doing her thing. It was the best way for her, the
best way to move forward somehow in life.

But the thought of somebody seeing her possibly changing a crime scene while in one of her trances bothered her
tremendously. She got up, had a quick shower, got dressed,

put on coffee, and then headed to her home office, where she kept the other sketchbooks. As she opened her big portfolio, out fell one of the most recent sketches that she had pulled from her sketch pad before giving them to the captain. She often took a knife and just cut them cleanly. These were the ones that she didn't want other people to see, the ones that showed things with a little too much detail, a little too intense, a little too much for her.

Not that it really seemed to matter to anybody these days. It wasn't as if she'd had anybody knocking down her door to try and get to her. And that made her sound pathetic, but she wasn't. She was strong. She was a survivor, and she had to be strong. However, everything else that went on in this world was just too much at times.

So much so that sometimes she needed to disappear into her artwork. It was a sane and sacrosanct space for her. She honored it and kept it in that set-apart space because there was really nowhere else for her. It was always that kind of a thought process, that something else should be out there, and she was just missing out. She didn't know how to make that make any more sense, but it's what she felt.

As she pulled out all the recently removed sketches, she took a slow and careful review of each one, realizing just how variable most of them were. Here was one where she was just getting into her trance, and most people were not even looking at her or even looking her way, which was a good thing. She went into another trance for other sketches, as she moved from one section to another. She could picture it as she slowly and carefully moved around the casino, as she sketched out everything she saw and everything the others didn't see.

By the time she got to several more of these removed

sketches, her heart rate was already up and pulsing with the pain of everything she had seen.

Finally she put down the pages and stared at the one in front of her. She reached out her finger and slowly retraced some of the lines, keeping her finger aloft just enough to not mar the actual pencil strokes. This sketch was one of those that was emotionally so specific, so hard, so difficult to take in, and yet so difficult to not see. She stayed in that position for a long time, wondering what she was supposed to do with this, wondering if these pictures had anything of value, when her phone rang.

Groaning, she looked over at her cell, picked it up, and answered it.

"I'm glad you answered," Porter said.

"If I'd known it was you, I wouldn't have," she snapped. She could sense his smile through the phone, even though she couldn't see it. "Stop smiling," she snapped.

He burst out laughing. "I think you're not telling me something."

She guiltily stared down at the photos on her desk and then glanced around her home office, wondering if he could have bugged it.

"And I'm okay with that to a certain extent," he admitted, "but I do feel as if you need to share something."

"And what would that be?" she asked in a harsh tone.

"I don't know exactly, but I sense … Do you have other drawings? Ones you didn't show the captain?"

She slapped the removed pages sitting before her. "Sure, I do. I only gave him the good ones."

"I want to see those too."

"And what if I don't want to show you?" she asked.

"That might have been something you could have gotten

away with before, but not now."

"And why is that?"

"Because another young woman died this morning," he said, "and we're pretty sure it's the same killer from the casino shooting."

"You haven't caught the mass shooter yet?" she asked, amazed.

"No, not that killer, the second one."

She closed her eyes and whispered, "Shit."

"Yeah, that's definitely a good word for it. I'm coming over. Confirm you're there when I arrive."

"And if I'm not?" she challenged.

"You're not working today, at least not in an official capacity," he replied, "and, if I have to, I'll call the captain and get you put on suspension."

She stared at her phone in outrage. "What good would that do?" she asked.

"Then I can get you to come sketch with me."

"Why the hell would I want to do that?" she snapped. "I still need to eat, and I've got bills to pay."

"Good. Then you won't have a problem coming along with me today. I'll be there in ten minutes." And, with that, he disconnected.

She stared at the removed sketches and realized that this was her chance to destroy any she didn't want him to see because she had no doubt he would bug her long enough until he badgered her into handing them over. She wasn't sure that she was ready for that by any means, but she also wasn't sure she had a choice, at least not now. He was clearly on a mission, and anybody who stood in his way would get flattened, including her.

"Hell," she pointed out to herself, "not just including

me, … especially me."

With that in mind, she sorted through the pictures, putting a few aside, a few that weren't as good, a few that showed a whole lot less clarity, but she left a couple in place. When she got up to answer the door, he asked, "Where are they?"

Wordlessly she led him to her home office and to the images he was so desperate to see.

He flipped the pages from the first sketch to the second one to the third, and then he stopped. "Good God. Do you see who you have here?"

She frowned at him, then came closer and shook her head. "I have no idea who that is."

"He's a serial killer who escaped about six years ago," he stated. "And, if you saw him at the casino, that completely changes this entire game."

"It's not a game," she corrected.

"For you and me, it's not a game, but for this man? He lives for that shit." And, with that, he lifted up the sketch and motioned to her. "Let's go."

"Where are we going?" she protested, as he led her to the door.

"First, we'll go see the captain, and then we'll start making some phone calls to see where the hell this guy is. They were supposed to lock him up and throw away the key," he muttered.

"Somebody probably let him out for good behavior," she suggested.

"And that would be a joke," he replied, turning to look at her, "because he had killed four people already."

She didn't even think, didn't blink, nor did it occur to her to restrain herself when she immediately responded,

"He's up to twelve."

PORTER DROVE KYLIE straight to the captain's office, but, so far, she had refused to elaborate on her source for the update on the escaped killer's murders to date. "You'll have to tell me at some point."

"No, I don't," she snapped.

He didn't say anything, at least not until they were half-way to the captain's office. "And what if I tell the captain you said it's twelve?"

"He'll think I'm full of shit, some of which will spill over on you."

"Maybe not," he murmured. "I know Stefan doesn't think you're full of shit." At that, she stiffened, and he noted it with grim satisfaction. "I'm not sure what's going on between the two of you, but Stefan's pretty adamant about what he thinks you can do."

"He has no clue what he thinks I can do. He's just hoping that I might belong to his little club of psychics."

"You already do. Whether you're an honorary member or a reluctant one," Porter stated, "you are a member, and so am I."

She froze in place and then slowly turned toward him. "Really?" she asked, her voice low and her gaze searching.

He nodded, letting her see some of the emotions in his gaze. "There's a reason my sister was in that hospital," he admitted, "and a reason why I feel so guilty about it because I couldn't protect her, even though I was doing my best."

"You were young," she pointed out. "Nobody should have expected you to look after her at that age."

He smiled. "See? You're already doing it."

"I'm not doing anything," she growled, as she turned and stormed ahead.

"The captain will want a little more of an explanation."

"I don't really care," she snapped, as she moved toward the captain's office. "I don't have an explanation."

"Maybe if you would stop turning that little tiny earring in your ear, you would." At that she froze, as expressions of pain, shock, and other emotions he couldn't quite define rippled across her face, before she locked everything down. He nodded to himself. "Sorry. I'm not trying to burst open all your secrets and bare them for the world to see, but there is a time and a place for them, and we do need your help."

Her gaze was stony, and he could tell there was no give to everything inside her. It was all locked behind that earring and would stay there. He couldn't really blame her. Being exposed as a crazy psychic in this world didn't help anybody. But he knew what it was like to try and close off that part of his personality.

He led her by the arm toward the captain's office and added, "I know you want to keep all this locked down and out of the public sphere, and I'll do what I can. However, a serial murderer is out there who appears to be on a killing spree, and we can't allow that to continue."

"Sure," she snapped, "and, when this murder is over, there'll be another one. And when that's over, another one, with still another after that."

He glanced at her face, hearing the woodenness in her tone, and nodded. "That is possible," he murmured, "but think about it. ... You could be part of the solution."

"Or I could be part of the problem, and I could get it wrong."

At that, his mind wondered just what had happened to

her. "How much of this is coming from your aunt?"

She struggled to catch her breath, once again stunned by the personal intrusion, and asked, "Did you have to investigate my life?"

"Of course," he stated. "You're working for the police, so that is a given."

"Maybe," she conceded, "but nothing that ever happened during that time with my aunt applies to this job."

"Maybe not, but it does apply if we have a killer out there."

At that, she turned very slowly, poked him in the chest with her finger again and again. "There's always a killer out there. That's one of the sad facts of life. There is always one more. One more case, one more killer, one more victim. There is no end." She was almost shouting by the time she finished.

He nudged her into the captain's office, and she appeared to be completely unaware that he had already opened the door and was ushering her inside, trying to keep her out of the public view as much as possible.

The captain frowned at her. "What the hell is going on?" he roared.

She turned, glared at him, and roared right back, "Nothing. This guy is off his rocker."

"I know that," he agreed, "but nothing I can do about it."

She just stared at him. "How is that even possible?" she asked, raising both hands in frustration. "He's making all kinds of accusations."

At that, the captain turned and looked over at him. "Porter? Is she correct?"

"Nope, not accusations at all," he replied. "Yet she's a

little unwilling to open up about certain aspects of her life."

The captain frowned at him and gave her a shrug. "I can't say that I blame her." Surprised, she turned to the captain, and he nodded. "I've known Porter a long time," he began, "and, in many ways, he's family. I know that some people would call it cursed that he's followed in his family line with certain gifts. I know some of the pain he went through. I know of the torment his sister went through. So, Kylie, if you are dealing with anything like some of this stuff that I have seen already in Porter's family tree, I agree. It's something you don't really want the public to know about." He raised a hand in a careless wave and rolled his eyes. "However, I'm not the public."

"No, but you're just as likely to toss me out to the public." She couldn't hold back the bitterness in her words and let the accusations fly. "You're just as likely to use me as you would want to use anybody else," she snapped, "and I'm not up for it."

"I wasn't planning on using you for anything," he shared, "except that your sketches are absolutely incredible. I wish to God they were prettier, but I understand why they're not. They'll be one hell of an evidentiary look for the court cases, but they aren't something I really want the victims' families to see."

"Right," she agreed, as she appeared to be trying to get a hold of herself mentally and emotionally. She walked over and slumped into the nearest chair. "And I don't know that I have any abilities."

The captain eyed her in surprise, then pointed to Porter. "Porter seems to think you do."

"Of course Porter seems to think I do," she noted, with a wave of her hand, "but that really doesn't matter because that's about Porter, not about me."

The captain gave her a halfway smile, and, for the first time, she saw what was almost a gentleness in his gaze. "That is true," he agreed, "and Porter can be damn irritating."

She rolled her eyes at that. "*Ya think?*"

Porter protested, "Hey, I've been really good."

She turned and stared at him. "Really?" she asked. "I guess we have different ideas of what *really good* means."

He rolled his eyes at her.

The captain intervened, addressing Kylie, "Look. I need to know if you have anything else on what's going on here."

"Yes, she does," Porter declared, "but she didn't really understand what."

The captain shook his head. "Kylie, you need to explain all these sketches and whatever else you have."

She shrugged. "When I did the images, I did a lot more than the ones I showed you, and then I went home, and I sorted through them to find the ones that were the best representation of the carnage that I saw," she explained. "But apparently, in some of the other sketches that I kept, which I tend to do a lot," she admitted in almost a self-defensive way. "It helps me to get into the swing of things, and I know that sounds bizarre, but apparently I drew somebody who Porter here seems to think is important."

And, with that, Porter brought over the sketch that he had in his hand and laid down the large drawing before his boss.

The captain looked at it, squinted several times. Then his gaze focused in on one face, and he stabbed at it with his finger. "Are you saying that he was there?"

"If it's in my sketch," she clarified, "then he was there. I didn't know who he was, not until Porter brought it up."

The captain stared at it in shock, then over at Porter. "Good God."

"I know," Porter murmured. "I understood that he had escaped at one point, but I thought he had been picked up again over the years. Obviously I was wrong."

"He did escape, and I'm not exactly sure where that investigation went," the captain murmured. "But it's something we need to figure out. He's still on the run, as far as I understood, and this would be confirmation of that."

Porter nodded. "You would hope that he wasn't given a pass for good behavior."

"That would never happen in his case. I remember him, and the son of a bitch annihilated an entire family. So, he's already got four kills under his belt."

Porter turned to look at her and nodded. She shook her head. He glared at her and then spoke. "She has something to tell you."

"No, I don't," she growled, crossing her arms over her chest.

The captain watched the two of them go back and forth. "Somebody needs to tell me what it is that she doesn't want to say. … Porter, you're up."

He hesitated at first. "When I told her that our escaped killer had four kills under his belt, she corrected me, saying, *He has twelve.*"

The captain's breath hitched, as if his chest had taken a hard blow. "Christ," he whispered, as he stared at her and then gave his head a shake. "I don't suppose you have any way of proving that, do you?"

She looked at him but didn't say a word.

"No, of course not." He scrubbed his face, as if all the years that he'd been on the force had coalesced into this one crazy moment. "You know that's not what I want to hear, right?"

She shrugged. "I didn't say anything."

He snorted. "The fact that you wouldn't say anything makes it worse, not better."

"What am I supposed to tell you? That number just came into my head. You know as well as I do that it would never stand up in court, and that won't get you any more budget money to fight whatever the hell is happening here."

He stared at her, fascinated. "Maybe not, but if there is any credence or way to corroborate that number, then we need to know."

"I don't know," she stated. "All I can tell you is that's the number that came up."

"And when numbers come up," the captain asked, "do they generally mean something in your world?"

She gave him a wry glance. "Generally, … yes."

"But not always, is what you're saying?"

"I'm saying that I can't prove it. I don't know where that number came from or how I got it. All I can tell you is that, in the past, sometimes the numbers would matter."

"Would matter?" the captain repeated. "You really don't like going out on a limb, do you?"

Porter winced at the stony look she gave the captain. Porter didn't understand everything that was going on, but considering how locked down she was about this whole psychic-gift mess, chances were, she'd taken a beating somewhere along the line due to her gifts and was not open to a repeat of it. He looked at the captain. "Regardless of how many he's got to his credit at this point, if he was at the casino, you and I both know that the posed woman victim would have been right up his alley."

"In what way?" Kylie asked, turning to face Porter. "You said he was a family annihilator before."

"Yes, but what I didn't tell you was that it was a kill for hire."

She stared at him, then whispered in shock, "Somebody wanted an entire family killed?"

He nodded. "Yes, and he was convicted, then somehow escaped on the way to a transfer."

She stared at him and shook her head. "See? This is why I don't like people," she announced.

"It's also why we don't always like people, but we can't judge everyone by the same stick," he reminded her.

"Why not?" she asked. "A lot of times there's really not a whole lot of difference."

"Regardless of whether there is or not," the captain added, "he was suspected of killing several others." He brought up his computer file and snorted. "In fact, according to this rather large file, we suspect he has ten dead to his credit to date, and, if he did take out that young woman at the casino and this additional woman, found this morning, his latest victims, that would be twelve so far."

Kylie didn't say anything, just stared at the captain.

He looked over at Porter. "How do you want to proceed? This is more your domain than mine."

He nodded. "I want to take Kylie to the crime scene of the woman who was killed this morning."

"You're thinking it was our escaped killer?"

"I don't know what to think at this point," he admitted, "but I think it could be beneficial if we did find out if Kylie gets any feeling from this newest crime scene or can draw anything from it."

"If the bodies have been removed, what is it you want

me to draw?" she asked.

"I don't know, but, when we get there, if you are prompted to draw something, I suspect you'll draw it. If there isn't anything to draw, then you won't."

She glared at him. "I don't always have control."

"I understand, and I suspect that earring of yours has something to do with it too." Instinctively her hand went up to the tiny metal stud in the groove of her ear at the very top, almost indiscernible, but still there. "I would love to know the story behind that earring."

"That's nice, but I don't plan on telling you."

He nodded. "That will be something that bugs me forever then, but I don't have any way to force you to tell me, so we'll leave it for now."

"We'll leave it forever," she snapped, glaring at him.

The captain clicked away on the computer keyboard. "So, let's focus on the woman killed this morning. We don't have much, outside of the fact that she was potentially posed, and we're not sure if that's accurate at this time. Porter, you've been at the crime scene, correct?"

He nodded. "I have, so I was going to take Kylie with me this time."

"Good." Turning to Kylie, the captain explained, "I know you won't like this, but I guess a part of me would very much like you to follow Porter's instructions and see what you might tell us from the scene."

"I'm happy to go there and draw the crime scene," she replied, her tone softening. "Anything I can do to help the victim is something I will do, but I just don't want to play games over this."

"Maybe not," the captain stated, "but, until we can figure out exactly what's going on here, it would be helpful if we could put some controls on your sketches. So, if Porter asks you to do something, … then maybe you could just do it."

She stared at the captain in surprise. "You have an awful lot of trust in him."

"I do to a certain extent," he admitted, with half a smile. "As I said, … he's kind of family, and we've been through a lot together already, so I have more of an inside look into all this woo-woo stuff than a lot of people."

"So, let me guess. You also know Stefan?" she asked the captain.

"I know of Stefan."

"So, then yesterday when I asked if you knew who Stefan was, … you lied to me. I had asked you if he's the one who recommended me to you. He wasn't. That was Porter."

The captain nodded. "Your question came out of the blue, and I wasn't sure how to respond. I know that Stefan has helped Annalise quite a bit. I will always be grateful for that, for everything he can and has done for us."

She stared at him, sensing something much deeper. Then she turned to Porter. "And Annalise is your sister," she said.

Porter nodded. "Yes, that's correct."

Then she stared at the captain. "Wow, and Annalise is your wife."

He looked at her, then at Porter. "Yes, that is correct. We haven't been married all that long," he shared, glancing from her to Porter, "and it took a bit to even get her that far, but, yes, … she's my wife."

Such love and compassion filled the captain's tone that Porter smiled. He looked over at Kylie to see a sense of confusion on her face, as if she didn't understand.

"Not all psychics are hated," Porter shared. She stared at him and didn't say anything, but he still saw her confusion. He could understand how she didn't quite know how to put the pieces together. "Not every gifted person is treated the way your aunt treated you. Regardless, … if you're okay, let's go grab your sketchbook."

"I've got one."

"And these three standalone sketches, we'll keep here in the captain's office, if you're okay with that."

She stared at them and then nodded. "A couple others are in that batch too," she admitted, then turned to Porter. "I don't know if you noticed."

"Other sketches or other images of this guy?" Porter asked.

"I don't know if there are other images of this guy," she said. "I'm just telling you there were other sketches that I withheld, with other people who I drew."

"Right," Porter noted, "and that's a fine distinction too."

"I don't know if it is or not," she muttered and glared at him. "All I can tell you is that sometimes I know what I'm drawing, and sometimes I don't."

He smiled. "In this instance, I quite believe you, and that's why I'll ask you to do something a little bit different when we get to this next site."

She glared at him. "Just remember that I'm not some trick pony."

He laughed. "I would never make that assumption. Besides, I think you would get a little too angry at me."

"I would, so keep that in mind."

"Absolutely."

He led her out the captain's office door when the captain called out, "I'll want to see those other sketches."

She turned to him and nodded. "We can pick them up sometime today."

The captain looked back at Porter. "The sooner, the better."

Porter nodded. "Agreed, I'll get them as soon as I can." And, with that, he led her out to his car.

When they got into his vehicle, she asked, "Was that really necessary?"

"Yes. I'm not sure where all the resistance on your part comes from. I can hazard a guess, and I'm certainly not in a position to judge, not after I saw what my sister went through, but I'm here to tell you that I'm not trying to make your life difficult. All I want to do is catch a killer."

"Sure, you want to catch a killer, but then you'll want to catch another killer and another after that. At some point in time, I just can't catch killers anymore."

CHAPTER 7

K YLIE STAYED QUIET until they got to the latest crime scene. Then she got out, grabbed her sketchbook, and noted the place was empty.

Porter stopped her at the entrance. "I don't want you to go in yet."

She frowned at him. "Why? You think I haven't seen what's in there before?"

"Unfortunately, I'm sure you have," he replied.

When he pulled out a blindfold, she immediately shook her head. "Oh, hell no."

"It's as much for the captain and for everybody else that'll be involved than anything else."

"No, absolutely no way." She glared at him. "I already told you that I'm not a trick pony, remember?"

"I know you're not," he murmured, "and I knew I would get some resistance, but I was hoping you would understand why I need to do this."

"Nope, I don't understand, and I don't care what your reasons are." She headed to the front door, yet something prohibited her from walking inside. She felt as if a 2x4 beam stopped her. She turned to glare at him. "Are you doing that?"

He looked at her in surprise. "I'm not sure what you're asking."

She hesitated, looked back at the door, and then at him. "Are you doing anything to stop me from entering?"

"No, I would never do that."

She frowned at him, asking, "Why do you want me to put on a blindfold?"

"Because I want you to sketch whatever it is in your mind that you're seeing, versus what you could see here."

"You don't understand," she began. "I have to get into a certain zone before I can sketch at all. If I'm at a crime scene, I don't get involved in any of the photos. I step out of that. At the mass shooting at the casino, because just so much carnage was inside and I needed to do so many sketches, I immediately dropped into a trance. Yet only one dead body is here, so chances are I won't need to do anything in preparation."

He nodded. "I know it's a call on faith, and I know it's about trust. All I can tell you is that I think this is really important."

She eyed him for a long moment. "What is it you're really asking me to do?"

"I just want you to put on the blindfold and keep it on while you sketch."

She stared at him. "So, what do you expect me to sketch?"

"I guess it's what I expect you to think you're seeing versus what you're seeing."

"So, you think I'm making up these images?" she cried out in horror.

"No."

She shook her head. "I don't understand."

"I know, and that's the main reason why I'm asking you to do this. You don't seem to acknowledge the gift you have."

"Jesus," she muttered. "Fine, but asking an artist to sketch a scene without seeing it makes no sense."

"I know," he agreed, with a gentle smile. "Just humor me."

"Why come here at all? We could have done this at the station."

"Exactly," he agreed. "So we'll take five minutes and do this silly experiment. Then you can go about your business and do your thing."

She glared at him while he put the blindfold around her eyes. "Look. You can still see the presence of light. I'll lead you into the room where she is."

Kylie shivered at his words and whispered, "Why the hell would she still be in there? That makes no sense."

"Okay, so the body has been moved to the morgue. Just her outline remains on the floor."

"Right," she grumbled.

"Now I'll lead you into the room, and then you can do your thing."

"Whatever my thing is," she stated bitterly.

"I just—"

"Whatever," she snapped, cutting him off with a wave of her hand. "I'll prove it to you in a matter of minutes."

He led her into the room and handed her the pencil, opened up the sketch pad for her, and said, "Okay, now sketch what you see."

"You mean, what you think I'm seeing or what I think I'm seeing?"

"Exactly. I know I'm not being very clear."

"No, you're not," she snapped. "Now, step back because I just need a few minutes to figure out what it is you think

I'm supposed to be drawing."

He laughed. "If nothing comes, nothing comes."

But images were already forming in her head, as if she could see outside of the blindfold. She had seen things like this before but had more or less ignored them all her life as an overactive imagination or just day terrors. Who needed crap like this going on in their mind 24/7?

As soon as she stopped the internal argument with herself, her pencil hitting the paper, she sketched a woman lying on the floor. Kylie remembered what Porter had mentioned about following the MO of the second killer at the casino, involving some posing. Her pencil kept moving steadily. She wasn't sure how close Porter was or if he was giving her space. However, she suspected he was right there beside her, watching everything that went down on her paper.

When her sketching slowed, she unclamped her hand and groaned. "Now, take the damn thing off."

He immediately untied the blindfold, obviously standing right there in front of her, waiting for her to say that. "Now, take a look at your sketch."

She looked down at the sketch and winced. "Well, shit, guess I've got a great imagination, so thanks for that intel."

He opened up his phone and held up a photo. "Maybe so, but this is a snapshot from the crime scene that I took this morning."

As she stared at it, she felt some of the pain inside her tightening more and more. She took another look at her sketch and asked, "And?"

He snorted. "And it's exactly what you just did, blindfolded."

"Not likely," she replied, peeling her gaze off the screen on his phone. "Your picture is worse."

He gave a bark of laughter and nodded. "I won't argue with that because you're right. It is. Your sketch is so much clearer. It's scary clearer. Even though you couldn't see the original scene or this cleaned-up scene."

"So, what is it you're trying to say?" she asked, glaring at him.

"My guess is that you don't see the crime scenes at all," he began. "You're drawing something else, aren't you?" She just glared at him and didn't say anything. He smiled. "I know trust is a huge thing with you, and I get that, but right now it would really help if we had the truth."

"Why?" she asked. "None of my sketches are admissible as evidence in court. You can't use them for anything but to further your case along."

He smiled and nodded. "I know that, and that should give you a little more comfort, knowing that whatever you're doing is helping the victims, if for no other reason than to confirm we catch the killers."

"Sure," she agreed, "but your little trick doesn't prove anything except that I have a great imagination."

"Really? Including the necklace you drew?"

She looked down at the necklace in her sketch, then over at the photo still up on his phone. She winced. "Is that all you wanted? To bring me here and show me that I've been drawing visions inside my head instead of what's in front of me?"

"Yet you *are* drawing what's in front of you, but you are not limited to just that," he declared. "You're drawing layers past what the normal person can see."

Her shoulders slumped, and she didn't know what to say. In an uncanny movement that she wasn't expecting, he pulled her onto his arms and just held her.

"I think you've been alone for a very, very long time." She shook her head, but it was a movement muffled against his shirt. He smiled as he let her step back a little bit. "Yes, you have, and so much so that you're scared to let anybody in."

"Nobody can get in," she stated, her gaze stony as she stared up at him. Yet she wanted to step right back into his arms again, and that was dangerous. "People hurt each other, and they do it with joy. They do it with abandon, and sometimes they do it just because, in their mind, it's the right thing to do."

"And that sounds like your aunt speaking," he whispered. "She was a very broken woman in so many ways."

Kylie's eyebrows shot up. "How would you even suspect that? My aunt was very controlled, very contained, and very fearful."

"And why was she fearful?" he asked. "She had many of the same issues you did, but she squashed down her gift and made sure that nobody would ever know about them."

"No way," Kylie argued. "I asked her about that several times. She would have told me."

"Would she?" he asked. "Or was she so scared of you and what you could do that she made sure she completely avoided everything in your world that could bring up the discussion of psychics?"

"I don't know," she admitted, speaking slowly as she stared at him, "but it doesn't matter. I have zero relationship with her now anyway."

He nodded. "I get that. It's hard to have a relationship when somebody just wants you gone, isn't it?"

Her breath came rushing out in a whoosh. "Wow, you really did your homework, didn't you?" she asked sarcastically, hiding the pain inside. "She also taught me to be independent and to watch out for everybody, if only because she was so harsh."

"Of course, she taught you her fears, so that they would become yours, so that you would be a little more careful than she had been."

"Than she had been?" Kylie repeated.

Porter nodded. "Your aunt at one point in time helped the police. I found a police file on it, but the case went bad, and your aunt was blamed."

She shifted, realizing, if that had happened, it would have locked down her aunt.

"It was pretty dark and pretty ugly for a while, and she disappeared, I only realized who it was, when I realized who you were."

"Who I am?" Kylie repeated, shaking her head. "I'm nobody, and the sooner you realize that, the better."

"I'm looking at a woman who just sketched a crime scene while blindfolded, and she got accurate details that a camera got earlier, plus she got details that a camera didn't get."

"What do you mean?" she asked fearfully.

He pointed. "Look closer."

And because the camera had only taken a snapshot of that particular time, it hadn't necessarily picked up all the details clearly. The details were there, but in her sketch she had expanded them much bigger, much easier to see. "You can still put the photograph through a filter and enlarge it, make it bigger."

"Yes, and every time we do that, we end up with fewer details, don't we?"

"Sure, but this detail isn't necessarily something you

need," she stated, as she stared down at the photographic image. And yet what she had sketched had been uncannily accurate. She sighed. "You'll never let me live this down, will you?"

He let out a laugh which tugged at her own heartstrings, making her realize just how alone she had been and how different it was to have a conversation about this with somebody without being mocked.

"Seems you've been alone for a very long time."

She shrugged. "It doesn't matter. That time is long gone. I'm not a child anymore, and I'm not somebody living in my aunt's house on charity."

"I don't know if it was on charity alone," he stated, "or out of complete and total fear. Fear that you would ruin everything she had built up, fear that you would open yourself to the same hellishness that she had suffered, or, even worse, bringing her back into the same issues that had scared her so much. Agatha would have done an awful lot to avoid that."

"She did do an awful lot to avoid it," Kylie murmured. "She avoided everything to do with me and my life. It was a case of *Here is your food. Eat it. As soon as you're an adult, leave.*"

He smiled, then rubbed her back and her shoulders. "But, in many ways, she gave you a gift."

She stared at him. "What kind of a gift is that?" she asked in shock. "I was just a child."

"Yes, and you could have used more love and affection. You could have used an awful lot, but what she did give you was a skin tough enough to withstand what the world out there would do to you, if they found out, and they did find out, didn't they?"

She stared at him and swallowed hard.

He nodded. "I know you don't want to talk about it, and all the things that I found out about you barely scraped the surface. There's so much more to you, so much more to what you can do, and I understand that for you it's not anything you want to address. You didn't choose to do this, to be this, but for some reason you did choose to come in and start drawing for us."

She stared down at her sketchbook, realizing she could explain only so much. "I think it was a way to keep my abilities happy or quiet, yet at the same time protect myself. … I don't know when I sketch how much of it is me," she shared, pointing down at the sketch that she had just done, "versus what is really there."

"I saw you at one point in time at the casino," Porter admitted, "and your eyes had a very unfocused look to them."

She winced. "That was a very special case, and I figured I could easily pass it off as being in shock."

"I think we all were in shock, trying to make any sense out of that mess, which is asking a lot out of any of us."

"And yet you seemed to handle the casino murders just fine."

"No," Porter replied, "I didn't. Some souls there weren't very happy with their lives."

It took a moment before she realized what he'd shared. "Oh my God, did you see them?"

He nodded. "I saw some of them. I didn't speak to any of them, but I did show the light to a couple. When people pass over very fast like that, sometimes they go quietly, and sometimes they wander around in chaos, looking for the way back again. In a few of those cases, I can guide them."

"Does your partner know?"

"Somewhat but the details … God, no." Porter shook his head. "The captain knows a little bit, but I don't even tell him about those things."

She sank to the floor, thinking about how many souls had died in that twenty-minute shooting episode at the casino and nodded. "I can't imagine how they felt."

"Which is why sometimes I can help, and sometimes I can't. Learning to accept that I can't help everyone has taken me a lifetime."

She shook her head. "I can see that too," she murmured, as she stared around the area. "I'm not even in the same room where she was killed, am I?"

He crouched in front of her, a smile on his face, and nodded. "Right, you're not. Do you want to see it though?"

"Yes," she said, her voice stronger as she stood up again. "What was your purpose in bringing me into this particular case?"

"I'm pretty sure the killer has some connection to you," Porter shared, "and so I need to put him down forever."

She stared at Porter. "A connection?"

He nodded. "Yes, a connection."

"And why is that?"

"Because he's the same killer who killed that entire family and then connected with your aunt and ruined her life."

PORTER WATCHED THE color completely drain from Kylie's face, as she slipped right back down to the floor. She stared up at him in shock, and he nodded. "I'm sorry. It would have been easier if your aunt had mentioned something to you."

"How is that possible? She never gave any indication of having any abilities at all."

"And she did a damn-fine job of hiding her gift," he noted. "I don't know if you're aware, but she changed her name and yours."

"Mine?" Kylie asked, staring at him in confusion. "No, no, my name has always been Kylie."

"Yes, your given name has always been Kylie," he agreed. "But you were Kylie Macintyre. You are now Kylie Okovi."

She blinked several times. "What?"

He nodded. "The thing is, the family that was annihilated was yours." She started to shake, and he immediately dropped to the floor and hugged her. She soon was convulsing in his arms, as he watched the years of deceit and deception, done for her own sake, fall away.

With tears in her eyes and shock in her gaze, she whispered, "Please, no."

He nodded. "I'm so sorry, and I wish I didn't have to tell you." He pulled her into his lap, rocking her while she shook, the tremors almost convulsing her to the point that he wondered if he needed to get her some help.

Finally the tremors slowed, and she shook her head. "No way Agatha would have kept that from me."

He didn't say anything because he already knew that her aunt had done such a thing.

Then Kylie sighed. "Of course she would have. She never told me anything about my family, about the circumstances, just that my parents died in a car accident." She suddenly lifted her head. "You said a family of four."

He winced and nodded. "Your mother had just had twin boys."

She stared at him, her jaw dropping as she shook her

head. "No, no, no."

He nodded. "Yes." He watched as she confronted the shock and horror at realizing what had happened to her, but she still didn't understand it all yet.

"I don't …" Then she buried her face in her hands, the tears coming with so much pain and grief.

"You don't have to believe me," he said, "but I do have a file that you can read."

"Why didn't she just tell me?" she asked, such betrayal in her tone.

"I'm sorry she didn't tell you. I guess … she did it to protect you—and herself."

"From what?" she cried out. "What could she possibly protect me from?"

He hesitated and then replied, "For a long time I think she thought the killer would come back after her, and, therefore, after you as well."

"Come back after us?" she whispered. "Dear God, do I know anything about my life?"

He swallowed and pushed the hair off her face. He wiped the tears from her eyes and replied, "I know you'll judge her for it, but she was trying to keep you safe."

"By not preparing me for any of this?" she asked in outrage.

He winced and nodded. "And again we're judging her for something we don't have a way to understand."

"I understand," Kylie declared. "She's supposedly connected to a killer, the very one who had already killed my family," she muttered, staring at him, her gaze haunted. "A family I don't remember, a family I'm not even sure I believe existed, and you're telling me that my aunt raised me in a cold, unemotional way, and that was supposed to be for my protection?"

He winced at that too. "I don't know about the cold, unemotional way as being part of your protection," he replied. "I can tell you that she raised you to keep you safe, and she likely did whatever else she could handle or could do for you. I don't know the whole story. I just have bits and pieces."

"Good God," Kylie said, "it seems to me that you're writing a horror movie."

He smiled. "As horror movies go, this one would probably be a blockbuster."

She took several deep breaths. "You're telling me the truth, right?" she asked, her gaze hard. "This killer, … this guy who supposedly you're after … Wait. Hang on a minute. Why would he even be here? Why would he be in this area if—" Then she stopped. "No, no, no, that doesn't make any sense."

"What doesn't?" Porter asked, waiting for her to work her way through it.

"Why would he be here? What would he be doing in this area? How is he connected to my aunt?"

"We think he was hired to kill the senator's daughter at the casino the other day, and it could be a coincidence that he is in this area, or it could also be that he's looking for the one who got away."

"That would be my aunt, but I haven't seen or heard from her in so long. I can't imagine that he could even find her, since I have no idea where she is either." Porter nodded and didn't say any more. She stared at him and asked, "What are you not telling me?" He winced. "Come on. Out with it. Tell me," she snapped. "I'm not sure what's going on, but you're still keeping something from me."

"The one who got away is you," he stated. "You were in that vehicle at the same time."

"Good God. I was in the car accident with my family?"

"You were in the car accident," he confirmed, with a nod.

As she stared at him, he knew how hard this would be for her right now. He was rewriting her entire history. He didn't even know who she was really, but, as soon as he had come across her in that hospital, he realized that something profound was in her history. He knew at first sight that Kylie had abilities. Then seeing her aunt, he dimly recognized Agatha from a case she had helped the police with. That case had haunted him. He had to search it out to figure out what was going on. Now he had Kylie sitting here in his arms, staring at him in shock, as he told her the truth about her history.

"You can prove all this, right?" she asked.

"I highly suggest we do a DNA test, and that would prove it to you too."

"I would have to," she said, "but I don't know what DNA I'm supposed to compare it to, other than my aunt."

"We have the DNA of your family on file. I also have the adoption records and the name change records."

"Oh, Christ." She stared at Porter. "But the family annihilator wouldn't have known I was here, right? The killer doesn't know anything about me. At least not the adult me, right?"

"I don't know whether he does or not," Porter admitted, giving her a closer look. "To be honest, I'm not sure he does. I think he thought everybody in that vehicle died. I don't know if he realized that the four-year-old little girl was still alive."

She swallowed several times. "Why did he kill my family?"

He hesitated and then sighed. "The evidence that we have points to it being a hit, but we never did find out who would have paid him to do it."

"Good God," she cried out.

"I know. I know." He kept rocking her. "It's a lot to take in."

"A lot," she muttered. "You've just taken my entire childhood and thrown it up in the air and tossed it down into some strange horror movie that doesn't make any sense. Now you're telling me that the family I thought died in an accident was murdered, not only murdered but targeted. Somebody paid this killer to do it, and my aunt was somehow connected with the police hunt to find him."

"Yes."

"And, in the meantime, my aunt, crucified by the media for trying to help on a case she was not in any way equipped to help with, goes underground and what? Why did she change our names? Why did she know that this was something that she needed to do?"

He frowned. "I suspect, and I don't know this for certain, but there may have been some communication after the fact from the killer's holding cell via a woman. I'm thinking maybe an advocate for prisoners that the paid killer got close to. If I could find that woman, I wouldn't be at all surprised if she wasn't asked to take a letter to your aunt, saying that the killer would find her."

She stared at him and whispered, "So, if threatened, Agatha would be terrified, realizing we were both targets, so she decides to change our names and move."

"Yes."

"And somehow he now finds me here in Vegas? I don't believe that."

"I'm sure you don't, and I'm not sure I do either."

"The only thing that could make this even worse was if this killer is psychic too, capable of following me anywhere." When dead silence came from Porter, she stared at him, wide-eyed. "Please tell me that he's not."

"I don't know," he murmured, "but it is something I've always wondered."

"Wondered what?" she asked. "It's not as if he would have been tracking me all these years, or he would have already found me. After all, I've been right here, and it's not as if I've been hidden away. And if you found the name change files, he could have found them as well."

"I'm not sure he cared in any way," he explained, with a sad smile, "until you got involved with the police."

"Oh, God. Just like Agatha. Yet a child's face is not anything like the adult face they grow into, at least not to the layperson."

"I'm not sure it matters here."

"Why?"

"You are the spitting image of your mother."

"I am?" she asked. "I have no pictures of my mother. I have no idea what she looks like."

"You're the spitting image of her. Maybe he saw you in some news coverage and maybe understood that you could be the daughter. Then he would know that he had missed somebody."

"And why would he care?" she asked bitterly.

"Maybe he doesn't. Maybe it's professional pride, or maybe it's because of your aunt, who was instrumental in putting him behind bars. Maybe he's even afraid of her. I just don't know. You're asking questions I don't have answers for."

"Why don't you have answers?" she asked petulantly, and then groaned.

He chuckled. "At least your brain is back to thinking again."

"No, it's overwhelmed. It's confused and completely doesn't like this new reality."

"Of course not, and I get it." Porter gave her a smile. "I really do, and I'm so sorry. I didn't want to be the one telling you all this."

"And how long have you known?"

He shrugged. "In a way, I've suspected for a while, but it wasn't until these last couple months that I really started digging into it."

"Why were you digging into it?"

"Because I wanted to know more about you," he shared.

"Know more about me?" she repeated, glaring at him. "You just wanted me to come on board and do more work for you guys."

He laughed. "That could be it. Once I saw you in that mental hospital, I couldn't forget you."

"You saw me there?" she asked, staring at him. "And you're still talking to me?"

"I was there because of my sister," he reminded Kylie. "So I knew perfectly well that you were fine. I could sense that. I could see it," he shared, as he patted her hand. "I didn't want you to be tortured any further, but it's hard to get the conventional medical community to listen to anybody."

"God, when they get it into their heads that you're sick," she murmured, "they just won't leave it alone."

"And yet you fooled them," he stated, with a knowing smile.

"Did I?" she asked. "It doesn't feel as if I fooled them. It feels as if I'm still running, terrified that somebody will find me again."

"And that's always a concern when you have abilities that can make you seem odd, different, or strange."

She snorted. "Or all of the above. And it's not any easier just because people say you're safe around them," she declared, now glaring at him. "It really doesn't help."

"I know. I'm sorry. I pushed a lot of buttons, and I didn't intend to, but I also knew I had to shake you out of that reverie that you were in, in order to make it a little easier to communicate with you. Your walls are very strong."

"They've had to be," she stated. "Not only did my aunt not show me any love or affection, she also didn't show me any trust, acceptance, or anything along those lines either."

"Did she look over her shoulder all the time? Did she act as if the world would get her at any moment?"

Kylie considered that for a second, then slowly nodded. "She had an almost grim reality to her, that she would do whatever she could. Yet, when any situation made her feel unsettled, she became very cold and snappy, as if no answers were in the world, and it would all go bad very quickly. She was a downer, with almost no joy in her heart."

"I think she probably felt terribly guilty about your family too," he suggested, "because she had abilities and may have tried to say something to your mother."

"I don't know anything about my mother," Kylie noted, staring up at him before shifting off his lap and trying to stand up.

He helped her to her feet and added, "I do have some

information on your mother, but not a whole lot."

"Right. All these years and I never even thought to investigate any more about the accident, or who she was as a person." Kylie frowned at that. "I was more concerned with trying to survive my own reality because, without any sign of love or affection, I didn't have a whole lot of anything to make me want to do more. I know that sounds terrible, but—"

"Don't go there. Don't even think that. You were a child trying to survive."

"Sure, but I'm not a child anymore, and I haven't been a child for a very long time."

"Sure, and then your aunt was against all your abilities, so what did you do?"

"I hid them as long as I could, and then, when they wouldn't hide, I decided to help the police," she explained, rubbing her face. "That didn't go so well."

"No, it didn't," he noted, with a gentle smile, brushing the hair off her face. "So, the media got a hold of you again."

"Yes." She winced. "I really didn't think about it that much and just turned the other cheek and headed back into doing nothing, but my sketching was one avenue, one answer to support myself," she explained. "A way of trying to help and still appease the ability. I don't know how yours are, but mine? If I don't do something with them, it's as if they are forcing me into a weird state, so that I have no choice but to acknowledge them."

"I understand, and that was the same with my sister too. If she didn't use her abilities, she would become almost a zombie, as the abilities took over. You're supposed to control them—"

"But nobody ever shows you how," she interrupted.

"And yet you keep turning Stefan away." Her shoulders hunched at that, and she glared at him. He nodded and smiled. "Sometimes he gets that reaction from people. I've always thought he was easy to get along with." She touched the earring in her ear, turning it. He studied her while she did so. "What does that earring mean to you?"

"I don't know, but I don't take it off, not ever."

He nodded. "And did you put it in there?"

She shook her head. "My aunt did."

"Ah, that's interesting."

"Why?"

"She showed zero affection for you, so I have to wonder why she gave you that."

"I've cherished it in a way because it's the only thing she ever gave me. I also tend to forget about it because it's one of those little pieces of jewelry that's tucked away, and almost nobody ever sees it, including myself. It's easy to forget about, as I just leave it in."

"And it never gets infected?"

"No, never." He just nodded, and she stared at him. "Now you're making me question this too."

He laughed. "No, it's fine. I was just wondering because I've seen you touch it several times."

She shrugged. "Agatha told me it was my mother's, and in a way it's just that little bit of security, that little bit of a connection I've never had before."

"And that makes sense too," he said. He wrapped an arm around her shoulders. "Now …"

"Now what?" she asked. "You've completely bludgeoned me with the hidden truth, and I have absolutely no idea what I'm doing with my world now."

"I'm sorry. I didn't mean to hit you with such shocking

news, but no easy way to tell you."

She stared up at him. "The news was harsh regardless."

"Harsh, yes, but also necessary. Since your aunt didn't tell you, I'm the one left to do the dirty work."

"Maybe," she muttered, as she stared at the room. "Did you expect to tell me here?"

"No, not at all," he said. "I didn't bring you here to do that. I brought you here to see if I could get you to sketch without seeing the crime scene because it seemed to me that you had picked up so much more information from the casino than the actual photographs had. That is rare."

"It's not that I picked up more than the photographs would," she clarified, "but I picked up interpretations that the photographs couldn't."

CHAPTER 8

KYLIE LEFT HER experimental sketch with Porter, insisting that she needed to spend some time alone to absorb the very personal information he had just filled her in on. So he dropped her back home again, retrieving more of her set-aside sketches from the casino murders, as the captain had requested. She did tell Porter that she wanted a copy of her family's file as soon as she could get it. He agreed, but he had to get back to the office to get her latest sketches to the captain today. He also told her that he had two undercover cops assigned to watch over her here. She grimaced, but no way would she decline his help.

Inside now, she couldn't stop herself from locking the doors and the windows, as she turned and stared at her surroundings. She'd always had a fear of living alone, and she knew that came from her aunt. Her aunt locked up every-thing as soon as she got into the house, as if that would keep away the boogeyman. Aunt Agatha should have known that it in no way was effective, and that constant negativity probably attracted more bad energy than it ever repelled.

Forcing herself, Kylie now went and unlocked all her windows and doors, pushing everything wide open in order to change the energy in her home. As she stood here at the double French doors, staring out at her backyard, she looked around and whispered, "What the hell were you thinking,

Agatha? Why would you never tell me?"

But her aunt was still in hiding, of course, still terrified of everything out there. And, if she'd had some communication from Kylie's family's killer, it would make sense that Agatha was worried he'd find her, even now. But Kylie didn't have any of that information, not until now, because her aunt had never divulged any of that, had never warned her about any of that.

Kylie walked back inside and made herself a pot of coffee. With a fresh cup she headed to her computer, where she researched the name she had been born under. It didn't take long to come up with a very gruesome set of articles on the death of her family, just as Porter had told her. The killer had been caught, and it was a murder-for-hire, which detail the killer never divulged. The authorities never did figure out who was behind the murder either, only that the killer was a mercenary, and he admitted he had nothing against the target family personally. It was just a mark for him, and he was well paid.

And that just made Kylie feel even worse. No wonder her aunt had always been terrified. If somebody had cared enough to kill Agatha's sister and her husband and their children, that in itself was enough to set anybody's nerves on edge. Kylie had no memory of her twin brothers because they were literally newborns, on the way home from the hospital when they were killed in a car accident. A bomb had been set under their vehicle and had gone off when they were heading down the interstate. Nobody else was killed but the four of them, as Kylie had been thrown clear of the vehicle at the time.

She sat here, staring at the computer screen, feeling as if her entire world had coalesced into something new, something different. In a way it was as if she herself were new, as if she were different, and she was. The deaths of her family members just didn't make any sense. Her parents weren't rich or famous or hateful or criminal or politicians or drug lords. So who would want to kill them? None of this made any sense to her at all. Kylie felt this overwhelming sense of panic and fear, and she didn't even know how she survived the car bombing. Was it dumb luck or did her being here serve a greater purpose? Sometimes she had wondered if she was here for some greater purpose because her life hadn't been the easiest.

She had never been suicidal, but at times she understood what it had taken for other people to get into that depressive mindset and to not want to live anymore. As she clicked through the online reports on the death of her family, one article shared a photo of Kylie's mother. It could have easily been a current photo of Kylie herself. Even the way her mother stood there revealed a mannerism Kylie caught herself in at many times. Her mother leaned against the doorjamb, one hip hitched up a little bit, her arms crossed over her chest. Although a lot of people might do that, Kylie usually leaned her head against the doorjamb too and stared out at the world.

She zoomed in on her mother's face and stared, seeing the same eyes, the same tilt of her lips. Another picture was of her mother holding the newborns in the hospital, and she was glowing, absolutely glowing.

"Did you realize that, within a couple days of this photo, you would be dead?" Kylie murmured to the image. Upon seeing her mother for the first time, and then a picture of her father in a different news article about the death of Kylie's family, suddenly she felt the tears welling up. Without warning, she fell to the ground, sobbing uncontrollably as grief overwhelmed her. She didn't even notice when the sobbing stopped. She found herself lying on the floor, staring up at the ceiling, as if she were on a completely different universe.

She remained on the floor, turning her head to study the ceiling, wondering why it looked brighter, why the sunlight coming in from the windows shone with a different tint of color. It was as if she had a whole new perspective on her world. Not that it was any better but different. Her old one had been cold and empty, while this one? It didn't seem any better, but maybe it helped her understand her aunt, understand who Agatha really was on the inside and why she was the way she was.

Kylie slowly pulled herself into a sitting position. The cup of coffee she had poured earlier had gone cold. She made her way back into the kitchen, poured another cup of coffee, and slapped together enough ingredients to make somewhat of a sandwich. With that on a plate, she took both outside and sat down on her deck steps, where she slowly munched on her meal. She stared out at the world around her, wondering how everything could be so different and yet maybe not different at all.

"Did it change anything?" she murmured to herself.

Knowing doesn't change anything, silly girl.

Kylie's inner voice was strong, just like her aunt's. "No, maybe not."

From what Kylie now knew, a killer was still out there. Two killers in fact. One had been responsible for the mass shooting spree at the casino. She hadn't heard anything about whether the cops had caught him or not. And then there was the second killer who posed his victims—the young woman in the house today and the senator's daughter among the massive deaths at the casino. Possibly the same murderer who killed her family.

As Kylie sat here, still munching away on her sandwich, she felt watched, as if someone, somewhere, was checking in on her. She looked around, but she had a six-foot-high fence all around, and no face peered over the top, with no knotholes for somebody to peer through either. Nobody was out here. Yet she couldn't shake the feeling. She turned toward her house and bolted inside. She walked firmly and deliberately, wishing to confirm nobody was in her house either. Then slowly—half nervous and half determined to not let this beat her—she checked every corner, every closet. She even looked under the bed, just to confirm that no one was inside and that nothing was out of the ordinary. As it turned out, her house was empty. She found nothing suspicious here and nothing out of place.

When her phone rang, she answered it without checking the number, as she finished searching her house.

"I found you anyway. Nothing you can do." And, with that, the phone call went dead.

She stared down at her cell and checked for the last number dialed, but the ID read Private Number. She didn't even know what that meant or what she could do about it, but she quickly phoned Porter and told him what had just happened.

"Let me see if I can do anything, but chances are the call came from a burner phone."

"Right," she replied, as if she knew what that meant. And theoretically she did, but she didn't know why anybody would do that.

"So, you're saying you felt somebody around your place,

and then he phoned you?"

"Yes."

"You're sure the caller was male?"

"Yes," she reiterated. "For a moment there I wondered if it could have been my aunt, but, no, it was definitely a man."

"Right. I think your aunt has done a hell of a job ducking into the deep dark privacy of her current hiding spot, so, if you're trying to locate her, I wouldn't advise it."

"No, I'm not trying to find Agatha," Kylie replied. "If she wanted anything to do with me, she would contact me. When this is all over, and my family's killer is caught and behind bars—or better yet dead," she snapped, "I could send Agatha a message and tell her that she can relax. However, after all these years, I doubt if she's even capable of true relaxation."

"It would be good if she would, but you're right. I'm not sure she could recondition her response after so many years."

"I doubt she wants anything to do with me anyway. I think she thought trouble would always follow me."

He laughed. "You do tend to have that ability, don't you?"

"Maybe," she muttered, "but not on purpose."

"No, not on purpose," he agreed. "The captain wants to see you, by the way."

"That's nice, but I'm not sure I'm ready to see the captain."

Porter laughed. "It isn't a bad thing. At least he knows a little more about you."

"How is that a good thing? And what does the rest of the department think of this stuff?"

"They know about me, somewhat. My partner has always kept me on the straight and narrow, not letting any of this woo-woo stuff get to me."

"Meaning?"

"Meaning, Neil likes to joke about my unusual methods, but, when it comes down to it, he generally accepts what I have to say. So, we can move on and don't waste time discussing psychics and their methods."

"That would help," Kylie muttered.

"Besides, we still gather all the evidence as usual. We still follow the law, so nobody will take the stand and believe anything I have to say just because I say it."

"Right, I guess police procedure hasn't changed at all either, has it?"

"No, it sure hasn't. … You sound a little rough."

"*Ya* think? First I had a complete meltdown on my office floor, after finding articles and pictures online about my family. Then I made a sandwich. I was sitting outside on my deck steps, eating, when I had that horrible sensation of being watched."

"I have those two undercovers in your area. I'll see if they noted anything. And I was about to come to your place anyway," he shared. "So I'll pick you up and bring you back here to the station. Then we'll talk to the captain. He just wants to discuss the sketch you created while blindfolded, and we'll go from there."

"Sure, but I'll grab a quick shower first."

"Good idea," he murmured. "At least that should make you feel better."

"Says you," she muttered, as she disconnected. Time was short, so she didn't waste it, and headed up to grab a shower. She couldn't quite relax. Even as she was scrubbing down, she had one ear tuned for any unwelcome visitors. The trouble was, she didn't know whether they would be on a physical level or something else completely.

How had the killer known that Kylie was turning around in her backyard, looking to see if somebody was watching her? How could he possibly have had that information, unless … he was nearby, checking in on her?

PORTER HAD SPOKEN to his two guys on watch in her neighborhood. They saw nothing. With a shake of his head, he drove up to her place and watched as she stepped outside. She looked better. Her hair was braided in a ponytail, still damp, but it bounced as she raced toward him. When she got in his vehicle, he looked at her curiously. "That's more enthusiasm than I thought I would get."

She shrugged. "Can't toss that feeling of unease now."

He nodded, as he contemplated her house.

"Go, go, go," she muttered. "It's not that bad."

He laughed as he put the car in gear and drove back out onto the street. "Says you. I don't want you so afraid that you can't sleep in your own house."

"Too late for that now," she replied, giving him a wry expression. "Considering all the murders that have gone on recently, and the fact that I really felt a presence, followed by that phone call making it all very real, … I'm certain that he knows where I live."

"That is a concerning thought," he murmured.

"Yeah, it definitely is. And I get it. For you guys this is just more normal stuff," she noted, "but it's not quite so normal in my world."

"Not for us either … in this case." He drove through traffic, giving her a chance to settle her nerves a bit.

"Do you think the captain is upset?"

"I don't think so. Just curious and wanting to know more, hoping you have more."

She winced. "That's the problem with giving anything. As soon as you do, everybody wants more."

He had to agree with her. It was a casualty of the work that he did. "And yet we can't blame them. If we were the ones looking for answers, you know very well we would want more."

"Of course we would, but it would be up to us to get our answers. It wouldn't be up to us to get answers for everybody else, and that's where the challenge comes in."

"Have you been asked to get answers often?"

"Enough that I backed away after things didn't go so well."

"Like your aunt, *huh*?"

"Not that bad. I was in a test group with a disbelieving group of people doing a whole pile of tests. Someone decided to take the opportunity to shoot somebody within that group, thinking it would be a great time to prove to every-body that psychics weren't real. I did see something happening, and I did warn them, but they laughed it off—until the shooting started," she explained. "At that point, I went underground. They tried to contact me afterward, but I wouldn't have anything to do with them, and eventually they left me alone. That was after people got angry at me for not having done more."

"What more were you supposed to do?" he asked.

"You know what people are like. You always have to do more. It doesn't matter what you've already done. It's never enough. Everybody wants more."

"You've really been through it, haven't you?"

She shrugged. "For some that would be nothing. I just

didn't want to get any further involved, knowing that was how people would react."

"Of course, but that doesn't mean that all people are the same."

"No, they're not all the same, but the one thing they universally want is *more*."

He could hardly argue with that because he'd seen the same thing in his own world, and their captain was a prime example.

"Yes, he is," she muttered in acknowledgment.

Porter froze for a moment and then replied gingerly, "I didn't say anything."

"Yes, you did. You said, *The captain was a prime example*," she stated crossly.

He glanced at her and clarified, "Actually I didn't say it. I thought it."

She looked over at him, then shook her head. "Bullshit, I heard you clear as day."

"I know, and I'm questioning that now too."

"Of course you are," she muttered, adding an eye roll. "Christ, it feels as if I need to move again."

"Move again?"

"Yes, every time something goes wrong in this world, I end up moving," she muttered. "It just seems to be the safest way to deal with this shit."

"I don't know about the safest way, but it's one way."

"I won't sit here and listen to your criticism. I don't know how well you've done keeping all your abilities under wraps, but you've had a support system. At least the captain believes you enough that your teammates don't laugh at you."

"No, they don't laugh at me, but plenty of times they

look at me sideways, wondering just what I'm doing, saying, or believing. Another level of awareness happens."

She didn't say anything to that, but nodded.

As they drove up to the station and parked at the back, Porter added, "I didn't say that out loud—about the captain, I mean."

She looked over at him and shrugged. "You must have because I sure as hell can't read minds."

He avoided any further argument on this topic and asked, "Do you always carry that pencil with you?"

She clenched her fingers around it. "Yes."

"Any other things that you always have with you?"

"No, why?"

"I'm just wondering," he said, keeping his tone neutral as he watched her.

"Stop staring at me," she snapped irritably. "It makes me nervous."

He gave her half a smile. "It's all good."

"Yeah? Says who?"

As she walked into the captain's office, the captain stared at the two of them and said, "Finally." When she glared at him, he lifted a hand. "Okay, so maybe that's not the best way to greet you."

"Whatever," she muttered, as she threw herself down into a chair.

The captain studied her and asked, "Not a good day, *huh*?"

"Some truths were given, some enlightenment that I didn't ask for," she stated, with a hard glance at Porter. "I'm still dealing."

"Ah, yes, he told me about those."

"He told you about it before divulging all this though,"

she pointed out, "so you knew this time was coming. I didn't. So, for me, it came out of the blue, and I can't say I'm terribly impressed at having heard it at all."

"Would you rather have been kept in the dark?" Porter asked.

She thought about that for a long moment and then shrugged. "No, I just wish my aunt would have done something about it earlier."

"We do too," Porter replied, "but, for whatever reason, she felt she couldn't do that."

"I don't know what she was thinking," Kylie muttered.

"Or she wasn't thinking at all and was simply reacting, hoping that it would end up better than it was."

"Maybe. I don't know." Then Kylie turned to the captain. "What did you want to see me about?"

The captain lifted the sketch on his desk. "This."

"Oh, that." She stared at it glumly. "Yeah, I wish I could take that back too."

"You can't," the captain declared, "and I gather that you really aren't too interested in doing this work, but right now we obviously have a problem, and we're hoping you can help."

"Yes, but your hope means finding answers, and then you get angry when I don't," she said. "So I'm not sure that this is a good deal for anybody."

"You know who it's especially not a good deal for?" the captain asked, staring at her.

She shook her head. "What do you mean?"

"The next woman who's already in trouble right now, ... his next victim. We lost one this morning. We really don't want to keep losing them."

It was on the tip of her tongue to say, *Do a better job,*

when she realized that would just come across with all the hurt and anger that she felt inside. The captain wasn't the target. Her aunt was, at least in some ways, but maybe not. It was a confusing thing to even contemplate right now. "What exactly do you want from me?" she asked.

"Anything you can give us."

"I gave you that sketch, and I'm not sure what else there is. … Oh." She frowned, as something clicked. "Apparently there is something else." She picked up her pencil, reached for her sketch pad, and started scribbling.

The captain looked at her and then Porter. The captain opened his mouth, but Porter held up a hand.

"Good idea," she muttered. "Keep quiet until I'm done." And, with that, everybody settled into their respective positions and waited. When she finally released a heavy sigh, she said, "I guess I missed that in the first round."

"Something has definitely changed," Porter noted. "So, if you missed something, that's understandable."

"Is it?" she asked. "I don't understand any of this, so whatever." She resumed her sketching.

"What happens if I were to give you a different pencil?" Porter asked.

"I would use it, but I wouldn't be happy about it," she replied. "Why do you ask?"

"I just wondered if it has any talisman-type meaning to you."

She laughed. "If you mean, would it make my drawings any better or any worse, or would it not be psychically charged? I doubt it," she stated. "I have been using it all this time, and it certainly packs a punch, but I wouldn't say it was that special."

Porter just nodded and didn't say anything.

When she was done, she rubbed her face. "There. I don't know that it makes a damn bit of difference though." She handed her latest drawing to the captain.

He snatched the sketch and turned it around.

Porter walked behind him to stare at Kylie's newest artwork. "Look at that. You've drawn a person this time."

"Sure, you mean a person other than the victim?"

"Yes."

She shrugged. "But it won't be clear, and it won't be enough to help."

"How do you know?" Porter asked curiously, as he still stared at it. "You've certainly added some details about … I presume the killer?"

"I don't know whether it's the killer or not," she replied. "I didn't look."

The captain frowned at her. "Well then, look now, for heaven's sake."

She frowned at him, then got up, walked around, and stared at what she had drawn. She tried to hide her shock, but Porter wasn't letting her hide anything.

"See?" he asked. "Something has changed."

"Yeah, well, I don't know what's changed," she declared. "I don't know why it's changed either. So, if you were planning on asking me, don't bother."

"I wouldn't ask you about that at all," he said, his gaze warming. "I was interested to know if you had seen the change you made here, compared to your earlier drawing."

"No, … I haven't. I don't understand it either," she murmured. And she didn't. It was weird. She didn't quite understand the impetus to draw a second sketch of an earlier crime scene, but she saw more clarity, more details, and now a male figure stood beside the dead woman. "I don't understand what he's doing," Kylie added.

"Neither do I, yet," Porter agreed, as he looked at it, "but is he standing beside his victim because he just shot her, or does he have another purpose?"

"It's not sexual," she stated.

"That's a damn good thing," the captain muttered. "Nothing good about that."

"Nothing good about any of this," she added, looking at him. "It's all just plain bad."

"I get it, and, for you, this is particularly troubling."

"Yes, it is, and, as you already know, I don't like dealing with this. … I don't like any of it."

"Because it's criminal in nature, or just because it's violent?"

"It's because of all the shit that people do to each other," she explained, staring at him. "Who the hell wants to embroil themselves in that crap?"

"And what if you solved something and came to some finish line?"

"It hasn't happened yet," she noted. "And according to all the people I was working with in a study group, it can't because I don't have enough abilities, the right abilities, or something."

"Sounds to me as if you've been listening to a lot of garbage over the years," the captain shared.

"It's not as if I had any trustworthy people to listen to," she said, staring at him.

"What about Stefan?" the captain asked. "Or did you not know of him back them? So when you were involved in that study, did they say anything at all about your gifts?"

"Just that I didn't pass and didn't do anything correctly. *Nice try, but you don't have any abilities.* I knew I had abilities, but I'd been trying to hide them, having been cornered into doing this study in the first place. I was young and stupid and felt as if I had to prove myself. So I opened up and told them about the shooting that would happen. Then they all laughed at me and muttered, *Right.* Within five minutes the shooting started," she shared.

Porter watched her beating herself up about it. "So, you got scared then, *huh?*"

"Not the words I would use. Ever since that happened, I just shut down. People don't want to know or to hear what I have to say."

"I do," the captain declared. "I want to hear all of it." She stared at him and frowned, but he nodded. "I get it. I see the dislike of what I'm saying in your gaze, and I can even understand it. But that doesn't change the fact that I do want to know everything that you hear and see when it comes to this mess."

She shook her head. "You don't understand what that entails. It's more than just whatever I hear and see. It's a lot more."

"So, tell me," the captain prodded. "You saw this latest woman's death earlier this morning. Drew your first sketch on it. Then your mind came back to that same scene—while sitting here in my office—and you added a living character to it."

"Yes."

"How come?"

"I don't know," she fired back. The questions continued until she finally raised her hands and announced, "I'm not kidding. I don't know. I don't know why I came back and added it."

"Because we were saying there should be more or because you felt cornered? What?" Porter asked.

"I felt cornered," she confirmed, with a hard look in Porter's direction. "You'll just end up trying to corner me again and again and again, just to get more answers."

"No," Porter argued. "We're not. However, if you get more answers, if you have anything else to say or to offer, we would very much like to hear it." Her jaw worked, as she stared at him, and he continued. "It's really like pulling teeth with you."

She shrugged. "Yeah, I imagine it is."

He smiled. "And yet I suspect you aren't all that hard to work with."

"What do you know?" she asked, with a half laugh. "Stefan's been asking me to work with him for a very long time, and I keep saying no."

"Any particular reason why?"

"Yeah, I don't like being made fun of, for one. I don't like people making me into something I'm not or thinking that I have abilities that I don't. I mean, this latest sketch came out, but who's to say it is of any value to anybody?"

"And who's to say it's not?" Porter countered. "I get that you feel insecure and stressed, but you now have somebody on your case, somebody who contacted you and told you that he saw you, that he knows you're there. Doesn't that worry you?"

"Yes, it worries me, but I highly doubt it worries you," she noted, staring at him. "This is the problem. Somebody found out where I am. He doesn't know what I can do and is worried that I might do something."

"Tell us again what happened," the captain said.

She groaned and then filled him in on it. When he frowned immediately, she shrugged. "It felt as if I was being watched, but I didn't see anything. Porter's two guards didn't see anything. Nobody was at my house. So, it's fine."

"No, it's not fine," Porter stated. "Good God, you're being amazingly difficult." She glared at him, and he laughed. "If I could say anything guaranteed to piss you off, I think I just did it."

Her shoulders sagged, and she shrugged. "Maybe. I'm not used to dealing with people on this issue."

"You should be," Porter stated. "You're very gifted."

She shook her head. "You don't know that the person I added to this sketch has anything to do with the latest murder. For all you know, I just added it to piss off you guys or to send you off in a million directions."

The captain snapped at her, "Did you?"

"No, of course not," she snapped right back. "But you don't know that, and you have no proof of that, so nobody will believe this."

"Ah, I understand now, I think," the captain began. "So, as long as we can keep you safe from all that craziness in the world out there, plus keep you safe from the judgment of people likely to say you're a fake and a fraud, you might be interested in working with us?"

She frowned at him. "How the hell did you even get to that point because I didn't say that at all."

The captain laughed. "And yet I also know that you really love to draw."

She looked at the sketches still on his desk. "I don't know if I love these crime-scene sketches. I don't know that anybody can love them, but I feel as if I'm doing something here. I don't know exactly what that is."

"Something honest at least?" Porter asked.

Kylie shrugged.

The captain nodded. "So, maybe just give it a try and do a bit more and see where you go. If nothing else, your crime-scene sketches are absolutely top-shelf, but these additional two? These are incredible."

"Maybe," she murmured, "but they aren't easy on me."

"Do you feel a physical effect?" Porter asked.

"No, I wouldn't say that," she clarified. "It just, it just feels different. It feels as if I'm doing something I'm supposed to be doing."

"I agree because I think that is exactly what you're supposed to be doing," Porter shared. "You have a very unique gift, and I think you're picking up a hell of a lot more than you even realize."

"So what? Now you'll tell me that this latest sketch with another person in this one resembles the killer who's been on the run for years."

"It absolutely does resemble him," the captain admitted. "You captured the essence of who he is with just a few strokes, and I'm stunned because I don't know that even a camera would do that."

"It would," she replied, "but it would be different."

"Exactly, and this difference here shows me there is so much value in what you do."

She stared at the captain, wondering if she could believe him, but sincerity filled his tone, and something inside her started to settle. "Maybe," she muttered. "I don't know."

"You haven't been very happy with this gift of yours," the captain noted, with a gentle gaze. "I get that. I understand what you feel, particularly when you've been laughed at and mocked, and things didn't turn out well. Whether that's a lack of training or a lack of confidence, I don't know, but you might want to consider opening up a little bit more when these things happen, and seeing if you can get more."

"Because you want more," she stated, with a mocking glance at Porter.

"Not just me," the captain admitted. "I think everybody wants more, and I understand your viewpoint because Porter has argued with us many times over about the same thing. The fact that he can't just give us more all the time. Apparently something about that whole *more* thing drives people like you nuts."

She laughed. "I'm not even sure what *people like us* means," she said, hanging her head. "But, yes, this constant need for more, the constant pressure, that constant sensation of not being able to do enough, to help enough, to see enough makes my job harder. Yeah, it's incredibly difficult," she murmured.

"Why don't you agree to give us what you can, and we'll agree to work with that?"

She stared at him in surprise. "I highly doubt that anybody you work with will be content with that."

He smiled. "You let me worry about that. While you're here over the next while, you'll work closely with Porter and see if you guys can pick up things and find out where this asshole is and what he's doing in town."

"You mean, outside of killing people?" she asked, frowning.

"Do you think he's killing somebody? Is he here to specifically target somebody?"

"I think so, but I don't know who," she said. "For all I know, it's me, and I'm just not aware of it."

"What would it take for you to be aware of that?"

She stared at him, then shrugged. "I really don't know. I've never been a target before."

He nodded. "That's good to know."

"No, it's not good to know," she declared in a mocking tone. "It's one of those things sadder than hell to know, but it's never good to know."

JUST AS PORTER and Kylie walked out of the captain's office, Porter's phone buzzed. He checked his screen to see a text from his partner. Porter looked over at the captain. "I need to go talk to Neil."

He nodded. "Okay, then send him in here. I'll have him do something else while you're working with—" He nodded toward Kylie.

"I do have a name," she stated crossly.

The captain smiled. "And it's a beautiful name too. Just remember that Porter and I are open to working with you."

Porter nudged her out of the captain's office.

"And here I thought you told me how Neil was fine," she noted.

Porter shrugged. "I did. I do, but apparently the captain has a different take on that."

"And that's because Neil must have said something to the captain," Kylie suggested.

"Maybe, but I'm not going there right now."

"Easy for you to say," she muttered.

He laughed. "Come on. Let's go get you some food."

"I'm not hungry," she grumbled.

"Yes, you are. You're hungry and cranky and miserable. I can see past that whole facade you are scrounging up."

"Gee, thanks for that great image."

He shrugged. "Hey, I call it as I see it. Better get used to it."

"*Great*," she muttered. "Do you ever *not* do that?"

"Not often," he replied. "It's too difficult not to, especially in these situations. We have to protect ourselves the best we can."

"And are we literally protecting ourselves in this situation? Because, if we are, who are we protecting ourselves from?"

He frowned at her. "That is one of the questions the captain is worried about. If this escaped killer is now taunting you, then we must figure out what he wants."

"I don't know what he wants, unless it's my aunt, but I would never tell him anything." Porter didn't respond. "What?" she asked. "You don't believe me?"

"In ugly situations, people will say anything to get the pain to stop, and that includes handing over your aunt," he stated, with a shrug, "and nobody would blame you."

"She would," Kylie declared, staring at him. "She did raise me. She did give me a place to live, and I am a successful adult because of her."

He nodded. "I hear you. I'm just saying that, when and if this guy ever finds you, we want to confirm he doesn't have a chance to put that loyalty to the test."

Kylie's heart sank as she realized what he was talking about. "There is absolutely no reason for him to come after me. I have no idea where my aunt is. It makes no sense."

"Just like he had no reason to come after your family?" When he stared at her, shivers ran down her spine. "Nothing makes sense with this guy," he murmured. "That is something else to understand. I'm not trying to scare you or to send you into hiding, but the bottom line is that he's doing this for a reason. We just don't know why."

She slowly nodded. "It could even be somebody other

than him."

"Why would that be?"

"I don't know," she snapped. "I'm just looking for any answers that make sense."

"And does that make sense to you?"

"No, of course it doesn't," she replied, raising both hands in frustration. "However, neither does your theory that he wants something to do with me."

"I'm not the one who called you," Porter reminded her. "Your stalker did."

"And what are the chances it was somebody else making that phone call?" She waved at Porter's partner ahead of them. "Maybe Neil did it. Maybe he's jealous of the time you're spending with me," she snapped. "Maybe it's just as simple as that."

"That would be easy enough to find out," Porter stated. "I could grab his phone and check."

"Don't do it for my sake," she protested. "I'm just throwing out ideas."

"These ideas all have consequences."

"I know that." She glared at him. "I don't know what you want me to say."

"Nothing. How about nothing?" Then he walked up to his partner.

Neil stared at her and noted, "Wow, you guys are really an item now, aren't you?"

"No," she muttered, fatigue in her voice. "Apparently he wants more sketches."

Her tone was filled with such disgust that Neil had to laugh. "Well, it is what you do, right?" he said cheerfully.

She nodded. "It is. Whether I'll continue to sketch, I don't know." He frowned at her, and she just waved her hand. "Don't mind me. I'm just really tired. It's been an emotionally rough few days."

"God, that's for sure." Neil gave a headshake, looking over at his partner. "I was just checking in to see where you guys were and what you were up to."

"The captain sent us over to the latest crime scene," Porter shared, as he took a seat, motioning at the spare beside him for her. "He wanted Kylie to do some sketches."

Neil sat down. "Who knew we had budget money for this stuff?"

"Right, that's what I told them," she agreed, with feeling.

He grinned. "And here I thought you would be all over it."

"Not after that casino mess."

"Ah," he replied, with understanding. "I can see that too. That was a rough one for all of us."

"It was sure as hell rough on me," she stated, as she looked at him. "It's not my normal life."

"No, of course not," Neil replied, "though it's not normal for any of us, for that matter. Seeing somebody with such disregard for life playing it out in such a big way is rough." Looking over at Porter, he added, "They did find the mass shooter."

"Oh, good." Porter seemed surprised.

Neil nodded. "Outside of mopping it up, it's basically over with anyway. He offed himself. They found him in the back of his mother's place, inside the shed. He'd blown his head off."

"Good for that," Porter stated, with feeling. "Not that I want to seem unfeeling or anything, but wow."

"No, be unfeeling," Neil agreed. "We all feel the same

way. A whole lot less court-case drama with something like this. And it'll probably come down to somebody who was mentally ill, needing help, and couldn't get it. I know that's no excuse, but it's hard enough on all of us. Still, if he killed himself, that's just one less case we have to try and deal with."

"And yet we still have so much evidence to gather and so much work to do on the casino murders," Porter added, "that, in a way, his suicide is even more work."

"But with an end this time," Neil reminded him. "That's the thing to hang on to. An end this time because we already have him identified, and we know to some degree what happened."

"Do we have the full story?" Porter asked Neil.

"Apparently his girlfriend has come forward. He was struggling with depression, delusions, and his medications. He'd gone to the doctors multiple times, and they'd changed it up, antidepressants, antipsychotics, and whatnots. He got very, very depressed, and his mother was very ill. As the story goes, he didn't want her to suffer."

"Oh, man, so, he killed her?"

"He killed her and then apparently that somehow morphed into him killing a whole lot of other people because he was angry. Angry at the system, angry at the people who were making money. Simply angry at anything and anyone who seemed remotely happy."

"Ah, so that's where the casino comes in."

"People who were spending money without helping others—like him, his mother. He just got angry at the world at large," Neil explained. "He went crazy and decided that all of them were better off dead, including himself."

"Good God." Kylie stared at Neil in shock. "I understand how he could get so upset, comparing their abundance with his lack. Yet it's still sad to think that his way of dealing with the disparity and his envy and jealousy and his suicidal ideation was for him to brutally take everybody else with him, under the guise of it's being better for them. Yet that was never the shooter's choice. Those people were never given a choice."

"Exactly," Neil replied. "In the shooter's mind he may or may not have been able to give them that choice. The girlfriend mentioned he'd gotten stranger and stranger and a little more fanatical every day. She was contemplating breaking up with him but wasn't sure what would happen if she did."

"Are you sure she didn't?" she asked Neil. "That would be another trigger that would send him flying."

"And maybe she did and hasn't told us the truth yet. I don't know," Neil conceded. "But, if the shooter was as unstable as she's saying, it would explain some of what he did. Anyway the end result is that he's in the morgue downstairs, and we've got two other teams on it."

"Not you?" she asked him.

"No, because technically"—he motioned at Porter— "this guy is my partner, and we were assigned to the other case, the one from the more recent shooting, for the woman who apparently you went to see."

"I didn't go see the woman," she corrected. "I went to see the crime scene."

"What did you think of it?"

"It was disgusting," she stated. "What else it could be? That's what crime scenes are. They're impactful. They're snippets of moments in time when somebody's rage or hurt or anger or greed overtook them, and they changed other people's lives forever," she described. "It's terrible. All of it is terrible."

Neil nodded. "I can agree with that." He looked over at Porter. "Will you catch me up on things?"

"Yeah, I will." He gave a nod at Kylie. "I need to take her back home."

"No, I'm not going home."

He frowned, then shrugged. "Maybe that's best." Turning back to Neil, Porter added, "The captain asked me to send you in next, so maybe go deal with him first, and then we'll catch up in a little bit."

Without any argument, Neil hopped up and walked toward the captain's office.

Kylie whispered to Porter, "Will Neil really be moved out of this case that easily?"

"No, he won't, and, if the captain is smart, he won't hint at him being out. I think he'll just attach him to someone else temporarily, the same way the captain's attached you to me."

"*Great.*" She rolled her eyes. "The last thing I want to do is make another enemy in here."

"Another enemy?" Porter asked.

"Yeah." She nodded. "A couple people here don't really like who I am or what I represent or something," She sighed, followed by a shrug. "It's not as if I understand why."

He looked at her quizzically. "I hadn't been aware of any animosity toward you."

"I'm new enough that I don't know that anybody has really noticed any of it either," she added, "but I presume some people were let go in the latest layoffs, and yet somehow I've just been brought on."

"Ah." Porter nodded. "That's very true. I'll give you

that. And it is something that could have caused some confusion, and we aren't ..."

"Of course you're not sure if you're keeping me," Kylie stated in a mocking tone, "and some people here would totally agree with that decision."

He frowned at her. "You seem eager to get out of here. In some ways, I would think you don't want to be here."

"In some ways, yes," she muttered. "In other ways, maybe not. However, now that I'm involved in this case, and I have this asshole contacting me, I would just as soon get it resolved so I can move on."

"And what would that look like?"

"I don't know," she snapped. "I really don't know."

"How many times have you moved in the last few years?" She just glared at him and didn't answer. "Quite a few I imagine."

"Doesn't matter. If I have to, I do. I've gotten used to it."

"Then what? You move from town to town, road to road, like your aunt?"

She stared at him. "That's hardly fair. My aunt is surviving the best way she knows how. So, whether you or I approve of her method or not, it's kept her alive."

"I won't argue with that," he conceded, "and I mean no insult, but I would hate to see your life become as lonely and as hard as Agatha's has been."

Kylie shrugged. "It doesn't really matter what you want though, does it?" she stated, with an attempt at mockery, failing badly.

"No, not at the moment, it doesn't." And, with that, he added, "I need to go down to the morgue and get the scoop on the autopsy. I want you to come with me."

"Why?" she asked, her heart sinking. "You know that morgues are terrible places for me."

"Oh, I didn't know that, but I guess if I'd thought about it long enough, I would have. … That's not necessarily an issue."

"It is for me," she declared, staring at him. "That's just not something I want to deal with if I don't have to."

"Have you tried to go inside one lately?"

"Not sure I've tried to go into any of them. I have a reason for that too, remember? I shouldn't have to explain that part of it."

"I don't understand that," he admitted, looking at her. "Are you telling me that you're a sensitive as well?"

"I don't know what I am." She frowned at him. "I draw pictures. And sometimes those pictures are pretty, and sometimes they aren't."

"Ah, so you don't know what would happen when you go to the morgue. You're assuming it would be bad."

"Yes, I'm assuming it would be bad," she stated, with an eye roll, "as you should be assuming the same thing yourself."

He shrugged. "I am not very good at assumptions. Let's go find out for sure. At least with me, you're in a safe environment. So, if you pass out or something, I've got your back."

She stared at him as he half dragged her toward the elevator. "You really think I want to go into a morgue?"

"You work in a police department," he noted, casting her a casual glance. "It would be aligned with your job."

"And yet I feel as if something more is behind your actions."

"Yeah, but you always think something more is behind

my actions," he replied, with a gentle smile. "You must be great fun at parties."

"I don't do parties," she snapped, glaring at him.

"No, I don't imagine you do." He sighed. "You missed out on a whole lot of life."

"I didn't miss out on anything," she stated, glaring at him. "Most of what I didn't do was by choice."

"Or by fear because that's what your aunt drilled into you."

"Sure, but look at what my life is like," she pointed out, "so, to a certain extent, fear makes sense."

"Fear, yes, caution, yes, but overly fanatical about it? No, that's not a way for anyone to live."

"I'm hardly fanatical," she argued. "You can't say that."

"Whatever," he muttered, as he opened the door. "Just remember the coroner doesn't know anything about you. If you want your sketchbook …" She held up a small one. "Oh, good. I would've suggested you grab one, but I wasn't sure if you wanted to or not."

"I keep one on me always."

"You want to tell me why?"

"No."

He studied her and asked, "A story is in that too then, isn't there?"

She sighed. "You're very irritating."

"Yes, I understand I can be. Yet I'm also a good person to have in your corner."

"Are you though?" she asked, scrunching up her nose. "Right now, it doesn't feel like it."

He led the way to the morgue, and, as they got closer, she felt her insides shivering. "How come you're not affected by this?" she asked.

"You mean, because I'm psychic? Because I talk to the dead sometimes?" he asked. "As I told you, if I can help them cross over, … I do. Although that's not necessarily the easiest of jobs, it is rewarding when I can help them though."

"Do they not know what they're doing?"

"Sometimes. Sometimes they think they know, but they're too scared to move. Sometimes they don't want to leave loved ones who are still in this world."

"Which makes sense," she acknowledged.

"It does, and yet nothing more is for them here, so they need to move on," he explained. "So, that's definitely one of those things to be dealt with, and the sooner they face it, the better off they are."

"Maybe," she muttered. As they got closer to the morgue, she whispered, "I really don't like this."

"It will be fine," he replied.

"And if it isn't fine?"

He stopped to face her. "Then maybe you should know exactly what you can do down here."

"What do you mean, what I can do? I can do nothing down here. I'm pretty sure you understand the same as I do that these people are dead and gone."

He smiled and nodded. "Absolutely they are, but I always find one or two who want to hang around and party." Maybe it was perverse of him to tease her, but she'd led a completely locked-down life in so many ways that she was afraid of all aspects of her gift—to the extent of not realizing what her gift even was or what she could do. Yet he suspected she could do a whole lot more than she currently was. She just didn't know it. She didn't even know it was an option, and that part just blew him away. He had seen a little bit of her gift, every once in a while. Not everybody had a supportive environment growing up, and, in her case, it had been the exact opposite.

She'd hidden her abilities, and then, when she'd finally gotten free from her aunt, Kylie had gone a little bit crazy trying to utilize them, but she was out of control and hadn't learned any better. It didn't help when things backfired, and she'd gone back into hiding. Porter understood that, but hiding for a little while was one thing. Yet hiding for a long time was a completely different story. As far as he was concerned, she needed to get out and live a little. She might not agree with him, particularly after this session in the morgue, but he could only hope that she would be good with it in the end.

And, with that, he pushed open the door and nudged her inside.

CHAPTER 9

As Kylie walked into the morgue, she looked around nervously, hoping a line of bodies wouldn't be in her view. Since she'd had no exposure, she didn't know what it would be like.

"They aren't just lying around," Porter shared, trying to lighten the thick tension bubbling around her.

She hoped so, only to stiffen as she caught sight of the coroner, standing over a body and talking into a recorder.

The doctor heard them enter and shut off his recorder. "There you are."

"Hey, Doc. How are you doing?"

"I'm fine." He looked over at Kylie. "I don't believe I know you."

"I'm Kylie, one of the sketch artists," she said.

He smiled, then nodded. "Welcome. This is my studio."

She smiled, as if understanding what he meant, and, with that, she seemed to relax a little bit.

"So, what do you want to know?" the coroner asked Porter. "I mean, outside of the fact that I'm completely drenched in bodies, and I could use a whole lot more time than you've given me."

"I understand, but I did wonder if you had come to the one woman who had been posed at the casino."

"Ah, now she's an interesting one," the coroner noted.

"Unfortunately, given her identity, I'm sure she'll get a lot more attention than the others."

"Maybe," Porter conceded, "but it won't be because of her identity but because of the abnormality in her killing versus the others."

"Right," the doc replied. "So let me begin. She's healthy, outside of the fact that she's got some bullet wounds. She was posed, then shot in the ankles and hands, which is already an oddity compared to everybody else in the casino, who were just randomly shot. Apparently she deserved extra bullets in that way." He shook his head. "You just really never understand the mindset of these killers."

"And is that what her killer was up to, getting supposed justice," Kylie asked, "or was somebody else pulling his chain?"

He turned to her. "I'm not sure what you mean there."

Porter explained, "She's just wondering, as am I, if we have a completely different killer in this casino case. The MO with the senator's daughter was very, very different than all the others who were killed, and that's a concern."

"That did cross my mind. I don't have any proof that you have a different killer, but I do have proof that she was killed by a completely different method. If that's what you're asking for, then yes. I've got something there." He went through the list of injuries she had sustained from the bullets.

"While she had been shot, her cause of death was a stabbing to her back, right between the ribs, high up and right into the heart," he stated, indicating a wound on the body. "She would have died instantly, so the bullets were a surprise. I'm waiting on ballistics to see if it's the same bullets, the same gun that shot her and the others in the casino."

"That would be interesting too," she murmured.

"Wouldn't it though?" he asked, nodding at her with approval. "Either way, something was very specific about her shooting versus anybody else's. Do you want to tell me what's going on?"

At that, Porter hesitated and then replied, "Somebody of interest was seen at that crime scene before the shooting started or around the same time of the shooting. We don't really have a timeline as of yet, and the question is whether he may have had something to do with the senator's daughter's death."

"So, who is he, and why do we care?" the coroner asked.

"Keefe Hogan."

As soon as Porter mentioned the shooter's name, the coroner's eyes lit up. "Good God, seriously?"

He nodded. "Yes, seriously."

"It's been a long time."

"I know, a very long time." He hesitated, then looked back at Kylie and added, "We do have some reason to believe he might have been at the casino."

"Oh, if he was, then all bets are off on the senator's daughter's death. The others were shot, some randomly, some by accident," he noted, as he motioned to a child off to one side, the coroner's face creasing with sorrow. "Then some just appeared to be helter-skelter, as if he shot wildly."

"Which is what we suspect the casino shooter did anyway," Porter stated. "He's been ID'd as John Smith, a local. His real name too."

"And then we come back around to the one woman who appeared to have deliberate shots fired in a completely different way, depicting a crucifixion."

"Yes," Porter agreed. "Of course the staging also indicates that either we had the mass shooter trying to cover up this one woman's murder among the series of murders, or we have a second murderer there."

"I vote for a second murderer there," Kylie noted.

"I do too, but that's for you guys to prove," the coroner replied, with a smile in her direction. "I'll send you a report as soon as I have it done. However, remember that I've got a crap load of victims here, and I won't get it written up anytime soon."

"Still, can you put a rush on it?" Porter asked.

"No, not really. I know she's a senator's daughter, and I know you'll pull as much rank as you can, and you want as much information as you can get," he explained, "but I still have a lot of bodies to work with."

"Yes, but she was killed in another manner," Kylie pointed out, "so she takes priority because her killer is still out there, and that we cannot have."

The coroner frowned at her and then shrugged. "I'll see what I can do, but no promises."

And hearing the same words that she had echoed not so long ago, she nodded. "That's all any of us can do." She looked over at Porter and asked, "Anything else or are you good now?"

He laughed. "I'm good." He looked over at the coroner. "Stay in touch, Doc."

"You too." As they were about to leave, the coroner called out, "She can come back anytime."

And, with that, the doors closed behind them. She looked over at Porter. "I'm sorry. Did I jump in where I wasn't supposed to be?"

"No," he replied easily, "you did exactly what you were

supposed to do."

"And what was that?" she asked in a mocking tone.

"Be yourself. Just be yourself. That's always the best an-swer to anything."

"It's also damn hard sometimes," she muttered. "This isn't my world, and I'm still very uncomfortable in it."

"Of course," he agreed, "but I think you're wrong in saying it's not your world. I think it's more your world than you realize." He gave her a warm smile. "It'll just take you a little bit of time to find a place to call home and to be comfortable."

"Maybe," she muttered, "but God knows it's not been the easiest so far."

"How long have you worked for us?"

"A few months," she said.

"Funny how you seem to have been a mouse this whole time."

"I have been staying in the background, trying rather hard to avoid all the potential drama that goes with the officers," she admitted, with half a smile, "and then you came along and dragged me out into the public eye anyway."

"Yep, there doesn't have to be drama all the time, but it sure helps if you can get out from under it all and see the world around you," he stated. "Good things can always occur, but you have to get out in the world for them to happen. You can't just hide away."

"Hiding has kept me safe," she declared.

"Hiding has kept you hidden," he pointed out, "but it didn't keep you alive. You kept yourself alive, but you're hardly living. And, as far as your stalker guy is concerned, he wants to confirm you don't get to live at all."

"You don't know that," she argued, frowning at him.

"Maybe not, but I don't really want you to take any chances and end up in a situation that you are unable to get out of."

"That's a little depressing to consider," she said, staring at him. "I wasn't really planning on that."

"I understand," he replied. "All I can say is, when it comes to guys like this, there really isn't an easy answer or an easy way out. So, you have to be careful every step of the way."

"I was planning on it," she noted, "and even now I'm exhausted and just want to go back home again."

"And I'm happy to take you, but—"

"But what?" she asked, eyeing him warily.

"I want to confirm that your place is secure and that you won't do anything stupid."

She snorted. "What the hell am I supposed to do? I hardly have another place to go to, and you've made that location a whole lot smaller."

"Did I? I don't think so. That was all you." She glared at him, but it didn't faze him one bit. He smiled and added, "Or we could go out for dinner."

She stared at him in shock. "You mean, like a date?"

He burst out laughing. "I don't know about a date, seeing as just the thought of that appears to make you want to run for cover."

"It does make me want to run for cover," she admitted. "Something is very scary about you."

He stopped to face her. "Seriously?"

She shrugged. "You're a force that won't be contained. You don't listen to anything I say, and you obviously want your own way in anything you do. It's not the easiest environment for me."

"Wow. I hadn't really considered any of that, but you're right." He gave her a tender glance. "So, I can take you home if you want, or we can go out for dinner and get some food, and you can relax a little more. Either way," he shrugged and added, "It wouldn't hurt both of us to get out a little more." She wasn't sure what to say to that. As they got into his vehicle, he asked, "Chinese or Italian?"

She automatically answered Italian and then shook her head. "See? I'm just no good at this."

"Why aren't you any good at this?"

"Because you just got that answer out of me without thinking."

"That's because you trust me, and you don't have any reason to *not* go out with me."

"Are you sure?" she asked, with half a smile. "You're damn scary."

He laughed. "No, I'm not."

They were still arguing as he pulled up to a restaurant, and she looked at it and smiled. "This is one of my favorite places."

"Oh, so you do go out," he teased.

She shrugged, "Not very often." As they walked into the restaurant, she froze.

"What's the matter?" he asked, nudging her forward.

In a hoarse whisper, the words strangled in the back of her throat, she whispered, "He's here. Dear God, he's here."

PORTER'S GAZE ENCOMPASSED the entire restaurant. "Are you sure?" he asked in a low voice. "I'm not seeing any likely suspects."

"His energy," she whispered, "I can feel it."

"Feel it as in right now, or feel it as in maybe it's lingering?"

She gave an irritable shrug. "I don't know," she snapped. She pressed a hand to her forehead.

"Do you get headaches often?"

"No, I don't. Well, sometimes, yeah," she corrected herself.

A waitress walked up to them and asked how many was in their party. He hesitated, wondering if Kylie would be okay to stay.

Kylie replied, "Two."

The hostess nodded. "Follow me, please."

Porter followed, keeping a close eye on Kylie, yet scanning the entire restaurant. Kylie hadn't pinpointed where her stalker was, nor had she provided any other information about him. And that was dubious at best, but, if she was catching energy, it could be old energy, just that sensation of somebody having walked over your grave. It didn't necessarily mean that her stalker was here right now, and that was yet another challenge.

As they went past an empty table, she stiffened and spun to look at it. Porter caught her by her shoulders and asked, "Here?"

She nodded. "Here."

He nudged her forward to follow the hostess to their table just a little beyond. Then he asked the waitress, "Was somebody recently here at that table?"

She looked back and frowned. "Yes, he must have just left. I hadn't even given him his food yet." She walked back over to the table, where a large tip had been left, and she shrugged. "It happens sometimes."

Porter asked, "I would appreciate if you could describe

what he looked like. Can you?" She looked at him suspiciously, and he smiled. "I'm a cop, honest."

At that, her suspicions grew even deeper, almost as if she wanted to protect the man who had left her such a substantial tip. After he produced his badge, she began in a fairly noncommittal tone, "Tall, slim, late forties, maybe early fifties, hard to tell. In good shape, very polite, friendly." She shrugged. "That's all I can tell you."

"Beard, no beard, anything that made him stand out?"

"No," she replied, as she placed the menus on their table. "I'll be back in a few to get your order." And, with that, she disappeared.

Porter turned to Kylie, sitting there, almost trembling, visible sweat on her face. "Do you need to leave?" he asked.

She lifted tortured eyes in his direction and whispered, "No, I'm scared to go out there."

"Why?" he asked, leaning forward.

"I think he knew me," she shared. "I think he recognized or sensed me or something." She looked at Porter, the sweat glistening on her face. "Did you have any particular reason for picking this restaurant?"

He raised his eyebrows, then shook his head. "No, it's a place I love to come to."

"I do too," she replied, "at least I used to. I'm surprised you're not outside chasing him down."

"He's already gone. Otherwise I would."

She sagged into her chair. "What's he doing here?" she whispered.

"I would hazard a guess and say that he was getting food. But, when we walked in, either he sensed us or saw you or me and decided it wasn't a safe place to stay."

"But I didn't even see him go past us," she muttered.

"True, but there are other pathways. If he had gone around the tables off to the side, you wouldn't have seen him either."

She looked around and then nodded. "I guess, but I don't remember seeing anybody as we walked in."

"No, but he doesn't do what he does without having a lot of skill in making himself fairly innocuous."

"I suppose," she whispered. "Christ." She raised a trembling hand to her forehead. "For a minute there I thought I would puke."

"Better now?"

She looked up at him and whispered, "Yes, except for the fact that he knows I'm here, and it feels very much as if that was of interest to him."

"So, you didn't get a sense of fear from him?"

"God no, no fear, … but maybe something more dangerous."

"What's that?"

"Interest," she stated, looking sick. "A very strong interest, as if he wanted to know more about me."

"That would be an interesting scenario," Porter muttered to himself, "but I'm not at all sure it would be a good one though."

Her reaction was something he wasn't particularly comfortable with. He'd never seen her like this. True, he didn't know her all that well, but, up until now, she'd been fairly contained and completely capable of handling whatever was thrown her way.

Her stalker had sent lots of shock waves through her planned and ordinary life. At the moment she was still trying to deal with all that, and Porter understood. She'd held firm so far, and now he could tell from the look on her face that things were starting to get shakier. "Take a deep breath," he suggested. "Just hold tight."

"I don't even know if we should stay," she whispered, looking at him in shock. "Maybe we should just leave."

"You still need to eat, and so do I," he pointed out, "and our leaving won't get that done."

"Maybe," she muttered, as she took a deep breath, then waved her hand dismissively. "Okay, I'm starting to feel better. Maybe just give me a few more minutes."

When the waitress returned, instead of ordering wine or anything alcoholic, he ordered coffee for both of them and water for her. The waitress returned fairly quickly with both, and then they were left in silence again.

Kylie looked around cautiously. "His energy is so strong."

"That's another issue," Porter noted. "Why is it so strong for you?"

She looked back at him. "Meaning that, once again, you think there's a connection?"

"We already know there's a connection."

"I don't like anything along this discussion. You know that."

"Still, it doesn't change the fact that it's a discussion we need to have, considering that you are sensing this guy, when nobody knows what he looks like these days."

She picked up her water glass and downed about half of it. Then she picked it up again and finished it.

"Easy on the water too," he offered, not sure what any of this meant.

She stared at him. "Does the water matter?"

"I don't know," he admitted, "but it seems to be a strong response, and I'm not sure why."

She gave a broken laugh. "I don't know either. I don't know anything at this point. All I can tell you is that the man who killed both of those posed young women just walked out of here, and you didn't care."

"Oh, I care," he clarified. "I also noted cameras in this place and cameras outside, so we can access those, as soon as you're feeling better."

She stared at him in shock, and then her shoulders slumped. "See? I'm just not cut out for this."

"Why? Because you didn't note the cameras? It's not part of the work that you do," he pointed out. "However, it is part of what I do."

She took several deep breaths and then nodded. "I am feeling a bit better." She glanced around. "I'm not sure staying here is a good idea though."

"Do you think he'll do something?"

She frowned. "Yes, he'll do something, but I don't think it'll be here, and I don't even think it'll be now. I don't know what he's planning, but he'll definitely do something."

"Interesting," Porter murmured, just a hair above total silence.

She stared at him. "You don't have to believe me."

"I do believe you," he said. "I can sense your fear, and I can sense something shifting in the energy. I get an odd feeling to the place now."

"Yeah," she agreed, "and it's not a good feeling."

He laughed. "I can understand that, but we also won't run."

"Are you sure?" she asked, with a wry look in his direction. "What if we step out of the restaurant right now, and he's there, waiting to shoot us down?"

He stared at her for a long moment. "That's a damn

good point." He pulled out his phone and motioned for her to stay. "I need to make a call."

"Yeah, you go do that," she said. "I'll just sit right here and have a breakdown."

He grinned. "You won't do anything of the sort. You're handling this like a real trooper."

She shook her head. "You have no idea how nervous I am on the inside."

"Nervous is good," he replied, with a smile. "That means you're being reasonable and sensible. We don't want anybody going off half-cocked in this scenario." He pointed. "I'll just walk over there so I can make this call. You just stay put."

She stared at him, her jaw working, and then she shrugged. "It's not as if I have any place to go to that he doesn't know about."

He stared at her, realizing that she was fully expecting to have some repercussions from this. "Let's not hang on to that thought. We'll get through this. Let me make a call, and I promise I'll be right back." As he stood up, he added, "And order me the lasagna when she comes back, will you?"

And, with that, he walked to a coatroom area and quickly dialed Stefan.

CHAPTER 10

KYLIE WASN'T SURE who Porter was calling, but she had a damn good idea. Honestly, at this point in time, she wouldn't mind making that call herself. This was scary. It was unorthodox, and everything inside her screamed to get the hell out and run. Yet everything else was telling her to stay put, to not give the stalker an advantage, to not let him know that she had picked up on him. That he might already know that Kylie had picked up on his energy was something that hadn't escaped her attention either. But this was all about maintaining sanity in a situation that had gone crazy.

The waitress came back and brought her more water, so she quickly ordered the lasagna for both of them. With the orders taken, the waitress disappeared, and Kylie turned to stare back where her stalker had been sitting. There was almost a cloudiness around his table. It was weird and just added to the mystery of who he was and what the hell he was doing here. And why he was here. It was the why that bothered her. If he'd already killed two people, surely there weren't that many contracts to kill people daily. He didn't just advertise contracts by air, as in thinking, *Hey, I'm popping in. Anybody you want me to drop?*

That didn't make any sense to her. So, he was either hanging around for a personal reason, which felt very much like what this could be, or something else was going on.

Either way, she didn't like it.

When Porter returned, she looked over at him. "And? What did Stefan have to say?"

He smiled. "How do you know it was Stefan?"

"Who else would you call?" she asked in exasperation. "He's the king of all psychic phenomena, isn't he?"

"Is he now?" he asked, with half a laugh. "I don't know about that, but I do know that he's definitely somebody you want in your corner when the chips are down."

"I'm not sure the chips are down that badly. At least not yet," she muttered.

"What do you have against Stefan anyway?"

"Nothing," she said, with a groan. "Honestly, I really don't have anything against him. However, my aunt didn't have anything nice to say about him."

"Did your aunt have anything nice to say about anybody?" Porter asked curiously.

She eyed him, then shrugged. "No, she didn't. I think she hated the world." He just nodded, as that confirmed what he suspected. "She was still good to me to the extent that she could be," she pointed out, "and I can't forget that."

"You don't have to forget it," he noted, "but do keep it in perspective."

She shrugged, not exactly sure what that meant. Her relationship with her aunt was complicated, and Kylie worked hard to try and not make it a big issue in her life, but obviously it was still something that she needed to work on.

He looked over at her and asked, "Did the waitress come by?"

"Yes, and I ordered you a lasagna, as instructed." He looked at her carefully, as if to see if she was joking or really put out by his request. She shrugged. "I'm having the same thing."

"It's very good here, isn't it?"

"Yes, it is," she agreed, with a smile, "and I sure wouldn't mind having a nice hot meal right now."

"That's why we're here," he said, "and I also phoned the captain and updated him and asked for permission to see the security tapes here."

"Oh, I'm sure that went over like a ton of bricks."

"I think it's better that he be aware that we have a problem."

"Do we have a problem?" she asked.

"Considering that you already got a phone call from your stalker, and then we walk into a restaurant, and he's sitting here? … Yeah, I think it's a problem."

"But are we the ones who have the problem, or is he?" she asked.

He looked at her, a smile forming on his face. "Now that was an excellent observation."

"I mean, when you think about it," she began, "we were the ones who came in here, where he was seated already. So he might not be terribly impressed with our choice."

"Maybe not," Porter agreed, "and that just means that he'll have a closer look at you."

"Why not you?" she asked. "Why must it always come back to me?"

"That's the question I have to ask you. Why does it all keep coming back to you?"

She glared at him. "I don't have anything to do with this."

"I'm glad to hear that, so we won't have any unpleasant surprises when we leave here."

She frowned and looked about. "Do you think he'll be

waiting for us?"

"I don't know. I guess I won't be surprised either way. He appears to be that kind of a guy, flexible, capable of thinking on his feet. So, if he's got some ax to grind, you and I both know something will happen, whether we agree with his methodology or his reasoning. He's got to have a reason to be here."

"I was trying to figure out why he would still be hanging around this part of town. He's already … double dipped, so how the hell does that work? It's not as if you just advertise, *I'll be in such-and-such location if anybody wants somebody dropped*, and instantly pick up two hits for his one visit."

Porter's lips twitched at the thought. "It's an interesting business model, but not exactly one I would have thought had a guarantee of success."

"No, I wouldn't either," she agreed, "but then again, I'm not in the business, so maybe things are done like that."

"I hope not. That would be a little too cavalier."

"And yet that's exactly what his killings are like," she stated, frowning at Porter.

"He is very cavalier, by the looks of it. It's a business to him, and, as long as he delivers, then he keeps getting business."

"He didn't mess up, right?" she asked Porter. "I mean, nothing was left at either crime scene to get him into trouble with his clients, I presume?"

"I don't know. I guess it depends what the arrangements were. If somebody is pissed off at him, it's possible, but I can't imagine that he would stick around and do another job if he felt someone was on to him."

"Right." She frowned. "It just doesn't make any sense that he's still here."

"It does feel as if it's personal."

She winced. "I keep trying not to think that it's personal," she muttered. "That's not something I want to focus on."

"No, maybe not, but it doesn't change the fact that he has stuck around, even though we have potentially two kills on him. The fact that he even did two at once, in the same basic location, bothers me," he admitted.

"Unless one was *pro bono*," she suggested, "and again … maybe personal."

He stopped and frowned at her. "*Hmm*. That is something I hadn't considered."

IT WAS ALSO a good thought. As soon as they were done with dinner, Porter would head back to the office and see what he could roust out.

"I can see the wheels in your brain turning," Kylie noted in a casual remark a few minutes later. "I'm not sure what you're musing over though."

"Just your comment about one of the hits being personal. I hadn't considered that. We need to track the histories of those victims and see if we can connect them somehow."

"You really think he would do a personal job?"

"Absolutely. We all do professional services for ourselves every once in a while," he shared, "or at least for friends or special businesses. In this case, I doubt your stalker has much in the way of friends because of what he does, but that doesn't mean he doesn't have a reason to want somebody specifically taken care of just for himself."

The lasagna arrived then, along with big, thick slabs of garlic bread. He sniffed the air appreciatively. "This is some of the best food in town," he muttered, as he cut into the lasagna. He watched as Kylie reached for garlic bread and took a big bite, smiling in happiness. "And it's good to see you eat."

She frowned at him. "I eat," she snapped. "Don't go making me sound as if I've got some eating disorder now too."

"Not at all," he said. "It's more about confirming that you'll be prepped and ready for what's ahead."

She just stared at him and slowly put down the garlic bread. "What is ahead?" she asked, her voice faint. "Maybe you should clarify that, so I have a little warning."

"I don't know, but it's been quite a ride so far, hasn't it?"

"I'm not sure I like the way you say that," she muttered.

He laughed. "Of course not, and nobody would, but it doesn't change the fact that we have something going on, and it could get ugly. We just don't know yet."

"I've already seen enough ugly today."

"We both have," he agreed. "The good news is, the mass shooter is dead. The bad news is, we still have a lot of victims and survivors struggling in the aftermath of what happened to them and their family and friends."

"I also have to wonder if my stalker had something to do with that."

"I've been wondering the same thing," Porter acknowledged. "We should have the second shooter on camera here, so we know that he's been here and is basically doing his thing, but we don't know what his connection is to the first shooter. I do have several other coworkers trying to run that down."

"Right," she muttered, "because you have a team."

"I do have a team, and it's important."

"I just never imagined being in a situation like this," she muttered, as she started to eat her lasagna.

He let her eat for a bit, wanting to ensure she had something solid in her stomach because, even if she hadn't figured it out yet, no way she could go home alone tonight. Not if this guy was out there and tracking her. Porter didn't think she had come to that conclusion yet. She was probably thinking along the lines of being independent and still able to say no, but that wouldn't work anymore.

The captain had been pretty outraged that Porter hadn't gone after the guy, but, when he explained what shape she was in, the captain mellowed out pretty fast. Porter had also explained that the guy had been long gone very quickly and that Porter felt any attempt to chase him down wouldn't have made a difference in any way. Plus it would have left Kylie all alone and vulnerable. That made sense in a logical way, yet for anybody trying to track down this second shooter, it was depressing to think Hogan had been right here, so close.

The captain had put Neil onto searching the restaurant's cameras and the nearby street cams. They should have answers soon as to what the second shooter looked like now and what he was driving and then getting out an APB for everyone to hunt him down. A vehicle can give them a lot of information, but, with a pro like this hired serial killer, chances are his getaway vehicle had been stolen. Still, Porter was willing to take whatever information they could get and run with it. Enough things were going on that needed answers and clarity, and Porter was quite concerned about Kylie's mental health as well as her safety.

"What are you staring at?" she muttered.

He was literally sitting here, staring at her. He smiled.

"You're beautiful."

She stopped and glared. "Oh no you don't. No flirting."

He burst out laughing. "Why not?" he asked. "It's not as if the world has stopped turning."

"It should," she snapped, glaring at him. "Everything should stop. Besides, this isn't a date."

"Nope, it isn't a date," he agreed, with a smile in her direction. "It's just a meal among friends."

"Are we friends?" she asked, her fork pausing partway to her mouth, as if contemplating such an option, and he realized just how alone she had been for so long.

"There really are nice people out in the world."

"I'm not sure I agree," she retorted, with a heavy sigh, "but I'll take your word for it."

"I'll have you meet some of my friends when this nightmare is over," he suggested cheerfully. "They are a lot of fun."

"Sure, a lot of fun for you, but I highly doubt they would understand somebody like me."

"If they accept me," he added, with a wry look, "I don't think they would have much trouble accepting you."

She stayed silent, reminding him that friends were a different world for her, one that she didn't necessarily have any exposure to. He asked her, "What was school like for you?"

"I had to be good at school. Otherwise I wasn't allowed to stay," she stated.

"What do you mean, you weren't allowed to stay?"

"I wasn't allowed to stay at home. I had to be the best and clean up, do the dishes, and everything else in order to not piss off my aunt and get my ass kicked out of the house," she explained.

"Was there ever a threat to that degree?"

"No, but it was always in my mind," she shared. "It was always implied."

"Right," he murmured, wondering what that would have been like for a teenager, when she should have been out there making friends and enjoying life. Instead she was living in constant fear that her world would collapse again. "I'm sorry. I wonder why your aunt was even given custody."

"She was family." Kylie shrugged. "They always get the first contact, and, when she accepted, it was a done deal. I know that she didn't love me," she stated in a contemplative tone.

That rote reply made Porter really take stock because she was acting as if this were a prepared script, as if something in the back of her mind made it easier to listen to this stuff than to investigate further.

He didn't push it, thinking she had enough on her plate right now, but it was something he certainly would have appreciated a better understanding of. She would have been a beautiful child, although traumatized after the loss of both parents. And, even though she hadn't had a chance to know her twin brothers, it would have affected her in some way. Particularly as sensitive as she was.

"Do you ever do readings for people?" she asked him.

He laughed. It was almost as if she had read his mind. "Nope, enough people out there do that stuff. I try to avoid anything of the kind."

She nodded. "That makes sense."

"Why would you ask?" he asked curiously.

"I just wondered about my brothers, whether they're okay or not."

The fact that she mentioned her brothers and not her parents surprised him. Maybe it's because she felt terribly guilty about her brothers' deaths. "Maybe when this is over, we can find out," he suggested. "If it's something that you're questioning, then maybe it's something we should take further."

"You're awfully quick to say *we*," she noted, studying him over her fork again.

She had this habit of using the fork almost as a barrier between them. Probably another learned behavior. He smiled and nodded. "You've made a friend, so you are stuck with me."

Her eyes widened at that. "I don't know why you would want anything to do with me." She shoved a big bite of lasagna into her mouth, chewing furiously, studying him as if he were something very odd and unique.

"Because you're not a bad person," Porter replied, "and I kind of like you."

She shook her head. "Nope, that doesn't fly."

He burst out laughing. "You can't hide forever."

"Yes, I most certainly can," she stated defiantly. She put down her fork and looked around the restaurant. "I don't suppose I can get this to-go, can I?"

"Sure, you can. Haven't you ever done that before?"

"No, I usually come in starving and eat every bite," she confessed, staring down at her plate, which was still half full.

"And yet not today?"

"No. … Let's just say the conversation and the energy around here is not conducive to a good meal."

"Sorry to hear that, and, yes, we absolutely can get it to-go. You'll probably enjoy it later."

"I will," she said, with a small smile.

"Maybe I'll take mine too, and we can eat it together later." She stared at him, almost in horror. He burst out laughing. "If I had any less self-confidence, you would have torn me apart already," he noted, in-between chuckles.

She didn't know what to say to that.

"Have you not figured out that in no way can I allow you to stay alone tonight?" he asked.

"Why not?" she asked, almost in a groan, but she already knew the answer to that. She was just being prickly and irritable.

"This guy left as soon as we walked into the restaurant. So either he knew who you were, sensed trouble, or is well into the whole *coming after you* thing," Porter explained. "So you alone at your house is not doable."

She shook her head. "I'm fine," she muttered. "You don't know anything about me."

"I do know something about you," he countered, with half a smile. "I know that the thought of being alone with this guy terrifies you and that you'll just accept that tonight and every other night—until we get this resolved—I'll be staying at your place."

CHAPTER 11

WITH THE REST of their meals packed up and a quick sweep of the outside area confirmed as safe by two local uniforms, Porter paid, and she got into his vehicle without saying a word. She was still in shock. A part of her was incredibly relieved that she wouldn't have to go home to that empty house all alone tonight. And yet another part of her was terrified. She'd had relationships, but it had always been her at the other person's house overnight. She'd never gotten so close or wanted the type of relationship where they'd lived together. She felt odd having Porter in her own home.

She was only starting to realize just what an influence her aunt had had on her after all. As if fear was something that ruled her life from the shadowy depths of her soul, without Kylie even realizing it, and that terrified her almost as much as this asshole stalker out there. This in-depth look at her world was not comfortable. It was certainly not something she would choose to do, and honestly wasn't something she had wanted to start in the first place, but Porter had other ideas. Whether it was out of the goodness of his heart or not, a process of unraveling had begun, and it was all Kylie could do to contain the ends of her world as the stitches came apart.

She didn't want everything in her world to be destroyed,

but it felt as if she was on a self-destructive path that she couldn't get off of. It was uncomfortable, soul destroying, and to even believe that so much in her life wasn't as she had thought it was, and made it all a lie, was incredibly distressing. To find out she'd even had brothers she had missed out on, brothers she didn't remember, broke her heart. They had only just been born, so they hadn't had a chance at life at all. They hadn't even made it home from the hospital, according to Porter and the online articles. It was just incredible to think that the killer hired to kill her family had escaped prison and was killing more people, making his recapture an ongoing issue. Kylie shook her head, thinking how her aunt had been involved in capturing this guy.

No wonder Aunt Agatha had always kept them hidden and had moved a lot, but why had Kylie ended up safe? Had Agatha been that good, or had this killer not cared that much until now? And why out of all of this had Kylie ended up right here in this location, nowhere near her aunt as far as she knew, and yet the killer was here too. Kylie struggled with the concept of coincidence, particularly in something like this. It felt more like divine intervention, almost as if some cosmic joke. Yet she'd been capable of turning her back on everything up until now, and now that she couldn't anymore, it slapped her in face. *See? I told you so. You need to deal with this shit.*

But how did one deal with shit that Kylie hadn't even been aware of that her aunt had been hiding? And who knew how Agatha was so good at it?

When they pulled up in front of her house, Kylie got out without a word and walked up to her front door, or maybe stomped was a better word. As she got to the house, she unlocked the front door, pushed it open, and stepped in.

Porter followed, then snatched her back, and pulled her right out of the house.

She didn't say a word, still dealing with the shock of the smiling gunman in front of them.

"That answers one thing," the gunman said in a genial tone. "You really don't have any abilities. Otherwise you would have seen me coming a mile away."

He was right. She should have seen him coming a mile away. Dear God, she should have. What the hell was wrong with her? She'd been so consumed by everything else in her world that she hadn't even seen him coming.

She stared at him, her throat working as she tried to get words out, but she froze, seeing that snub-nosed revolver pointed her way, knowing that this man killed with impunity and would cheerfully do it all over again. "Why do you care?" she managed to whisper.

He gave half a shrug. "I'm just checking. If you don't know anything, it's all the better for you."

She wanted to rail and scream at him, *Did you kill my family? And, if you did, … why? Who paid you?* But she couldn't do anything but stare at him. Porter stood behind her, holding her tight. She wasn't sure what he thought she would do, but any movement on Kylie's part was beyond her. "What do you want from me?" she asked in a slightly stronger tone of voice.

"You? I don't want anything from you," he stated, with a negligent shrug. "I'm not even sure who the hell you are or what you're doing in this mix," he muttered, as he stared at her curiously. "But I learned long ago that anomalies must be checked. They can't be allowed to run free, not without some logical reason for their existence."

She blinked at the conversation, almost a theoretical

Newton's law, a conversation she had not expected from him.

He studied her closely. "Where is your aunt?" When she stiffened, he nodded. "Now we're onto something."

"I don't know where she is," she replied.

He frowned at her. "I hardly believe that."

"I don't know where she is. I haven't had anything to do with her since I left years ago."

He studied her, as if wondering at the veracity of her words, then sighed. "Of course she would have run, as if that'll make a damn bit of difference," he muttered. "All I ever wanted was answers."

"Answers for what?" she asked faintly.

He waved her off. "None of your business, and, if you don't know where she is, you can't help me."

He raised the gun as if to fire, and she spluttered, "Wait, don't do that."

"Why not?" he asked, looking at her. "You're nothing to me, so why would I care?"

She didn't even know what her next words would be, but she opened her mouth, prepared to speak. Yet Porter beat her to it.

"She's your family," he said. "Are you sure you want to kill her?"

The man stared at him in shock, real shock. He took Porter's words as if a visceral blow to his body, almost a swing forward to hit him. Time came to a complete standstill for all of them. Then the gunman suddenly disappeared into the shadows at the back of her house.

Immediately Porter told her to stay hidden in the bushes at the front, and he would be back in a few minutes. He half shoved her behind the big cedars around the front steps. She sank to the ground, feeling the hardness of the concrete wall behind her and the chill of the cold ground beneath her and the harshness of the cedar branches as they scratched her face, shoulders, and arms. However, none of it mattered. None of it had anything to do with the reality of what Porter had just shared.

What the hell did he mean? That she was family? The killer's family? How? Surely not. It couldn't be. That was not something she wanted to contemplate at all.

Dear God. She closed her eyes, her heart slamming against her chest, as everything in her world shifted once again. Surely Porter meant it as a joke. Surely he just tried to shock the gunman. It had to be that, nothing else. There couldn't be any other explanation. At least that's what Kylie hoped. Hearing a noise coming from the front, she turned her head sideways. She felt almost numb, seeing Porter racing to her.

He bent down over the landing to stare at her. "Are you okay?"

She nodded. "I'm okay," she whispered, "as much as I can be." He winced at that and helped her to her feet. "Where is he?" she asked.

"He's gone. He left a vehicle running in the back alleyway. He had just enough of a head start that he's gone. And it was a truck this time, most probably stolen."

"Of course." She stared at Porter. He led her into the house, and, as soon as the door was closed, she turned and looked around. "You're sure?"

"Yes, I'm sure, but we'll go through every inch of the house to confirm you understand that and can see it for yourself."

She shook her head. "You don't have to do that," she

whispered. "I can sense the emptiness."

He nodded. "Good, your instincts will keep you safe more than anything."

"Will it? He was right about one thing. If I had any abilities, I would have seen him coming a mile away."

Porter half chuckled, half groaned. "If you weren't still dealing with major trauma and things in your world unraveling without your permission or control, maybe you would have, but right now? I don't think so." She sat down on a nearby chair, and he said, "I'll go get you a hot cup of tea."

She barely heard him, her mouth frozen by so many questions, all ready to bubble up and to demand answers. When he came back, he crouched in front of her. "The teakettle is on. I'll get you a hot cup in a few minutes." She stared at him. He stared right back and then relented. "I know. You want answers."

"Damn right I want answers. I need answers. Was that just a shot in the dark? What the hell was that about family?"

"Kind of, yes," he admitted. She stared at him, and he shrugged. "I don't have all the answers. Do I think you're blood related? No. But I do think a connection is there that he's not aware of. Yes, it was a shot in the dark, but I don't think he's family."

She sagged back into her chair, her hands covering her face, as the relief washed over her.

"But I do think he'll consider my words and be back."

Her eyes flew open. "Good God. He will be back, won't he?"

"Yes, I suspect so. Maybe it wasn't the best thing to tell him, but I didn't have any control over myself at that moment, and the family angle just seemed to be the best answer to give him."

She didn't know how to respond to that. "Best answer? You just made me a target."

He winced and nodded. "You're right. I did, and, for that, I am sorry. However, it worked to save your life tonight."

She announced, "We could use it." He stared at her, and she shrugged. "We know he's coming back sometime, somehow, somewhere. He'll walk into our lives, and we need to be ready for him." A note of admiration slipped into his gaze, but she didn't want to see it. She was trying to think like a cop, to think like somebody who wanted to be out of this nightmare. "You have no idea how grateful I am that it was just a shot in the dark," she shared, shaking as if to expel some nasty thing. "Of all the things that I could possibly survive, knowing I was related to that monster is not one of them."

"You would survive," he stated firmly. "You are strong. You've had a pretty crappy upbringing, and I'm not sure how much you even remember about it, but you survived. We're all survivors, but you really have done well."

"No," she argued. "The only reason I'm still surviving right now is because I don't necessarily understand what the bottom line is here. I'm trying hard to adapt, but it's not the easiest thing."

"No, of course it isn't," he agreed, "and that shouldn't be easy. All kinds of things in life are a little harder, and that's okay too. These aren't necessarily answers that anybody can grasp quickly."

When he got up and returned to the kitchen, she realized the teakettle was whistling in the background. When he brought a cup of tea and set it down, he again asked her, "Are you okay?"

"I will be," she murmured. "Yet … I can't say this has been an easy evening."

"No, of course not," he agreed, then smiled. "Yet you've handled yourself very well."

She waved her hand. "Stop with the compliments. I need to know what the hell is going on."

"I think there's a connection that we don't really understand between him and your aunt."

"No, no, no, no."

He continued. "We already know of one connection because she's the one who put him away."

"Right," she said in relief, "so maybe it's hatred." Then she winced. "Dear God, do you think he raped her?"

"I don't know anything," he replied, "so let's not even go in that direction. We need to understand why she had so much of the world shut off, as if it was not to be trusted. I don't imagine anything was to be trusted in her version of the world where she lived," He sighed. "We still don't know anything about it."

"Right, and I think maybe it's time we tried."

"Meaning?"

"We should contact my aunt."

He smiled at her and nodded. "Good. I'm glad you're suggesting it because I was about to."

"Of course you were." She glared at him. "Like everything else, you've been waiting for me to come up with the answers, and then you get to pat me on the back. Meanwhile you were waiting to tell me all about it in the first place."

He shook his head. "Don't take it the wrong way. I'm really just feeling my way through all this mess too."

"Are you though?" she asked, staring at him. "Because it seems to me as if I'm a puppet on a string, and you've been the puppet master this whole time."

His gaze darkened, and he crouched in front of her and snapped, "Don't ever think that. I'm not here to pull your strings. I'm not here to hurt you or to upset you. I've had the difficult job of telling you about some horrific information about your past that was kept from you. I don't enjoy being the bearer of bad news, and I certainly don't enjoy being the one who gets blamed for it," he muttered.

She got all that but still wasn't reassured by hearing him say it.

He remained crouched by her side. "I understand that you'll hold something against me because of all this, and that's fine. You do what you have to do," he said. "However, don't hide and don't fool yourself into thinking this is deliberate on my part or that I have any ulterior motive or any harmful intent for you because I don't."

"I'm glad to hear that," she muttered, still not sure she should believe him. She took a sip of tea, her gaze wandering around her living room. "Do you think he'll be back?"

"I thought you wanted to set up a trap because he *would* be back," he stated, frowning at her.

"I know. I know. I guess the question I'm really asking is, will he be back tonight?"

"I don't think so, but we can't be sure. So, I will be staying here."

"Of course you will," she said, without any rancor. "I guess I would have been surprised if you weren't."

"That's progress," he muttered. "I'll take that at least."

"I'm not that hard to get along with," she stated, eyeing him over her teacup.

"No, but it hasn't been easy for me either."

"No." She winced. "I realized you were the bearer of bad

news but that you weren't the creator of it."

"I was not," he confirmed, "and I'm still worried that you haven't quite processed all of it."

"Of course I haven't," she declared, staring at him. "How could I? Just think about everything you've told me. How my entire history has been rewritten. The fact that my parents were murdered, and it was a hit, a killing for hire. And the fact that I had twin brothers I didn't even know about." She shook her head, her jaw working. "Do you know how guilty that makes me feel?"

"You were a child. Remember that too."

"I don't care. It just makes me feel horrible."

"I know, and emotions do take over."

"Of course they take over. … Do you think my stalker left anything behind?"

The words came right out of the blue, and he stared at her for a long moment, then stood up, looked around, and asked, "As in what?"

"I don't know. I just … it's probably nothing."

"No such thing in our world as *probably nothing*," he stated, glancing behind him, then at her again. "So, tell me. What is it that you're thinking."

"I'm just wondering if he left something behind."

"What exactly do you mean by something? Would you recognize if he had?"

"I don't know." She slowly stood up. "I wish to God I hadn't even thought of it."

"Now I wish to God you hadn't either," he replied, with a smile, "but you did, and now that's on the table."

She pinched the bridge of her nose, and then it hit her. "The kitchen."

"I was just in there," Porter said. "I didn't see anything

specifically that looked as if somebody had left something behind."

She followed him into the kitchen and stood in the doorway. She got no sense of somebody having been in here. The energy wasn't that easy; it wasn't that clear. But she still felt a sense of wrongness, and that's all she could explain to him.

"Okay, we'll start from there," he began. "When you say *a sense of wrongness*, what do you mean?"

"It just feels wrong," she stated.

"Because somebody was in your house?"

She frowned, contemplating his words, and then nodded. "That's part of it, that sense of violation."

"Okay, but that's completely different in another way."

"It may be the same thing. I don't know," she replied. "I'm not used to doing all this."

He smiled. "Hang on." He walked back into the living room, picked up her sketchbook, and handed it to her. "So, sketch it."

"Sketch what?" she asked, staring down at her book in confusion.

"The crime scene," he replied. "A crime happened here, so sketch it."

She shook her head. "It doesn't work that way."

"How do you know?" he asked, giving her an encouraging smile. "You haven't done it."

"Of course I haven't done it," she snapped waspishly. "And it won't do any good."

"You don't know that. Sit down and try."

Glaring at him, she returned to the living room. Sitting down, she stared at her sketchbook, opened up to a page, and shook her head. Looking back at him, she declared,

"Nothing will come."

"And that's fine. If nothing comes, … nothing comes. Then we'll tackle it from a different angle."

"I don't understand," she muttered. "This doesn't make any sense."

"Breaking and entering is a crime, and it happened right here. That makes it a crime scene."

She rolled her eyes at that and pulled her pencil from her pocket and set it to her paper. Almost instantly she fell into a weird fugue of images, and her pencil started moving, and she was barely aware, as the pencil shifted back and forth on the page. She couldn't stop it and could only surrender to whatever was happening.

She sensed Porter coming behind her, to stand and to watch, wondering what it would look like if she could even see herself doing this. This had been one of the things that her aunt had been absolutely distraught about when Kylie had shown signs of abilities. Then her aunt had gotten angry and cold, as if Kylie were the devil's spawn or something. It made life even more difficult for them, and Kylie had done her best to stifle everything to keep her aunt happy, to make herself seem more normal, whatever the hell that meant.

Suddenly she blew out a very long sigh. She opened her eyes and stared down at the page that she had been completely covered. She glanced up to see Porter staring at her images, his gaze narrowed as he studied it. "Does it mean anything?" she asked lightly.

He frowned at her. "Do you recognize it?"

"No, I sure don't. See? I'm not very good at this. It's supposed to be my house because this is where the crime scene was."

"Maybe, or it's another crime scene you haven't visited

yet."

She stared at him. "That's not what I want to hear. That would mean I'm picking up crime scenes before I've even seen them."

"Yeah, and I wonder." Porter squatted before her and took the book from her hand to study it. "What would it take for you to see a crime scene before the crime happened?"

PORTER KNEW HE'D shocked Kylie. Hell, he'd shocked himself, but this sketch, drawing, or whatever she wanted to call it, was not of her house. And that surprised him too. He had expected to see the crime scene here, expected to see something that would pinpoint the same man they had been chasing and who had shown up in their space instead of them into his. Porter looked over at her and held up her sketch. "Do you recognize this location?"

She looked at it and shook her head. "No, I don't."

"It's somebody's living room. Have you ever lived in a house like this?"

She frowned and shook her head. "I don't think so. And this scene is not violent at all. It's just a room."

"Doesn't have to be violent in order to be a crime scene. Remember that," he pointed out. "Even here you had a break-in, but he didn't do anything other than terrify you."

"It was a violation of my privacy."

"Right, and that's important too, but it wasn't like the crime scenes you have been drawing for us."

"No," she said, studying her sketch. Then she frowned. "I don't know but maybe ..."

He looked at her and nudged. "Maybe what?"

"It might be the house I grew up in—or at least one of

them."

"One of them?"

She nodded. "Honest to God, there were a bunch of them."

"Of course there were. Your aunt moved you a lot, didn't she?"

"Yes."

"And did she ever explain why?"

"No, she just told me that I was bad." He stared at her in shock. She shook her head. "I don't know if it was true or not, but she took it quite seriously. I heard her time and time again saying that I was the reason we had to move."

"But she also took looking after you quite seriously too, didn't she?"

"If you say so." Kylie shrugged. "I'm just not sure what she thought at the end of the day. She never talked or told me about anything. We always had a nebulous relationship, where I didn't have a whole lot to go on. I was good because it kept me alive and gave me a place to live, but, beyond that, I didn't have anything."

"Fascinating," he muttered.

"I'm glad you think so because it wasn't exactly an easy childhood."

"And yet you probably didn't know that you were suffering, did you?"

"No, I didn't. That was the one thing she used to say to me. Things like, *You're doing just fine. It's not as if I've beaten you or tortured you or anything.* She said something else. What was it?" Kylie tilted her head to the side and added, "Something about *I have done everything to the letter.*"

"Everything to the letter," he repeated, staring at her. He looked down at the image and then back at her. "I don't suppose you care to clarify that, *huh*?"

"I wish I could, but I don't know what she meant."

"Everything to the letter. What does that mean?"

"She never explained. And then, as soon as I turned eighteen, I was kicked out."

"Also fascinating when you think about it."

"I don't want to think about it," she stated, with indignation in her tone. "This is BS, and I really don't want to hear about it."

He smiled. "And I get that, but it is fascinating."

"No, … it's not fascinating," she snapped, as she pushed herself to her feet and started to pace the small living room. "This doesn't feel like my home anymore."

"I'm sorry. That is the sense of violation coming through. Somebody unwanted and unwelcomed came into your home, threatened you, was here before you got home, and was here waiting for you when you walked in, making it even worse."

"I know we were distracted and all, but how come we didn't sense him?"

He shrugged. "I don't know. I'm not sure, but maybe he has abilities of his own."

"That would suck," she muttered. "It's tough enough to nab criminals without their having the same abilities."

"Sometimes it happens that way."

"Nobody should be having this conversation."

"We're having it," he pointed out. "Lots of people like us are out there."

"And now you're back to talking about Stefan again."

"Stefan is one of them. And there is also Maddy and a few others I know."

"Yes, I've met Dr. Maddy, and she is lovely."

He turned and looked at her.

She noted he was standing to the side of the front windows, looking out into the yard from the window's edge, so that nobody could see that he was there. "You're expecting him to come back inside, aren't you?"

"No, not necessarily." He turned to her and asked, "You were saying you knew Dr. Maddy?"

"Yes, Dr. Maddy is a wonderful human being. What about her?" Kylie asked.

"I mentioned the name, but I didn't say she was a doctor. How did you know her?"

She sighed. "She came to the institute."

He smiled. "And that's exactly how my sister was helped too. What did Dr. Maddy tell you?"

"She gave me hints on how to pass the testing so I didn't appear crazy," she shared. "Yet I didn't put much faith in her process, and I didn't pass. … I got more of the same. We talked about healing or whatever else she did, but I definitely needed help to get out of that institute, so I finally took her advice. Even though it all seemed so crazy, some of it made sense."

"She's good at that," Porter declared, a warm smile lighting up his face.

"Your sister, how is she handling life now?"

"Much better. As the captain told you, they're married, and he looks after her. She's the most precious thing in his life, and I absolutely love seeing it."

"It's hard to imagine. He doesn't look the type."

"But he is the eternal protector. When he fell in love, he fell pretty hard, and my sister has benefited greatly from his love and affection."

"I'm happy for her. I doubt very many people would

have taken kindly to a psychic."

"Maybe not, but the captain already had me in his world at that time. My sister was just an add-on he'd known forever, but, somewhere along the line, they fell in love." Porter smiled. "I couldn't have been happier for her. They needed each other."

"So, she has her own protector."

"Absolutely," he agreed, smiling at her. "That's a good word for it. The captain doesn't tolerate any rumors or judgments or any negative comments, and she needs that too. She works with rescue organizations, helping animals and children in need, plus immigrants who have traveled through very difficult times to what's considered a whole new world, but are finding the adjustment pretty rough. As a matter of fact, she looks after any stray—human or animal— that she comes across. It's as if she attracts them, but she is somebody that's there for all of them."

"I can think of a lot worse things in life," she murmured.

"So can I. Now, how about getting some sleep?"

She frowned and shook her head. "I'm not sure I'll ever sleep another wink."

"I think you might surprise yourself. I know I'm tired."

"But aren't you staying up all night?" she asked, with a wry look. "Isn't that what heroes are supposed to do when they rescue a damsel in distress?"

He laughed. "Maybe, but that's not what I'll do because I need sleep too. So, we'll both go upstairs and grab some sleep."

"How will that protect us with you asleep?" she asked.

"The captain has two people on watch outside. Plus, Stefan will keep an eye on us via his special gifts."

She frowned. "I'm still not sure I'll even close my eyes."

"And again I think you'll surprise yourself. Come on. Let's show you that all the doors are locked, and then we'll go from there."

"What difference does it make to lock the doors when he came in anyway?"

"That's a good point. Come to think of it, how did he get in?"

"He'd already figured it out," she muttered crossly.

"I don't suppose you keep a key outside, do you?"

"Yes, I do, and I know you'll slam me for it."

"And now your armed stalker probably has that key, right?"

She glared at him but nodded anyway.

"Any reason why you keep a key outside?"

"Because I don't like carrying metal around," she snapped, glaring at him.

He frowned at that and asked, "Any reason?"

"Of course there's a reason, but not one I'm prepared to divulge."

He smiled and nudged her up the stairs. "You go first."

"That's not very hero-like, is it?" she asked sarcastically. "What if he's hiding under a bed upstairs?"

"Well then, we're about to find out, aren't we?" Her footsteps slowed as she reached the landing, and he added, "Bravado will only get you so far, sweetheart. I promise I will look after you."

She shook her head. "Not sure with my stalker around that anybody can make that promise," she murmured. "It's just not doable. He's like a ghost."

"Nope. Everybody gets caught at some point."

She laughed. "And you yourself know that's a bald-faced lie. Lots of people have gotten away with murder. Sometimes they've confessed on their death beds, and sometimes they've never been caught. This guy is happy to go to his grave in exactly the same way."

"I thought so, but now I think he'll want more answers."

"Sure, and that's because you made me a target," she snapped. "Remember that part? So, how does protecting me work with that bull's-eye on my back?"

"I'll keep you close to me, and we will work it out," he shared. "I've already got the captain working on a plan to keep this guy on our radar. Remember all the cameras that guy should show up on? Then we do some facial recognition, matching him to street cams, and voila. We can pick him up and talk to him."

"Pick him up and talk to him?" she repeated, grimacing. "Do you really think he'll allow that?"

He gave her a one-arm shrug. "No, I really don't. I think there will be a shootout. I'm counting on his being shot, not you or me."

"That's an awful lot to count on," she noted, staring at him starkly. "This guy has a long history of taking people out. Hell, he's paid to take people out."

Porter nodded. "Yes, but this one is personal, and that's how we will get him. I promise."

Kylie shook her head, but he placed a finger against her lips and whispered, "I promise that he will not get you."

"You can't promise that," she whispered, staring up at him, "I wish you were able to, but I know in my heart of hearts that you can't, and, therefore, you also need to look after yourself."

He shook his head. "Just because you think you know everything about me doesn't mean you do. I have a few tricks up my own sleeves."

"Yeah?" she asked in a challenge. "Then why didn't you use them when he was here?"

He smiled at her. "What makes you think I didn't?" He could see the wheels turning in her head. "He didn't shoot you, did he?"

"No." She frowned at him.

Porter nodded. "He didn't shoot you. He didn't shoot me. He turned and walked away. So think about it. Who do you think made him do that?"

"Why would you let him walk away?" she asked in exasperation. "That would be daft. We needed him caught."

"Sure," Porter agreed, "but I also didn't need him to shoot anyone. I have tricks, but not a load of them."

"I would have cheerfully taken bullets," she stated, "if it meant taking him down. He killed my family, and I won't ever forget that."

CHAPTER 12

KYLIE WOKE UP the next morning with a start. She had slept in yoga pants and a sports bra, just on the off chance that she would have to get up and run from an intruder. She rolled over, felt decent, and had slept well surprisingly. Frowning, yet delighted, she got up and headed for a shower. After scrubbing herself top to bottom and feeling a whole lot better, she got dressed in jeans and a T-shirt, pulling her hair back into a ponytail and heading down to the kitchen to put on coffee. Porter was in the kitchen already, sitting there with a cup of hot coffee.

He looked up and smiled. "You look better."

"Right," she muttered, with an eye roll. "Regardless, I do feel better."

"You were pretty rough physically last night," he noted, "emotionally as well."

"That I was," she admitted. She walked over, poured herself a cup of coffee, and then leaned against the counter to face him. "Was it a quiet night?"

"It was." He smiled. "You seem surprised."

"I am surprised that I slept. I didn't think I would."

He nodded. "And sometimes"—he picked up his cup—"sleep is the best thing for you."

"Oh, it absolutely was the best thing. I just didn't think I would get any." She brought her coffee over to the table and asked, "What are you working on?"

"Researching your aunt," he replied.

"Oh, that's probably completely boring. I'm telling you, the woman didn't have a life," she muttered.

"She did though. I just think it's a life that she wouldn't share with anybody for whatever reason."

"Because she was scared of the killer who realized she was helping the police? Maybe my stalker is that killer. He did say he was looking for my aunt, so he knew who I was."

"Yes, maybe he realized that—or not, considering your aunt might have any number of nieces and nephews."

Kylie frowned. "So, are you thinking that maybe my stalker didn't know I was the one whose family he killed?"

"That's possible," Porter acknowledged. "We don't know exactly what he knows and what he doesn't."

"But we'll assume that he knows a hell of a lot because he's clearly not stupid, since he's still free after escaping while being transported to prison so long ago."

"Exactly," Porter agreed. Just then his phone rang. He looked at the screen and noted, "It's the captain."

"Probably wants to know if we're still alive," she muttered.

He tossed her a quick smile. "Probably," he agreed cheerfully. "I'll take it outside." Hopping up, he answered it and carried on, walking out to her deck.

She wanted to follow and get details but figured it would be rude. Then deciding that she didn't care if it was rude or not, she headed out onto the deck a few minutes later, just as he was ending the call. "And?" she asked.

"Everything is quiet so far. No sign of him, and, so far, no more killings."

"As I mentioned earlier, I can't imagine he's put out a

blanket call, looking for work, not while the police know he's here."

"Wouldn't be a smart way to run his business," Porter conceded, "but it doesn't mean he isn't doing something along that line regardless."

"He did say something about my aunt."

"I know, and again I'm not sure how to take that."

"Did you tell the captain about your theory that I am somehow family to my stalker?"

"I did," he admitted. "He's not very happy with me either."

"Oh, good, finally we agree on something."

Porter let out a sigh. "The captain agrees, though that it could make for a good opportunity to try and catch this guy."

"Sure, I always love being the bait," she said in a mocking tone.

"It's not that bad," he replied.

"No, of course not. How bad can it be? He's just a mercenary, after all, so what do I care?"

He frowned at her. "Are you really upset with me?"

"No, I'm not really upset at you," she stated in frustration, raising both hands. "I'm upset at him. He's destroyed my peace and quiet in the nice little cocoon of a world I had built up."

"Ah, that kind of upset."

"What did you expect, genius? That I would wake up, and everything would already coalesce into something I could understand and deal with? Resulting in a sketch maybe?" she asked, her tone rising an octave. "If that's what you were hoping for, I'm sorry to tell you that it didn't happen."

"I think you probably came a whole lot closer to it than you realized."

"Maybe, but that doesn't mean I've had two seconds to even ask questions or to come up with the questions that I would want to ask," she explained.

"Whatever you come up with then, you can always ask," he suggested. "I've been waiting for you to get up. So, do you want to cook breakfast here or do you want to go out for breakfast?" She frowned, and he frowned right back at her. He shrugged. "Hey, I need food."

"*Great*," she muttered, as she stared down at her coffee. She chugged back the last of it and asked, "Is it safe to go out? I haven't done enough grocery shopping lately to feed you."

He laughed. "We have multiple sets of eyes on us, so we can go outside."

"*Right*," she grumbled. "So I can be bait."

Porter ignored that and added, "We can stop on the way back and pick up some groceries."

"That's fine," she conceded. "You'll be back at your house anyway."

"Not until we've caught this guy," he stated, his tone hard. "So don't even try to talk me out of it. The captain firmly agrees."

"That's because you got yourself insinuated into my life," she noted, glaring at him. "Now it'll be hard to get you out."

At that, his face split into a big boyish grin. "You could be right. Come on. Let's go. I need food." And, with that, he nudged her toward the front door.

"And where is it you want to go for this food?" she asked in exasperation, now out the door and walking to his car.

"I don't know. Do you have a favorite brunch place around here? I'm talking about a big breakfast with the whole works—pancakes and eggs, sausages, ham, and bacon."

She frowned at him. "How are your cholesterol levels, ham-boy?"

"Just fine," he said, with a beaming smile. "My body is more than happy with all that good food."

"*Good* my ass," she muttered under her breath.

"Yeah, your ass is pretty darn fine too, now that you mention it," he replied cheekily.

She glared at him. "That was highly inappropriate"— then she laughed—"but thanks."

"You're welcome," he said, with a chuckle, "and, oh, by the way. I am now officially on guard duty, assigned to look after you."

"Oh, *right*." She gave him an eye roll. "That'll make everybody bloody damn happy to hear the budget money was allocated for me."

"Most people don't know about it," he noted.

"What about your partner? Neil probably already feels left out."

"Yeah, I'll touch base with him today," Porter replied. "He'll understand."

"Will he?" she asked. "I've been worried about that."

"I wouldn't worry about him. He's been through a lot already, and he knows who's on his side and who isn't."

"That doesn't sound good either," she muttered. "You guys are partners, and you should be there for each other."

"We should be, and we will be." He waved his hand about. "Most of the time we are, but right now I have to fix this. I'm the one who got you into this, and I'm not leaving until it's solved."

She groaned. "Of course, since you made the mess, I hope you'll clean it up."

"Exactly. I'm glad you understand."

"No, I don't understand. That's the same motto my aunt used all the time. If there was a mess to be cleaned up, and I made it, believe me that I cleaned it up, and I cleaned it up fast."

"She sounds like a real winner."

Kylie shrugged. "And I'm probably doing her a disservice. It was a cold and lonely upbringing, but I was safe, and I had food and a roof over my head," she explained. "Sometimes I think I had it better than a lot of kids had."

"And you probably did. Some kids have it way worse, but that doesn't make your situation any easier just because other people were worse off," Porter noted. "That's one of the things you have to remember. Just because other people have it bad doesn't mean that you aren't entitled to recognize that your own life was pretty rough too."

"Whatever. It's over and done with, and I, for one, am very damn glad."

"Me too." Porter smiled. "After brunch, I want you to contact your aunt so we can talk to her."

"Oh, that's just peachy. I hope you have her number because I don't. And you still don't understand. She doesn't want anything to do with me."

"Let's give it a try, and we'll see."

He drove to the restaurant she suggested, another place she went to every once in a while. As she got out, she asked, "Have you ever been here before?"

He nodded. "Yeah, most of these are places I'm fairly well-known in."

"Interesting. I've come here a couple times, but I don't think I've ever seen you."

He nodded. "That's just a sign of the universe arranging things as they should be."

"What? So that we *don't* see each other?" she asked, laughing.

"Yeah, but now so that we *do* see each other all the time," he noted, with a beguiling smile. "Come on. Admit it. I'm getting under your skin."

"I don't have any trouble admitting that," she snapped. "Of course you're getting under my skin. I was just hoping that you would take a long walk and disappear for a while and leave me alone."

"Not happening," he declared, with an easy smile. "I won't leave you in danger, especially not when I put you there."

"Oh, so now we have guilt at work too." She sighed. "That'll get damn irritating as well."

"Yep, it certainly will," he said. "I'll make sure of it."

She groaned, as he laughed and opened the restaurant door for her to walk in. She walked in a few steps and stopped dead in her tracks.

He leaned in and asked, "Anything?"

"No, it's fine, but isn't that your partner?"

Porter looked over to see Neil sitting there at a nearby table, all alone, nursing a coffee and staring out the window. "It sure is." Porter walked over and smacked his partner on the back.

Neil looked up, and a big grin crossed his face. "There you are. I wondered what the hell happened to you." He noticed Kylie there and smiled at her. "I heard what this genius here did. Sorry about that. He tends to act first and think later."

"*Ya think?*" she quipped, sliding into the booth across from him. "He needs more self-control and to learn when to put on the brakes."

"I could tell him that until I'm blue in the face," Neil replied, "but he doesn't listen to me. Maybe he'll listen to you."

She laughed. "Not likely or more like never. This guy definitely won't listen to anybody."

"Hello? I'm right here, you two," Porter stated in a mocking tone.

"Oh, really," Neil replied, "and here I thought you were somewhere else."

Porter laughed. "Seems you two are off to a great start." He called over the waitress and said, "I'm starving."

She rolled her eyes at that. "I think I heard that the last time you were here."

"Maybe," he noted and quickly ordered breakfast. He looked over at Kylie.

She shook her head. "No thanks. I'll just have coffee."

"No way," he argued, then quickly placed an order for her too.

When he was done, Kylie glared at him. "That's pretty high-handed of you."

"Of course it is," he agreed, "because, if you get your way, you won't eat. Then later today you'll start moaning and groaning and crashing when things get tough, and I won't have time to feed you then."

"I've been looking after myself for a very long time now," she declared, glaring at him. "I'm hardly a child."

"Nope, you aren't," he confirmed, admiration in his tone as he grinned at her. "I can see that for myself."

She closed her eyes, feeling the heat rushing to her cheeks, and Neil's laughter broke the spell.

"Wow, look at that," Neil said. "You two are great together."

She turned and glared at him, but Neil was laughing too hard to pay any attention. "Don't you start," she muttered. "That'll just get Porter going again."

"He's not getting me going … again," Porter clarified, "because I never stopped."

"You're supposed to though, anytime now."

"Oh, I could, but I probably won't."

The waitress came back just then to bring their coffee, so Kylie stopped huffing at Porter. She really didn't have any reason to be upset. Compliments were coming all around, but just something about Porter still pricked at her every time. She turned to Neil and asked, "So, what have you been working on?"

"One of us has to work," he declared, with a look in his partner's direction, "so I've been assigned the case of the dead woman found in her apartment." Neil turned to Kylie and added, "Your latest sketches that you've drawn to date."

At that, Porter leaned forward. "Did you find any connection with the other posed woman?"

He nodded. "Yeah, they were good friends," he murmured, keeping his voice down. "So, your supposition could be correct."

"Meaning?" Kylie asked.

"I had two theories. I wondered if he'd killed the wrong woman or if the second one had witnessed him killing the first one," Porter began. "If both women were at the casino …" He turned and looked at Neil, and he nodded.

Neil added, "According to her father, she had been

there, and she came home hysterical, saying something about having seen her friend killed."

"Damn." Kylie shivered. "So, the two women knew each other. And the second woman was killed because of witnessing the death of the first woman, both posed after death by the same killer?"

"That's what we're wondering," Porter shared. "It would mean that the second shooter saw her, then followed her and took her out at home."

"Damn," she muttered, as she thought about what that young woman went through. "I mean, she was already horrified at having survived the mass shooting, seeing her girlfriend killed like that, then to be killed by the same guy?" Kylie shook her head. "Sometimes life is just out to get you."

"And sometimes it's not," Porter declared, "as in, not out to get *you*."

"Sure," she muttered, as she again rolled her eyes at him.

Neil jumped back in again. "I've spoken to the second woman's father on the phone, but I'll go to his place after breakfast and have a deeper talk with him. He's pretty shook up. His daughter was upset over the casino murders, and then it just seemed to coalesce into her murder as well. Her father's pretty confused and stressed about it all."

"And no wonder," Kylie noted. "She survived that horrific mass shooting only to come home and get taken out as well."

"Exactly, and that's something we all need to take a closer look at," Porter said.

"But it was your hypothesis," Neil pointed out, "and you were correct. So, if you've got anything else in that brain of yours that we can use …"

And that's when Kylie realized Neil knew about Porter's

abilities and often questioned or relied on him for direction or ideas. "It's nice that you can do that," she said.

"Hey, we can't use it in court, but, if Porter can help us sort out what these assholes out there are doing, I'm all for it," Neil admitted, looking around. "It isn't so cut-and-dried in this world, and I'll use any help I can get."

She had to admire that. "At least you understand it."

"Hell no, I don't understand any of it," he said, with a choked laugh. "I don't have any abilities myself, and I don't have any interest in having them. From what I have seen, they seem quite torturous."

At that, Porter leaned closer and whispered to Kylie, "Neil also knows my sister."

"Ah, one of these days I would like to meet her," Kylie shared thoughtfully. "It sounds as if we have something to talk about."

He smiled. "When this mess is over, it will be my absolute pleasure to introduce the two of you," he said, with a smile. "She can always use another friend."

She looked at him. "She has a cop for a husband and as her best friend."

"Absolutely, but it's not the same thing as somebody in her own field."

She frowned at that. "Does she have any connection to Dr. Maddy?"

"I don't know. I've never really quizzed her on that. I know that Dr. Maddy had something to do with my sister back when she had been sectioned but since then? … I don't know. Why?"

"I'm not sure. I just thought that maybe, if Annalise has been into helping all these animals and people in need, then maybe Dr. Maddy had given her some pointers on how to help them further."

"Maybe," he said, eyeing her, "but it's a good idea if she wanted to do more."

"Doing more is helpful," Kylie stated. "It gives you that sense of purpose that is often missing otherwise."

"*Hmm.*"

At that, Neil spoke up. "Can you guys describe him? Your stalker who may be our serial killer?"

She gave him the same description she had given Porter earlier, but Porter stopped her and added, "Now, think about what you saw, then repeat that to me."

She looked over at him and frowned. "Why?"

"Because I think you have this image of him in your head, but it may not match the person we saw at your house."

"But that could mean it's a different person," she noted.

"No, I'm pretty sure it was still him, but I think you've learned to do things by memory, and it may not necessarily be matching up with what you're seeing before you."

She frowned at him and shook her head.

However, Porter continued. "You describe him then, the stalker standing in front of you at your house, holding a gun on you." Porter nodded at his partner, knowing they both had seen the shooter while on trial and later in prison, before his escape.

Kylie frowned. "Late forties, fifties, potentially a little older. He was very well put together. His beard was trimmed, his mustache was trimmed, he looked good, and he appeared to take care of himself," she began. "It was the look in his eyes that really set him apart."

"Yes," Porter agreed, "that I-don't-give-a-shit attitude."

She nodded. "Definitely something about his eyes was

very different," Kylie agreed. "I'm not even sure I can explain that part, but he was dressed in black jeans, a black pullover, and had some hat over his head, but it wasn't a baseball cap, more like a fedora."

At that, his partner's eyebrows shot up. "Seriously?"

"Yes," she confirmed, "and that would make him fairly distinct, so he probably ditched it as soon as he left my house."

Neil nodded. "That's possible too." He looked back at her and asked, "Anything else to add?"

She sighed. "The anger and the shock he exhibited when Porter said I was family or related or whatever revealed even more about him. He was holding the gun as if it was an extension of his hand," she described, "and it was so shiny. That really surprised me. I kept staring at the handgun pointed at me, as if it would explode. And, of course, it was about to," she said, "but it had a different look to it."

"That was a silencer," Porter interjected. "And it looked to be a custom job too."

At that, Neil leaned forward. "Can you tell me anything about it?"

Kylie shrugged. "It was long, bigger than I imagined. When he held the gun along his thigh, and he took off, it was, I would say, a good four to five inches long."

"*Huh.*" Neil thought about that for a long moment, and the two men continued to discuss it.

Kylie grabbed a napkin and took out the pencil that she always kept with her and started to sketch. Very quickly she had a picture of the entire handgun. She turned it around and said, "This was it."

Porter snatched the napkin from her and took a closer look, then nodded. "Actually that's very close," he murmured. "Nice job."

She shook her head. "There was just something about it."

"What about it?" Neil pushed.

She winced, then added, "I think a lot of it was … If I say *energy*, would that be understandable?"

"To me it would," Porter replied, "but not necessarily to Neil."

"Energy? What does that mean exactly?" Neil asked.

"Energy clung to that gun," she said. "In other words, if you get ahold of that weapon, you'll find it's been used in several crimes."

"Which we already know," Porter pointed out, "and, of course, it would be nice to confirm with forensics, but we have to get it first. These guys are well known for ditching their tools."

"Not this one," she argued. "My drawing pencils are something that I hang on to, even if it'll be a problem. I still prefer to use my own than to get a new one. Same for our shooter."

"So, your stalker had a favorite weapon," Neil stated. "That's not uncommon."

"No, it's not," she agreed. "I'm just saying that this one is special to him. You want to piss him off? Then you've got to grab that gun and take it somewhere and deep-six it because, for him, … it's almost his lucky charm."

Neil nodded. "Let's hope we get a chance to take it from him and to really piss him off. Maybe, if he doesn't have it, it'll be like clipping his wings a little bit."

"I don't think so," Porter countered. "Something about the way he moved, the way he walked, makes me think he's done martial arts. I would swear to it. So, while he may use weapons most of the time, I wouldn't be at all surprised if he doesn't have the ability to take us out very quickly and easily with just his bare hands."

"And yet he doesn't," Neil stated, staring at his partner. "He didn't engage you, and we don't have any records of him going after anyone *without* a gun."

"Have you looked though?" she asked. "It's a different MO and not what you've been finding so far."

"Maybe." Neil made a note to himself on his phone. "I'll take a look when I get back to the office. You guys take care of yourselves, okay?"

"We can certainly try."

"Try harder. I'm not sure what you're doing about it at all, but let's not have any more deaths around here." And, with that, Neil tossed back the bulk of his coffee and got up and left.

She watched him walk toward the door and then bolted to her feet. "Neil!"

He spun around, just as a bullet shattered the glass window beside him. He dropped to the floor as if a rock, while the place erupted into shrieks, and everybody scattered. Under the table now, Kylie stared around her, as everybody froze, waiting for the next bullet, wondering who would be shot next and how to ensure it wouldn't be them.

Porter yelled at her to stay there, and this time he booked it out the back door. She wasn't planning on going anywhere. Yet no way could this shooter be her stalker asshole because he wanted Kylie, not Neil. However, if it were her stalker, why did he go after Neil? Maybe as a warning because that would be a connection to Porter, and Porter had pissed off her stalker.

And one thing she was quickly learning was to never piss

off a serial killer.

PORTER RACED OUT the back of the restaurant and around to the front, hearing tires squealing as the shooter took off. The driver gave Porter the middle finger in the air as he drove past him. No point in hiding his identity because it was perfectly obvious who he was. *Keefe Hogan.* And that meant Hogan didn't give a shit who saw him. An unhinged killer was something they really didn't want to deal with, but nothing was stopping Hogan now. Porter noted that the shooter had ditched the fedora, now wearing a different hat.

Hogan was a chameleon in appearance and seemed to switch in and out of facades quite comfortably. He also appeared to have absolutely no problem stealing vehicles quickly and efficiently. Porter knew this getaway vehicle would be dropped in a heartbeat and another one picked up as he moved along. This shooting made it all the more important to go talk to Kylie's aunt, even though Agatha refused to have anything to do with Porter's previous phone calls.

Porter made his way back inside the restaurant, as the patrons slowly came together again, having heard the gunman take off in a squeal of tires. Porter found Neil sitting down now, having a second cup of coffee beside Kylie. "Are you okay?" Porter asked Neil, as he reached them.

Kylie looked up with relief when she saw Porter. "When you took off, I wasn't sure what to do."

"The good thing is you did what you were supposed to do, which was stay put," he stated, with a note of humor.

"Did you see him?" Neil asked.

"I did. He gave me the finger as he drove past me. He

was in another stolen vehicle, and he had changed to a cowboy hat."

"Oh, that's right," Kylie said. "He has that weird ability, doesn't he? He blends in and out very quickly, and he's very good at changing somehow, fitting in wherever he is."

"Exactly," Porter agreed. "That just makes it that much harder to stop this guy because it's harder to catch him."

"We certainly didn't expect him to be here for coffee," she pointed out, staring at him, her face ghostly white.

He smiled. "No, but that's not a mistake we'll make again."

"What's that? Coming to eat?"

He could tell that she was still rattled, and why wouldn't she be? There'd been a shooting in the restaurant. It was a conversation that everybody here would talk about for days.

Even then, the waitress ran over. "Are you okay?" she cried out excitedly. And she looked at Neil. "How about you? Was he trying to shoot you?"

"I think it was a warning shot as much as anything," Neil replied.

And Porter agreed with that totally. It was a warning shot that they would be foolish to ignore. He looked over at Kylie, whose face paled even more. "Can you bring us some more coffee?" he asked the waitress. She nodded and quickly came right back with a pot, refilling Kylie's cup.

Neil shook his head and gestured to Porter. "None for him. He's had enough excitement and doesn't want the jitters all day after the shooting."

Kylie laughed as if it were the best joke ever, and it was obvious that now that all the danger was past, it would provide a steady stream of excitement all day.

"Best thing they've had happen to them all week," Neil

noted.

"All year," Kylie muttered. "God, I'm totally okay to not have that happen again. If hearing it was awful, I can't imagine being in it. I can't believe that you just managed to duck out of it, Neil."

"It's also why I think it was a warning shot," Neil stated, and he gave his partner a hard stare. "He could have shot me. That warning was for you, Porter, not me. So you need to watch your back."

"I know," Porter said, with a slow nod. "You better go tell the captain what happened."

"Yeah, that'll be fun. You can expect he'll want your sorry ass in his office."

"I'm working the case, and I'll come in when I have something to tell him. Right now we have nothing, and, until we do, really no point to call," he explained.

With that, Neil got up and headed out the front door again. Several people watched and waited, and then, when he made it through the door safely, a rush of people followed behind him.

She watched the exit and sighed. "I don't think we needed that today."

"I don't think anybody ever needs a shock like that in their day," Porter noted, with a smile. "The good news is, it was literally a warning shot."

"Yeah, but it'll be the only one you get."

"And, if that's the case," he said, studying her intently, "what is it he wanted?"

She frowned at him. "I guess that's the real question, isn't it? If it was a warning shot, why? What would it tell you, outside of *Watch your back* and *I can get you anytime*?"

"That's a pretty good one," he admitted. "Also that he's

pissed off at what I said, and he wants answers."

"But you don't have answers to give, do you?"

He laughed. "Sure I have some answers to give," he said, eyeing her strangely, "but they won't be any answers that he's happy to hear."

"Right, so, in other words, you've got a pissed-off gunman after you," she noted, with an eye roll.

"Maybe. Are you ready to go?"

"I thought I was getting more coffee?"

"Let's get it to-go," he suggested.

"Where are we going now?" she asked, as she stood up.

He quickly arranged a coffee to-go with the waitress, and then he turned to face Kylie. "Going to your aunt's now."

"You know where she lives?" Kylie asked. When he nodded, she stared at him. "Ah, shit. I was really hoping you would forget about that."

"I know you were," he murmured, "but you and I both know that we can't. It needs to happen, and it needs to happen now."

"Maybe," Kylie muttered, "but God help you when she finds out who you are and why you've come because that will piss her off."

CHAPTER 13

P ORTER PULLED UP thirty minutes later outside the small townhome. It was one of the middle units in a row of six, and it sat where nobody could really see or disturb the central occupant.

Kylie studied it and nodded.

Porter shared, "Even at this stage, she's protecting herself."

"Do you blame her?" she asked. "You realize that, if this Hogan guy has followed us here, he'll come after her?"

"Let's hope he doesn't know that we're here. She refused to answer my calls, to get back to me at any time," he noted, "so what else am I supposed to do?"

"Yeah, but normally you wouldn't have contacted her in the first place, would you?"

"Absolutely I would have," he declared, looking at her. "She has a very defined connection to this guy. No way anybody looking into Hogan's case will miss Agatha's connection to him."

"And that has always been her problem," Kylie said. "Agatha's been trying to put this all behind her, but instead of that, ... it keeps coming back around and around."

"And it will keep coming around, as long as he's out there," Porter noted. "I would love for her to finally have peace of mind and not have this be ... such a big issue for her. Yet, until he is dealt with, you and I both know he won't stop."

"Or," she muttered, more to herself than him, "he'll end up continuing to kill at leisure and disappearing whenever he wants to."

"Exactly, and he's got it down to a decent art now," Porter acknowledged. "He's making money at it, and there always seems to be a market for those who want somebody taken out."

"I just can't fathom that. And now I know that my entire family died at his hand," she whispered. "Good God, what kind of animals are these people?"

"Ones who have ulterior motives, I suspect," Porter replied. "And, in this case, we really don't have any way of knowing what was going on because we don't know who paid for the killing."

"Which is a scary thought in itself," she stated. "He took out all four of them. There is so much that I want to know. Was he supposed to take out all four? Was he supposed to take out five? Was it just the luck of the draw that I survived?"

"That is a mystery. If it was supposed to be all of you, then you would think it wouldn't have been quite so easy to have appeased his client with less than five kills. And that is something we don't know, and we may never know," he shared, thinking about it. "You'll torture yourself to death on that one, if you're looking for that answer."

"Maybe, but that is definitely hard for me to let go of. I'm sure you can understand that."

"Absolutely," he murmured. He got out, walked around to her side, and held the door open for her.

"If she sees us coming, she won't answer the door."

He frowned as he looked toward the townhome. "You could be right. She really is protective, isn't she?"

"*Paranoid* would be a good word for it," she murmured, "and I never understood it until now."

"But now you do, and so now you're being protective of her."

"Is that wrong?" she asked, staring up at him. "I mean, if you consider everything she's been through, it seems to be the least I could do."

He didn't say anything, while staring at the townhome ahead of him. "I just wondered," he murmured, "if she hasn't seen us, does she work?"

"I don't know. I have no idea if she's doing anything right now. I wasn't kidding when I told you that I have had zero contact with her since I left her home as I turned eighteen."

"Which is understandable," he replied, as he reached an arm around her and tucked her up close. "We could just look as if we were engaged to be married or something."

"She wouldn't believe it," Kylie declared.

He stared at her. "Why?"

"Yeah, I was pretty well warned off men from an early age," she explained, with a mock smile. "We never really discussed any of the personal stuff, but she was against any and all men right from the beginning."

"Wow." Porter stared down at her. "That's very unusual."

"Which just implies that she had a very difficult personal life and wanted to save me the hurt."

"Maybe," he conceded. "It's definitely something for us to contemplate. Let's see if she'll even answer the door."

"I'm really worried that we're passing her location on to

that asshole."

"Honestly, I'm beginning to worry that he's already been here."

"What?" she asked, staring up at him and then turning to look at the townhome. "Seriously?"

"Yeah, it's not as if she's hard to find, not to that extent. Plus, remember the crime scene you just drew at your place, which you didn't recognize?"

"Good God." Her footsteps raced ahead of him as she ran up the sidewalk toward her aunt's place.

"Have you ever seen her in this house?" he asked.

"No." She turned to face him. "I didn't know she was here. This is a new location. I've never even seen it before."

"How often did you guys move when you were little?"

"It's hard to say when I was very little," she began. "It was a lot when I was in school. I kept asking her to not move anymore because I really just wanted to spend time in the same school and make friends, and she told me that friends were useless and that they would turn their backs on me anyway."

"Wow, she really was paranoid, wasn't she?"

"I don't know whether it was paranoid or something else," Kylie corrected, "but it was just one of those teachings that always slipped out of her mouth, and I took it to heart."

He didn't say anything, and, as they got up to front door in question, he rang the doorbell.

Kylie shook her head. "She won't answer."

"No, I don't think she will either, but what I don't know is whether she can."

Kylie stared at him, her jaw twitching. "I really don't like what you said."

He smiled. "And I'm sorry. Just me being honest. Obviously it's not what I was trying to get across, but, if Agatha can come to the door, that's a whole different story than if she can't."

She winced. "Could you be a little less honest next time?"

He smiled at her. "You wouldn't appreciate that either." He rang the doorbell a second time and then a third, but nobody answered.

When the neighbor's door opened, and a woman came out, purse and keys in her hand as she locked up, she looked over at them and shared, "Oh, Agatha isn't here. She left in a hurry."

"Do you know when?" Kylie asked.

"No, no I don't," she replied. "She left me her cat to look after, which she's never done before. I'm not really a cat person. I do love animals though, so I wouldn't say no."

"Thank you," Kylie said.

"Do you know her?"

"Yes, she looked after me when I was little," Kylie replied. "I came to say hello, but apparently she's not home."

"Yeah, she's definitely one of those people you don't come up on out of the blue." The neighbor laughed. "I made that mistake once, and, boy, she tore a strip off me. You definitely have to make an appointment to see her," she added, with an eye roll. "But good luck with that anyway." With that, she gave them a small wave and headed to her car, parked on the side of the street.

Porter looked back at the door and asked Kylie, "Well?"

"What? It's not as if we can just break in there."

"No, of course not," he said, as he kept staring at the door.

"Oh, God, you really think something is wrong, don't

you?"

"I want to know for sure that she's not in there and injured."

Kylie poked around under the mats. "She always left a key. That was how I always got inside because she never gave me a key." Kylie sighed. "Either I wasn't to be trusted or something along that line." She quickly found a key taped under the mat, then waited for the other car to drive away. Once it had, she quickly unlocked the door and stepped inside.

Porter stepped in beside her and froze.

"He's been here," she muttered softly.

"I know, and we need to know if your aunt is still alive."

"Please, dear God."

"Stay here." With that, he raced upstairs to the bedroom. He went through the entire upstairs but found no sign of Agatha. He came down and shook his head. "I don't see her."

"That's a good thing then, isn't it?" Kylie asked.

"Maybe." He looked around and frowned. "It feels empty, cold and empty, but she also thought she would get away. Either she didn't quite make it or he found her and brought her back. We need to check the hospitals to see if somebody has not been identified." She stared at him, the color dropping from her face as he nodded. "I know. It's a bit of a shock, but I don't want to leave any stone unturned, not now." He quickly locked up, replaced the key, and muttered, "Let's go."

As soon as he got in the car, he phoned Neil. "No sign of Agatha, but a weird energy surrounds her place."

"So, what are you thinking?"

"Can you check the hospitals, see if any Jane Does have

showed up?" he asked, staring at Kylie beside him. For not having had any affection from her aunt, Kylie was going through symptoms of grief right now.

"Will do," Neil agreed. "I mean, this guy is really cutting a wide swath, isn't he?"

"Yeah, he is, and he doesn't appear to be done yet either. Watch your back."

Neil snorted. "It's not my back, dude. It's yours. You watch your back. And keep Kylie safe. I don't know if she's the end target Hogan's after, but I sure wouldn't put it past him to confirm there weren't any witnesses left."

"Which is exactly what he's already done once. So, yeah, I hear you." Porter ended the call. "We're heading to the station."

"What about my aunt?" Kylie asked in a faint tone.

"Neil is checking hospitals, and he'll call us if he finds anything. In the meantime, we're heading back to town to give the captain a brief update," he added. "We don't know what the hell is going on at this point in time, but we sure need to get ahead of this thing."

"He's got her," Kylie said. "He absolutely must have her."

"You don't know that," he stated firmly. "For all you know, she escaped, and she could be hurt somewhere." Kylie stared at him, and he winced. "And I get it. That's not a whole lot better."

"No," she snapped, "it isn't a whole lot better. I wouldn't wish that on anybody."

"No, I wouldn't either," he agreed, with a hard sigh. He drove steadily to town, and, when his partner phoned him back, he was a bit cagey. "What's going on?" Porter asked Neil.

"There is a Jane Doe. She showed up at a hospital yesterday morning, in rough shape." He gave him an address and added, "She's unconscious and has been since a few minutes after arriving. So that could be Agatha. She matches the rough description you gave me. You might want to do a drive-by to see if it's her."

"We are on our way." With that, he ended the call. Porter turned the car in the correct direction, then spoke to Kylie. "Presumably you're okay to go to the hospital."

"Absolutely," she murmured. "All I can think about is Agatha lying somewhere, waiting for this guy to come kill her. And then he finally shows up, and now she's fighting for her life somewhere."

"Let's not think about it that way," he murmured. "We don't know what's happening here. Let's just keep an eye on it." He pulled into the hospital parking lot and added, "Now remember. Don't say anything, and don't do anything. We're just looking for your aunt, who may have gone missing."

"Right. I can't tell anybody anything, can I?"

"We can tell them a little bit, but we won't tell them much. We sure as hell don't want to set off any alarms just yet," he pointed out.

They walked up to the reception desk and spoke to them, asking about the Jane Doe who had come in. He quickly pulled out his badge, and the receptionist wrote down the room number for him.

"Still no ID for her," the nurse shared, "so anything you can do to help us out would be great."

"We might have an ID," he offered. "I think this is her niece."

"Oh good." The woman seemed relieved. "Go check it

out please, and then get back to me. I'll set about doing notifications, once we can get that positive ID." With that, she returned to her work.

That left them to head to the elevators and then up to the designated room. As soon as they got out of the elevator, Kylie headed toward Jane Doe's room. "It feels … it feels as if maybe he was here already."

"Maybe," Porter conceded, "but let's not put that energy out there."

They found the room and walked in, and Kylie gasped, raced to the bedside, and picked up her aunt's hand. "Oh my God, Aunt Agatha, are you okay?"

The other woman didn't respond at all. She appeared to be unconscious.

Kylie turned to Porter. "This is my aunt."

He walked to the bedside and studied Agatha's features with a critical eye and asked, "Are you sure?"

"Yes, I'm sure. I know it's been a while since I've seen her, but I'm sure."

He nodded. "You stay here. I'll go speak to the receptionist."

Kylie waited in place, talking to her aunt, wondering what had gone on with Agatha. When Porter returned, he shared, "They're satisfied that you've identified her. They'll see if anybody else was in her life. They also want any information from you too. I've given them her home address."

"What happened to her?" Kylie asked.

"Apparently Agatha was running and fell and smashed her head pretty hard."

Kylie winced. "She was trying to get away from him, wasn't she?"

"That would be my take on it, yes," he confirmed, with a gentle smile, "but it looks as if, once again, she has survived, and you've got to remember that."

Kylie nodded. "She's ever the survivor." She went silent for a moment, caught up in a memory.

"What are you thinking?" Porter asked.

She smiled wistfully. "Just … she used to do exercises faithfully, old-school calisthenics. And wanted me to do them too. Every single time I asked why or complained, I got the same response. *Because you never know when you'll have to run for your life.* I always chalked it up as one of her quirky sayings, but, God, I feel so selfish now. There were all these hints, all these little bits and pieces of conversations that I never put all together," she murmured.

"Selfish, no," Porter corrected. "You did amazingly well with somebody who was working very hard at keeping you out of her life. For whatever reason, Agatha was trying to keep you uninvolved, whether that's because she was worried about you or because she didn't want to explain the mess that she had gotten into. Didn't you say she had zero interest in psychic abilities and was angry when you ended up with some?"

"Yes, and now I understand why."

"You mean, because she had them herself?"

"Yes," Kylie agreed, "and that is an easy enough explanation."

He shrugged and stared down at her aunt. "It would have been better if she had given you some help to manage them."

"Maybe," Kylie murmured, "but obviously she didn't think that way. As far as she was concerned, I was better off without them."

"And that could be exactly what happened to her," he suggested, with a nod.

A slight movement came from the woman in the hospital bed just then. Kylie leaned forward and whispered, "It's okay. I'm here. I'm here."

Agatha slowly opened her eyes and stared at her. "Why are you here?"

Kylie winced, reflexively pulled back. "You were hurt. You are in the hospital," she explained. "You were found unconscious on the street."

She stared at her, shook her head. "I don't remember that."

"Maybe you don't," Porter interjected, stepping forward, "but you were brought into the hospital, and they didn't know whom to contact."

Agatha closed her eyes and moaned. "My head."

"I'll call the nurse for you." Kylie got up and went outside, catching one of the nurses and asking her for pain meds for Agatha.

"She's awake, is she?" the nurse asked. "I'll bring the doctor along right away." And she walked rapidly down the hallway.

Returning to Agatha's side, Kylie asked her aunt, "Are you okay?"

"Of course I'm not okay," she stated waspishly. "I'm in the hospital. How does that even beget a question."

"That's not quite what I meant."

"Of course it's not what you meant, child."

"I wondered if our serial killer found you," Kylie stated.

Her aunt froze, her gaze opening wide as she stared up at her. Then Agatha frantically checked out her hospital room in a blind panic. "Is he here?"

"No, he's not here, at least not right now," Kylie said in a soothing tone.

Agatha stared at her. "What do you even know about it?" she asked, the fear still evident in her voice.

"I know that he escaped prison, remains free and clear, and that's he's recently killed two people in town," Kylie replied. "We're trying to stop him."

"What the hell do you mean, you're trying to stop him?" she asked in disbelief.

Kylie shrugged. "I work for the police. I'm a sketch artist."

Her aunt struggled to comprehend, the pain clouding her vision as she shook her head. "That makes no sense," she murmured. "They have photographers."

"I keep telling them that too," Kylie confirmed, "but some people just seem to want more."

"Everybody wants more," Agatha complained in the same bitter refrain that Kylie had heard all throughout her childhood. "Everybody wants more." And then in a more formal tone, Agatha stated, "You can leave now."

Kylie winced. "I told Porter that you would say that, but he didn't think so."

"He doesn't know me, does he?" she declared, staring at Kylie. "I'm fine, and I'll be home soon."

"I highly suspect that Hogan found you at your house," Kylie noted, "so you may not want to count on that."

"I don't count on anything," Agatha snapped. "I haven't had a whole lifetime of this for no reason at all. You just go take care of yourself and leave me be. I'm better off alone anyway."

Kylie wouldn't argue that point because her aunt had repeated this over and over throughout Kylie's entire life. She looked back at Porter, who studied her aunt with a hard look.

"What is your relationship with the serial killer?" he asked.

"Who are you?" she snapped, glaring at him. He pulled out his ID and showed it to her. She sagged back and muttered, "Whatever. I don't have any information for you."

"We need to know what your relationship is with this Hogan guy."

"You already know what it is, or you wouldn't be here," she snapped bitterly. "It's never good trying to help people, particularly the police." She turned to glare at her niece. "You, of all people, should know that."

"Yeah, maybe so," Kylie murmured, "but I also needed to do something that made me feel good about myself."

Her aunt stared at her and snorted. "Right, as if that'll work." She sagged back on the bed. "I need to sleep." She gave them a wave of her hand. "Please leave."

Immediately Kylie stepped away from the bed, but Porter held her close by.

"I get that you had a tough life," Porter began, "and I'm not sure what your relationship with Hogan is, beyond the obvious, but you sure had a hell of a deal raising Kylie."

"I raised her fine. It's not my fault she's fallen into your clutches now," Agatha declared, with a knowing look in his direction. "The men of this world are all the same, all cut from the same cloth. You are all users," she murmured, "and you are not needed here, so go away."

Just then the doctor stepped into the room, his jovial tone exclaiming, "Ah, you're awake. That's excellent."

"It is excellent," Agatha replied, "and I don't want any visitors."

The doctor turned to Kylie and Porter.

Kylie nodded. "We were just leaving. Perhaps you could take a moment to let me know how she is afterward."

"Of course, of course," he agreed, beaming.

"No," Agatha snapped, "you will not tell her anything."

The doctor frowned, evidently confused.

Kylie sighed. "Never mind. My aunt has always been very contrary."

"That's not your concern," Agatha snapped. "What I am is tired and sore, and I don't want people here."

"We got the message," Kylie replied. "We'll talk to you later."

"No, you won't."

And, with that, the nurse ushered them out the door.

On the way back to the car, Kylie went silent, her heart confused, everything inside her a jumble of raw feelings at seeing her aunt and hearing the same nastiness all over again.

"Lovely woman," Porter quipped, as they stepped out into the fresh air.

Kylie laughed. "She is definitely not. I don't know whether it's a natural reaction or she just intentionally pushes everybody away. Yet I can tell you that was just a small snapshot of what my life was like with her."

"I'm sorry," Porter said. "Every child deserves love."

"Every child deserves parents too, but apparently I didn't get mine."

"And that's not your fault either."

"No." She turned to him. "I know exactly whose fault it is." An edge filled her tone that she couldn't keep out. "Every time I think about it, … I realize how much I owe this Hogan asshole for the pain and suffering he's caused me."

"Easy now," Porter muttered, "only so much that you'll

ever get back in terms of answers or reasons."

"What about revenge or retribution?" she murmured, staring up at him, the intensity of her gaze deepening as he shook his head.

"Nope, we cannot allow ourselves that."

"Why not?" she asked. "You just saw what I dealt with because of him."

"I know, but, as you told me, your aunt raised you, and you did survive. You are also much stronger and much better off without her in your life now," he noted. "So, as hard as it might be, you need to thank her and then move on."

"That's exactly what I did," she replied, "until you insisted on dragging me back and facing her again."

"What about her did you recognize?" he asked, giving her a searching look. "Step outside your feelings and think only about the woman in that hospital bed. Exactly what did you see?"

She stopped, thought about it, and began, "I saw a scared woman, somebody terrified, who wanted to leave the hospital as soon as she could, but also someone injured, who needed time to regroup and to come up with a new plan." She thought back, stepping into the moment. "The trouble is, I don't think she has a new plan."

"No, she probably doesn't, and you know why she's terrified."

"Yeah, because of him," she snapped.

"Yes, because of Hogan, but it also means that she survived him again. Isn't that something you want to question? Isn't that something you want to think about?"

"Not really. Agatha's been waiting for this opportunity, waiting for this moment all her life. For Hogan to come back, I mean. At least that's my take on it."

"Oh, it's my take too," Porter agreed, "but, if that's the case, maybe you should ask yourself why. Why out of everybody else that he's managed to kill has he left your aunt alive? Not once, but twice now?"

CHAPTER 14

PORTER'S WORDS KEPT Kylie occupied as she pondered the vagaries of serial killers and her aunt. Her aunt was an enigma. Agatha was somebody Kylie never understood at all growing up, and the woman had gotten colder and more locked down the older she got. Even now, Kylie didn't have any answers. She finally stirred from her thoughts when she noted Porter pulling into a driveway, but not one that she knew. "Where are we?" she asked, as she looked around. "Why are we here?"

"This is a friend's house," he replied.

"So we're visiting at this hour?" she asked, her tone incredulous as she stared at him.

"No, this is where we're staying. My friend's out of town, and he's totally okay with us bunking here for a few days."

"Why?"

"Because I don't want to deal with a serial killer at our front door every ten minutes when we need sleep," he explained. "And this will buy us a little bit of time to get another plan in order."

"What you said about Hogan, about him keeping my aunt alive, is just wishful thinking."

"Maybe." He hopped out, walked around, and opened up her door.

She stepped out, thanking him absentmindedly, as she tried to organize her thoughts. "I don't get it at all. I recognize that you seem to think you did something to stop him from shooting me." His lips quirked at that. "But there is also the consideration that now—twice—he has also left me alive."

"Ah, I wondered when you would realize that."

She glared at him. "I don't play games, Porter. Don't test me, thinking I'll come up with answers. Be honest with me. Feel free to jump in anytime."

He chuckled. "I jump in a lot, and you usually get mad at me."

Her shoulders slumped. "I suppose I do. It's not exactly easy to be resilient and roll with the punches right now," she muttered.

"No, it isn't, but none of this is easy." He walked her around the car, out of the garage, and into the house.

"You really think we'll be safe here?"

"We will be for a while," he said cheerfully. "Unless you have some tracking device on you."

She stared at him. "What? I wouldn't even know what that would look like or who would be adept enough to plant that, much less why."

"It's the *why* that always gets me," he murmured, as he stared at her with a quirky grin in his face. "But come on, let's go get some sleep."

"Sleep would be lovely," she muttered. She followed him into the house and found it to be truly beautiful. "Your friend is quite lucky to have this place."

Porter nodded. "Yes, he is. He's also worked for it for quite a while. This is his solace area. I think that's what he would call it. It's his man cave, but he just wanted a space where he felt completely at home."

"Yes, I can see that. It's hard to be out in the world all the time and not have a personal space to call your own."

He smiled as he walked into the kitchen, dropped his keys, then faced her. "The bedrooms are upstairs. I know we didn't bring bags with us, but we can always make do without for tonight."

She waved her hand dismissively. "That's hardly an issue tonight, and you're right. Sleep would be the better option, but you realize it's still early, right?"

He nodded. "I do, but you're also very tired, and I can see it clear as day. So let's grab some shut-eye while we can. Then we'll order in some food and go from there." He led her upstairs, as she slowly made her way up, noting just how exhausted she really was. Somehow even navigating the stairs was a challenge.

"How come I'm so incredibly tired now?" she whispered.

"Honestly, I'm not sure."

An odd element filled his tone, and it irked her immensely. "And if you do know something, don't tell me about it right now," Kylie ordered. "I have enough to deal with."

He chuckled. "Yeah, my thoughts exactly."

She groaned as she made her way to the last of the rooms and asked, "Here?"

"Sure, that sounds good. Three bedrooms are up here, so we'll take the two spares. I'll be right next door." He walked her into the bedroom, so she could see where she would be sleeping.

The great big bed called to her. Kylie groaned. "I won't do anything but crash." Not sure what was going on, she was fully aware that her energy levels were dropping. As soon as she got to the bed, she collapsed down face-first.

"Are you okay?" Porter asked.

She waved her hand and whispered, "I just need sleep." She didn't understand it, but something, something inside was draining her at a rapid rate, and she was crashing so fast that she had no time to say much. Within a matter of seconds, she was out.

PORTER WATCHED KYLIE go completely under, wondering just what was going on and why she was crashing so fast. He pulled out his phone, deciding this was a question for Stefan. He'd barely had a chance to start dialing, when Stefan popped into his mind.

Something or someone has tapped her. I can feel her energy going down in waves. I just don't know why or what.

I brought her to a place where I think she'll be safe, so she can recharge. However, the closer we got here, and the minute she realized she could go to sleep, she just dropped completely.

I see that, Stefan noted, his voice calm. *I'll just run a quick scan and see if something is happening. Did you pick up anything?*

Outside of the fact that something was very strange about her aunt, no.

And this aunt also has abilities, I understand?

That's unclear at this point. Kylie has had theories both ways. I don't really know the whole story, but I can tell you that some very funky things are going on, either with the aunt or with the whole story of the aunt's involvement with Keefe Hogan. I don't really understand it yet.

Okay, that's good enough for now. I am sure we'll sort it out.

Yeah, says you. Porter laughed. *I can tell you that the aunt is not interested in sorting it out.*

Which is also interesting.

Maybe, but I don't understand anything about Kylie's reaction right now, with this energy drain on her, so I'll just stay close.

Definitely stay close. She might wake up in a very different mindset.

Meaning?

I don't know, Stefan replied, his voice distant now, as if trying to sort out something. *I need to contact Dr. Maddy. I'll get back to you.* And, with that, he disappeared.

Only Stefan could ever do that, and every time Porter interacted with the man, Porter realized just how much more potential there was in the realm of psychic abilities. Stefan always did something or showed Porter something that made him realize just how different life could be if everybody would use these gifts for good, as did Stefan.

Of course it was a very strange thing to consider, but Stefan was incredibly talented, and at the same time quite infuriating. Porter felt unable to help Kylie, when she was fading so quickly. Porter stared at her for a long moment, then stepped out of her bedroom, leaving the door open, his mind going to Stefan's quick exit too.

Porter had first met Stefan at the institute where his sister had been committed. Porter quickly realized that Stefan was a lifeline out of the madness that Annalise had suddenly found herself in. Porter's sister responded so beautifully whenever Stefan was around. Porter had become increasingly aware that Stefan and Annalise shared on a level that Porter didn't really understand. Now that he did, it was pretty amazing to see. Stefan was in their lives, not all the time, but definitely sometimes. At least enough that he had been a huge help in times of crisis.

It was hard to argue with somebody who could do all the things that Stefan did on a regular basis, and who helped to the extent that he did. It was pretty amazing that Porter himself could even do what he had managed to learn. Only through his sister did he realize that the telepathic messages were the way Stefan had kept Annalise intact during all this—not only intact but following his cues. Thus she had survived the testing to get her out of confinement, where Stefan could then help her further. Through both of them Porter learned just how much of an issue it was to have people with psychic abilities caught in this mental health loophole situation.

Porter ended up working with Stefan to help his sister, who was an empath, and who felt way too much about the people around her. That had made her life so much more difficult, particularly when she was in an institution and could feel everybody's pain and confusion and fear. But now that Annalise was so much better, Stefan had turned his attention to Porter, making him realize just how much he had helped his sister fine-tune and direct her own energy, saying that he had a similar gift that allowed him to do that.

To him it was just love, and Stefan had chuckled at that. "But that's what everything good in life is born of, so intent is everything."

It had helped Porter over the last few years to come to terms with a lot of things he did understand and could do, and he'd worked hard to expand and to open up his gifts. Therefore, when it came to his work and the crime scenes he was dealing with, he could pick up helpful bits and pieces with his gifts. He still had a long way to go to fully utilize those gifts, but it was something worth doing, so he was open to all kinds of advances.

He knew just from looking at her that Kylie had abilities and was locked down. Something incredibly weird was going on about her, but because he himself wasn't all that much of a pro at it, he didn't understand. He still didn't understand how unique her own abilities were and exactly what she was doing because, in many ways, she didn't know either. That was part of the thing he kept trying to bring up, but he wasn't sure Stefan understood what he was concerned about.

A nod of acknowledgment came through his mind, which made him laugh because, if ever people would freak out, it would be when someone was in their heads, letting them know they heard and understood their personal thoughts. That was just another unique thing about Stefan that made everybody look at him sideways, at least those who knew about him. Porter's sister couldn't say enough good about Stefan because of all the help he had given her, and, in his own way, Porter agreed. Something had been very life-changing about meeting Stefan. Life-saving, perhaps. It was a moment that changed his world forever. Porter just needed a little more help to figure out what was currently going on with Kylie.

He wandered back downstairs, put on a pot of coffee, sent a text to his buddy, saying they were in the house and thanking him for the hospitality, and got a quick thumbs-up in return. Then again it was expected, as he'd also helped his friend out once when his friend's sister had been in rough shape. You never really knew who your friends were going to be, but a lot of them for Porter had come from work, from the work he'd done to help others. There had to be something good about that.

With a cup of coffee in hand, he wandered around the house, keeping an ear tuned to Kylie, wondering just what was going on and how that aunt of hers was involved in all this. He did see the same fear on Aunt Agatha's face that he had seen on Kylie's. He didn't have the same detachment that Kylie had, which was interesting. But, for Kylie, this was a woman who had raised her in a negative, cruel, and isolating way, then kicked her out the minute she turned eighteen. Kylie had made the break and didn't want anything more to do with Agatha, which was understandable, and yet there was more to it than that. Porter just wasn't sure what. Had the aunt been protecting Kylie?

That would make sense in many ways, and yet, for such a cold-hearted woman, why would she have chosen to withhold affection from an innocent child, unless she just couldn't handle any more loss herself? Of course he could drive himself mad by creating scenarios that would fit, yet still they may not be true, since he didn't know all the information. The fact that the latest victims were connected and potentially were killed by the same guy stalking Kylie just meant that the stalker was afraid he had been seen, and that was a loose string the killer couldn't afford to leave. It also meant that, after he'd been forced to kill the senator's daughter, he followed his true target to her home and killed her there, but then what?

Then the killer had been a busy little bee finding Kylie and then her aunt. Yet our serial for-hire killer again had left both of them alive. Was the killer losing his touch? That possibility would probably drive Porter absolutely crazy because the killer was only as good as his skill level, and Porter wasn't sure that the skill was even there at the moment. Maybe the killer had come out of retirement for this. Maybe the payout was so big that it was worth the risk. Or maybe it was something entirely different. Porter just didn't know. All he had so far was supposition. He preferred to get solid answers to his questions, but those would only come from the killer himself—Keefe Hogan.

Porter would not call him Keefe but Hogan, in order to depersonalize his actions. Something was so horrific about somebody who could kill and not give a crap. Hogan's scary gaze when Porter had seen him at Kylie's place would not leave Porter's memory anytime soon. Yet Hogan's gaze had also been filled with a strange curiosity and wonder. Porter didn't understand his impetus to tell Hogan that he was potentially family to Kylie. It had certainly shocked Hogan, and he'd taken off, which was great and was Porter's ultimate intention. Still, he didn't have an answer for Kylie herself as to why Porter had even offered that suggestion.

On the other hand, his comment did make him wonder if there could be such a connection. It didn't make a lot of sense, but as he kept going around the same circle again and again, a whole lot didn't make sense, and that was the reality of the situation right now.

Hearing a sound, he walked to the bottom of the stairs and listened. It sounded as if Kylie was having nightmares, which was no surprise. Nothing about this case would let anybody sleep easy for quite a while. Having Hogan, the killer, find and enter Kylie's home, then find her aunt at her home as well was horrific. Porter found it hard to sort it all out because he didn't really trust anything about Hogan and Aunt Agatha at this point.

With coffee in hand, Porter slowly walked up the stairs, wondering if Kylie would stay asleep or if she was rising already. She'd only been down for about half an hour. Yet, if she was powering up, that was probably all she would get.

He stepped closer to the bedroom, hearing her speak in a low tone. He drew closer and peered around the doorway to see she was sitting up, waving her hands, as if having an animated conversation with someone. Her eyes were open and yet not focused, as if seeing something in particular.

He listened to the conversation in amazement.

"I know. I get it, but I don't know what I'm supposed to do about it," she snapped. "I don't understand any of this. … Why, why are you here? Why are you tormenting me?"

His breath caught in the back of his throat as he realized she was talking to somebody, potentially the killer, and yet Porter saw no sign of Hogan. Porter sent Stefan a telepathic message. *Are you getting this?*

Stefan popped back into Porter's brain. *Yes, this is interesting.*

Interesting? Is that what you call it?

Yes, it is what I call it. I don't know what—Is she talking to Hogan?

She's talking to somebody, and she appears to know him well, but I don't know why. Do you think she is aware that she's doing this when she's asleep?

I don't know. Stefan sounded confused, with wonder in his tone too.

Do you think she has tapped into talking with the killer? Porter was not letting it go, and it was not doing him any favors either.

It's possible. You're asking me questions I don't have answers for. You can try to work it out yourself.

What am I supposed to do?

Listen to the conversation and see if you pick up anything helpful.

Great, Porter muttered. *Somehow I don't think she'll like that.*

Has this happened before?

You expect me to know this? I barely know her. Hell, what do I know? If she's doing this at night, it would explain why she wakes up so exhausted.

That's possible.

And is it every night or is this just a one-off of Hogan having a conversation with her?

Stefan hesitated. *Meaning?*

I'm just wondering if she contacted him or if he's contacting her.

A ghostwalker? Stefan asked.

I don't know. I didn't even know there was a name for that.

Yeah, multiple names, depending on what Hogan's abilities are. Yet it would explain why he can ghost in and ghost out of people's lives.

I was thinking about that. He killed this other woman, and we can pin it on him. I'm just wondering if he came out of retirement for that job.

Interesting thought, Stefan noted, *suggesting that he ran out of money and needed it or that somebody begged him to do this job, as if nobody else would be able to—maybe playing on his vanity.*

I don't know, but why would he suddenly come back after being dormant for so long?

In our business, we know that serial killers have patterning, where they often go quiet—asleep, so to speak—and then pop back up again.

I know, but this latest kill of Hogan's feels very different, and that makes me wonder how long Kylie has been speaking to

Hogan.

I'm hearing something in your tone that says you have a theory, but it's one you don't like.

I don't like anything that involves Hogan in Kylie's life, but then what are the chances … No, no, she wouldn't do that.

Don't be surprised at what she can and cannot do at this point. You're also assuming that whatever she's doing is coming from her full awareness, but this is her subconscious at work. So, if she is in any way split over something or has some issue in her life—

Which she does, Porter interrupted. *That aunt of hers is something else.*

Right, … so, if Kylie's conflicted, looking for answers, but not sure about it and unable to get an agreement from her conscious mind, her subconscious mind could easily be going in and dealing with this, without her even knowing about it.

Good God, isn't it bad enough we have this violent shit going on all the time without having to deal with the fact that our own subconscious mind might be betraying us?

It's not a betrayal, Stefan clarified. *It's a question of who has the dominant force here and what is the intent and actual will of the person? You must keep that in mind. The subconscious is only following orders. The conscious mind is often the one that plays the bad guy and makes it look as if it's doing one thing, yet the subconscious is doing something completely different.*

How is that any better?

It's not better. It just is. Think about all the people on diets, who then sabotage their own efforts by eating secretly at nighttime or in some dark closet where nobody can see them. They know perfectly well what they're doing. They agreed to go on a diet. They agreed to whatever those new circumstances are.

Yet they can't seem to help themselves from going into the closet and from secretly eating every piece of chocolate they can find.

Right, but, Stefan, this is hardly the same thing.

It's hardly the same thing, and yet it's exactly the same thing, Stefan stated. *It's a split, a disassociation between one part of her psyche and another part.*

So, you're saying that she could be doing something that is hurting her because another part of her wants something out of this?

In a weird way, yes, but I don't think they would be trying to hurt her. In this case, I think a part of her is just too scared to cause trouble, and the other part of her knows that a resolution is needed and has taken it upon itself, but—Stefan listened in on the conversation she was having, but it seemed to be going over and over the same issue.

"You keep saying that I know what's going on, but I don't. I don't know what's going on at all," she declared, her tone harsh.

Stefan noted, *She doesn't understand, and she's looking for an explanation, but the other person she's talking to is not giving her any answers either.*

How can she still be asleep? Porter asked Stefan.

Check out her eyes. She's not really awake. She's not there. She's in this very active lucid dream.

Yes, but a lucid dream is literally still dreaming.

Stefan laughed. *Yes, until you get into psychic phenomena, and then anything goes.*

What if she's talking to the killer?

That's possible, but he doesn't seem to be acknowledging her. So then you have to wonder if this is all in her imagination. Either that or, since he keeps saying that she already knows, it's possible that she is deliberately withholding information from herself because it's too horrific or because she has blocked it, even the horror of it.

I don't understand all these vague potential answers. Good God, is it always this nebulous?

No, not always this nebulous, Stefan replied, a smile in his tone. *We will get the answers, but they'll come in her time frame, not yours. You want answers now, and clearly she does too, which is why she's trancing at night into these conversations. Yet it's likely she is not aware of her internal debate or these night talks either. If this is her subconscious reaching out to the killer on an energy level, you have to wonder at the skill level she has. If she's doing this unconsciously, imagine what she could do with some control,* Stefan pointed out. *And she probably has no clue that she has this skill.*

But why wouldn't she be aware of it? Porter asked in frustration. *Look at her. She's flipping unbelievable. Have you seen the drawings she does, the things I've seen her pull out of nowhere?*

Exactly, and then you have to wonder why she isn't using those skills.

I don't think she understands that they can really be of value. I almost feel as if, some days, it seems logical to her, and then, other days, it doesn't.

Yes, I would say that's quite true.

I have to confess that, at times, I've thought she was just playing games, Porter admitted.

I don't think she's playing games at all. I think that probably some programming is in there that's still very dominant, and she hasn't managed to free herself from it yet.

And now I'll ask what that means.

Stefan laughed. *It just means that her mind is working free of something that has held her back for a long time. Whatever block or programming is holding her back is still in place and hasn't allowed her to move forward, to be true to herself, even to face her own traumas.*

So, are we talking about an actual block?

Sometimes, yes. I've had to use blocks myself on patients, patients who are so far gone, so damaged that they couldn't function with all these bad memories in there.

Such as, her being in the car when her parents and the twin babies were killed?

Exactly. She was what? Three or four? Those memories are there. We just don't know if it could be something the killer might have said to her at the time, and then, every time she sees him, it triggers the memory block.

So, as soon as these memories are released, then what?

It could bring her abilities into high focus. Her gifts could be revealed by anything really, not just about tearing down a block.

Porter watched as Kylie twisted her earring, something of a habit for her. *That earring bothers me*, Porter shared.

Stefan went silent for a moment. *What earring?*

It's in her left ear, tucked up under her curls. It's just a simple metal stud, but she's constantly playing with it. She's also very adamant about having her favorite drawing pencil with her. It's always in her pocket. It's short, so fits anywhere. Sometimes it seems as if, should she not have that pencil, she couldn't draw.

That is also very interesting.

We all have certain amulets or lucky charms that we think make life easier for us to do what we do. Some people lock in their energies on it, and, for other people, it's just a tool that makes them feel good, so they can complete their work. You can have a favorite pen, a favorite sweater. Whatever you have is something that works well for you, so you want to use it continually. Sports guys have favorite socks or whatever. It could be something as simple as that. Maybe the earring is more than that to Kylie.

At that, Stefan laughed. *That's why you have so many of these unanswered questions because you keep coming up with all these scenarios.*

Maybe. Irritated now, Porter tried to shrug it off.

If it bothers you, I suggest you ask her.

Yeah, I need to. I just can't imagine why the earring would be important, and yet I can see that it is to her.

Nothing else matters then, because if it is important, that's all there is to it. Just accept it and move on, unless you are thinking Kylie has another reason for it. Are you? Stefan asked, his tone curious. *I can see where your mind is going with this, as if the earring and the pencil are some connection to something, but I don't know that you'll get an answer quite so easily from Kylie.*

Maybe not, but just standing here and staring at her is definitely unnerving.

It is, and you're only staring at her because you want to know what's going on. How will she feel, knowing you're listening in on this nighttime conversation?

Not good, I presume. When I tell her what she was doing, she will probably want to know exactly what she said.

That's a good point too. You'll have to go by feel on this. I can't advise you because I don't understand a lot of how she'll feel.

It could go either way, if you ask me.

I suggest you record her for proof. If anything else should develop, let me know.

And, with that, Stefan left his mind, leaving it not with

the sense of barrenness that he often did. It was almost as if a resounding gap closed every time he left, but this time it was a soft close, as if a door had just gone *click*.

Almost at the same moment, Kylie turned her gaze toward him and then jolted awake. "Oh my God." Her hand went to her chest. "You scared me."

He smiled and approached slowly. "And yet you're sitting up, so I thought you were awake."

She looked around and frowned. "I am, aren't I? I wonder why? Maybe I heard you coming," she suggested, staring at him. "How long have you been there?"

"I've been here long enough to hear you have quite a conversation."

She stared at him. "A conversation? No way." She shook her head. "I don't talk in my sleep."

"I won't say you didn't talk in your sleep. I'm just telling you that you were having a hell of a conversation with somebody. It was quite a fascinating experience honestly. You kept asking him why he was here again, but I couldn't hear the other side of the conversation. Yet it seemed as if he was saying that you already knew why because you kept saying, *No, don't keep telling me I know because I don't*."

She stared at him, her hand still on her chest. Then she slowly sank back down on the bed, until she could stare up at the ceiling. "I don't remember any of that," she muttered hoarsely.

"I know, and I wondered whether I should have listened in or I was invading your privacy. I didn't want to do that, but I was afraid that, if I didn't give you an idea of what it was you were trying to say, it would bother you even more."

"You mean, even more than hearing one side of a conversation?" she asked, with a startled half laugh, half cry. She kicked off the covers and slowly sat up, wincing, as she made it back up to vertical.

"Take it easy," Porter said. "Whether you remember the conversation or not, an awful lot of energy was moving around."

"Sure, that's what energy does. It moves."

"It does, indeed," he agreed, "and, if you're ready to get up, I've got coffee on downstairs."

"I'm still so tired," she grumbled, as she rubbed her temples.

"If you think about it," he suggested, with a note of humor, "I'm not sure you got any sleep because you really were talking the whole time."

She got up slowly and headed to the bathroom.

When she stepped out, he assessed her critically and then nodded. "That seemed to help." Her face was still a little damp, the tendrils of hair at her temples curling after a quick wash of her face. He smiled. "Now, how about some coffee and food?"

"Maybe," she murmured, as she headed toward him, walking carefully.

A little too carefully for his peace of mind. "You're really not feeling that well, are you?"

She shook her head. "I'm not sure what's going on."

"Let's go downstairs and see whether you're okay to be down there for a bit or it's something much more serious."

She laughed. "It's not more serious. If anything it's just a headache. What else could it be?"

"Blocks," he replied.

She froze at the top of the stairs, turning to look at him. "What do you mean by blocks?"

"Either blocks you yourself put in place that may be getting rattled and ready to release or blocks that somebody else put in place in order to make your life a little easier. Yet they might be coming apart right now."

She grabbed the railing and slowly walked down the stairs, without saying anything.

He never quite knew from her reactions just how she was taking the new information, so he waited until she got to the bottom. "Does any of that make sense?"

"It makes sense for other people, but not for me."

It was such a typical response for her that he burst out laughing. She looked over at him, and, instead of glaring, she grinned, and it made him realize how much progress she had made. "Any idea who could have put a block in place?"

She shrugged. "Could have been anybody, I suppose. I was a pretty traumatized little girl, so it makes sense for anybody—whether a therapist, a doctor, a neighbor, whoever—who saw what I was going through."

"So, it doesn't bother you? I would have thought it would have freaked you out."

She shrugged. "And it might have, if I felt that sense of being freaked out, but it feels..." She stopped in the hallway, as if considering exactly what she was feeling. "It feels right."

"That's good." Porter pointed toward the kitchen. "At least that allows you to come to terms with it."

"Not exactly sure what to come to terms with," she noted, "but it doesn't feel as if I should be panicked about it. And maybe that's after having some sleep and a chance to rethink what was going on."

"Maybe," he murmured, looking at her cautiously.

"I won't explode," she said, glancing over at him. "You do seem to be a little worried."

"I am a little worried," he admitted. "A lot of stuff is going on. So, between your conversations in your sleep and the mention of blocks shifting, it's a lot."

She just nodded.

He poured her a cup of coffee, and, as soon as she had that, she carried it out to the living room and sat down on the couch, tucking her knees underneath her.

He gave her a few minutes to relax and to settle into the sensation of being awake. Just when he was about to say something, she spoke.

"Thank you."

He looked at her. "For what?"

"For giving me a few minutes to collect myself. I know you're looking for answers, and, once again, I don't really have any."

"Maybe not," he conceded, "but I think things are about to start unraveling in ways that you may not expect."

"Oh, I get that too," she murmured. "It feels as if something is there, something momentous. I just can't tell you what it is."

"And you don't have to right now. Hell, maybe we won't get any details," he noted, "but getting some would at least help you a lot."

"You're probably right." She took a deep breath and then slowly raised her arms and stretched her neck and shoulders.

He wasn't sure what to do with this much-calmer person, and he didn't know if it was just because she had gotten some sleep or if this was a result of any blocks.

"Now you're looking at me weird," she said, without even facing him.

He groaned. "It's not that I'm looking at you weird. I'm

just trying to figure out who this person is who's sitting on the couch right now because I don't think this conversation would have been received quite so easily a couple days ago."

She pondered that and then nodded. "Another good point."

"The way you're even taking that comment makes me wonder."

"Things definitely feel different. I can't really tell you in what way everything feels different, but something does. Something has shifted, but I don't know what that means. I feel as if something has been released. Not a release after I've been angry, but a release in the sense that something I've been fighting against for a long time isn't there anymore."

"I think that's a good thing," he murmured, as he sat down on the big easy chair across from her.

She smiled. "Maybe, and I do remember parts of that dream now, but not enough that I can give you details."

He just nodded and kept an eye on her.

She sipped her coffee and relaxed even further. "I don't even know whether I truly slept or had a short nap, as much as it restored something. I don't know how to explain it, but it feels as if maybe some pieces were put together." His eyebrows shot up, and she nodded. "I know. It sounds very strange."

"It also sounds very good," he stated. "Anything that makes you feel more whole is bound to be a good thing."

She shot him a wry look. "And yet I highly suspect that whoever put in these blocks—if blocks are there—would have been my aunt."

He studied Kylie and then nodded. "That makes sense. She was raising you, and she needed you to be a little easier to get along with and also less traumatized. So I guess it would make sense that she put them in there. Stefan did say that he uses blocks on some patients at times, just to get them to a point where they can get over their trauma."

"Right," she agreed, "because some of the things in my life just seem very distant. I can see them, but they're not, how do I say it? They're not something I'm emotionally invested in at this point in time. So it's a little easier to contemplate. I'll put the car accident in that category."

"Of course," he murmured. "So anybody who put a block in there to help you get over that …"

She smiled and nodded. "That would be a block I would thank them for. Yet I'm an adult now, and apparently something has decided to shake some of these blocks loose. The question is, what?"

He hesitated for a moment. "I don't think it's a *what* as much as a *who*."

She glanced over at him. "You mean, this killer." She frowned. "We keep calling him the killer. Isn't his name Keefe or something?"

He faced her and nodded slowly, "Yes, Keefe Hogan."

"Right." She stared off in the distance. "I know what I'm about to say doesn't sound very normal, but it feels as if …" She hesitated, as if not wanting to say it.

"Just spit it out," Porter said, "because anything that helps right now will help in many ways."

She smiled. "It feels as if he was at that car accident in some way. As if he came up and saw me, yet decided to let me live."

"Why would he do that?"

"I don't know. … Maybe he just felt as if he'd taken enough from me already."

"And that's possible. Remorse is real. Is that why he

went into hiding afterward?"

"I don't think he went into hiding afterward. I think that's when he was caught and put in prison, right?"

"Yes."

"Exactly, so maybe he saw something in me. Maybe he has his own abilities and recognized mine or something and didn't want to take out a kindred soul." She shrugged, picked up her coffee cup, and took a big sip. Smiling in appreciation, she shared, "Even the coffee tastes better now. Everything just feels different than it did before I went to sleep."

He sat back and smiled. "I would take that as a good thing then, because, of all the things that I was expecting to hear from you, I can't say it was this."

"No," she murmured. "I'm not even sure that the block has come off as much as it's fading, giving me a chance to integrate lost knowledge and memories, with time to make it easier on me. I can see the car accident now, but it's distant. I can feel the pain that my mother went through, but again it's more distant." Kylie shook her head. "All I can tell you is that, right now, everything feels off, but in a good way."

CHAPTER 15

KYLIE APPRECIATED PORTER backing off and giving her a little bit of time. They had arranged for pizza to be delivered, and then afterward she went up and had a hot bath, trying to de-stress a little bit more, then headed back to bed. She couldn't believe how exhausted she had felt earlier. Then she got some strength, but now it was dipping once more. She was ready to crash again. What Porter had mentioned about blocks made some sense, and she highly suspected her aunt had put them there.

She remembered various times, where she had not been as compliant as her aunt wanted, and Agatha sitting her down and doing something strange, but Kylie didn't understand it. Her aunt did something that was beyond Kylie's comprehension.

Apparently Agatha had a lot more going on in her world than she had been prepared to explain to Kylie. It saddened her because her aunt could have been such a great help to Kylie. Yet Agatha obviously didn't want to have a relationship, and that also made Kylie wonder why in the world Agatha had taken in Kylie to begin with. It's obvious Agatha didn't want anything to do with her.

Maybe Agatha took in Kylie as Agatha's only living relative or maybe because Agatha's sister had been murdered, or just because Agatha had helped put the killer behind bars.

Regardless, Kylie had to be appreciative of the fact that Agatha had been there when Kylie was too young to support herself. Yet now she felt herself running out of appreciation for Agatha very quickly.

Kylie chastised herself as she crawled into bed, then hooked up her phone to the charger and set it to Record. Should Kylie have any further sleepytime conversations which she wasn't aware of, she needed to know just what was going on. Obviously more psychic stuff was happening than she had expected in her world, and that had proven to be a bit of a challenge too.

Up until now, she had only utilized that special ability for drawing crime scenes. Sometimes she drew them with her eyes open. Even then she wasn't seeing anything before her. Yet she was in a visualization mode, and the drawings were coming. In a way they were just being downloaded from her psyche as to any information she was picking up. So far, nothing had been so far off the wall that it had caused anybody any issues.

But it also made her a decent police sketch artist for victims too. She'd only done a little of that and was more than willing to do more, but she had been wary of her own abilities and what it would look like if she zoned out in front of people, yet continued to sketch. The couple times it had happened up until now had been incredibly powerful, but it had also affected her, hearing the victims' stories and their breakdowns over the people who had attacked them.

She quickly nodded off to sleep, her dreams calm, quiet, with something almost peaceful about them. She woke with a start in the middle of the night and stared around the room, wondering what had disturbed her. Sensing nothing wrong, she slipped back into an easier restful position, only to remember that she had put the phone on Record. She shut it off, then listened to see if anything was there. She fast-forwarded and heard nothing there. With a sense of relief, she reset her phone to Record and went back to sleep, this time into a deeper and calmer space.

Almost immediately she was picked up and tossed into a nightmare, at least something she would have classified as close to a nightmare, with horrific screams and cries coming at her from all around her. She didn't understand but clasped her hands over her ears, trying to shut out the noise, as she ran as fast as she could away from whatever was happening. It was almost like a mass shooting, and, with that thought, she snapped awake, sitting up in her bedroom and looking around.

Seconds later, her bedroom door burst open, and Porter raced in. Seeing her sitting up in the bed again, he asked, "Are you okay?"

"Yes."

"What was that about?"

"I don't know." She stared at him. "What was what?"

"You cried out."

She shook her head. "I didn't hear myself cry out."

"You did. It woke me up, and I came running."

She gave him half a smile. "I'm sorry if I disturbed you."

"No, that's not what we're doing here," he declared. "I just need to know that you're okay. Do you remember what you were screaming about?"

"Yes, a mass shooting."

"Ah," he replied, understanding on his face. "You're not alone there. Lots of people who worked that casino case are having trouble sleeping."

"Of course they are," she whispered. "It's just so sad."

He nodded. "It is."

She looked at him and asked, "Did you ever find a connection between our serial killer-for-hire and the casino mass shooter?"

"The research team is looking into it, but I'm getting the impression that they're not finding anything. At this point, we aren't hopeful that they ever will. It's beginning to look as if it may have been random."

"How was that random? Did Hogan just take advantage of that opportunity at the casino?"

"I don't think so." He walked closer and sat down at the edge of the bed, looking at her closely.

"I'm fine," she repeated. "I was in a nightmare. … I was running. I heard all these screams," she murmured, rubbing her head. "It's just so awful." She hated that the tears had reached her eyes. "All those people gone, slaughtered, and for what?"

"For one very angry and mentally unstable man," Porter stated. "We see it over and over again, unfortunately."

"Which doesn't help," she pointed out. "I mean, nobody wants to see that happen. Yet it seems as if we have so few safeguards to protect people when somebody chooses to commit a mass murder. It's awful," she murmured.

"I agree, and I'm sorry that it's disturbing your sleep."

"It needs to disturb my sleep." She stared at him. "Nobody should get so comfortable about shootings that they can sleep through it all."

He nodded. "I won't argue with you on that. I just know that you're already dealing with a lot, and I would just as soon you get some sleep."

She rolled her eyes. "Did you get any?"

"I was doing just fine until you woke me up," he shared

cheerfully.

"Now you can go back to bed," she said, with a wave of her hand. "Go grab some more sleep, if you can."

"The operative words are, if I can," he noted, with a smile. "I just need to know that you're okay."

"What time is it?" she asked, reaching for her phone, then seeing the red Record light on. She shut it off. "I put it on Record, just in case." She stared down at it but felt such a sense of foreboding that she didn't even want to hear it.

"Maybe you should listen to it."

She winced. "I'm not sure I'm up for it."

"I'm right here," Porter said, "so it would be a good thing if we listened and confirmed nothing else is going on that you weren't expecting."

"I'm not expecting any of this," she declared in frustration. "Most of the time I sleep like a baby, and nothing ever bothers me."

He looked at her. "Even with the work you're doing?"

She nodded. "I guess that's odd, isn't it?" He gave her the gentlest of smiles, a smile that she was coming to recognize as tenderness.

He murmured, "Remember that we all have safeguards to protect ourselves. Don't judge any safeguards that have helped you get to where you are."

"Maybe."

"Let's just listen to confirm." He shuffled over to her, and she sat up, so they were both close enough to hear her phone, and then she hit Play. Nothing immediately came, so she fast-forwarded several times, until all of a sudden she heard a voice. Her voice.

She shook her head in astonishment, as she heard herself cry out, "No, no, don't! Please don't!" Then there was silence for a moment, and she started screaming and screaming and screaming. And then it cut off really sharply. She looked over at him, and she hit Stop on the playback.

"I don't like anything about that," Porter said.

"I don't either, but …" She winced. "It's almost as if I was there, thinking the killer would pay attention to me and—"

"Or it's just your conscious mind," he suggested, "knowing what is coming, and you're asking him to stop the killing."

She sighed with relief at that very logical explanation. "Thank God for that," she muttered. "I'm starting to wonder just what is going on."

"We all are," he said, "but we'll keep it calm and under control, so we don't go off half-cocked, with expectations that it's something other than what we're thinking it is."

She rolled her eyes at him. "You make it all sound so simple."

"Most things in life are. It's just the explanation that gets us," he murmured. "So, let's just relax and not go there."

"It is getting late."

"It is." He glanced at his watch. "Or early, as it's five o'clock."

"In that case," she said, "I'm getting up and staying up."

He smiled. "I'll go put on the coffee."

"You can go back to bed," she replied, turning to look at him.

He shook his head. "Nope, I'll sit up and have coffee with you." When she hesitated, he leaned over and gave her a quick hug. "You're not alone. Given the way you were raised, that is probably the last thing you would ever expect to hear from anybody, but I'm not just anybody. I do want you to realize that you are not alone in this." And, with that, he left.

She stared at the doorway for a long time, wondering if she had ever heard that before in her life. She hadn't realized how such a basic human necessity for friendships and for people you could count on had been missing in her life. Her aunt had done the absolute bare minimum to connect.

Kylie shook her head, got up, got dressed, and headed downstairs. She heard the coffee dripping and Porter tapping away on his laptop. She walked into the living room, and it struck her. "I suppose you're sending off progress reports to Stefan," she stated, with a wry look.

"Nope, but it's not a bad idea. You could also send him one."

"Nope." She felt the intensity of Porter's gaze, and she raised her hands. "I don't really have a relationship with him," she pointed out.

"And yet you could. You're in the same field."

"Same field?" she repeated, with a laugh. "My God, he's such a pro in all of this, and, besides, I don't want to disturb him."

"Aha, I hear you there, and I'm pretty sure that would just piss him off."

"You're telling me that he doesn't have hundreds of thousands of people already queuing up to contact him?"

"Maybe, but he also has a lot of people he helps. So, helping you for five minutes, then your time is up and you move on is what Stefan does," Porter shared. "Until you're capable of dealing with whatever is happening in your life, in my experience, Stefan has been there. He still stays in contact with my sister."

"She is very lucky to have him," Kylie said warmly.

"You would like her," Porter added, with a smile. "She's very much like you."

"Oh, I doubt it. I'm very closed down and extremely unfriendly," she added, ending with an eye roll.

"No, you're just very private, mostly because your defenses are so deep."

"Sure, they've had to be."

"Exactly," he agreed, "and I'm not looking to change that. I'm just happy that we're talking and managing to solve some of these problems, without triggering too much response on your side."

She frowned at that and then nodded. "I guess that's one way to look at it."

"It absolutely is, and, as long as it's all still working, then we can continue to be ourselves." He poured her a cup of coffee and handed it to her.

She hadn't even realized that he'd gotten up, made his way to the kitchen, and returned to bring her a cup. She shook her head. "You move so quietly."

"I didn't want to disturb your great brainpower, churning away on the problem."

She laughed as she accepted the coffee. "Don't know about great brainpower," she murmured, "but definitely churning away."

"And what part of the issue is currently bothering you?"

His question was curious, not judgmental, so she found answering was easy. "I think my aunt had done something. I'm pretty sure, as I look back on various things in my life, that she put in the blocks. Anytime I had trouble, I was forced to sit in a chair, and she would always stand beside me. I thought at the time it was to confirm I stayed there as a punishment. But maybe it wasn't. Maybe she had some way of putting blocks into me that I didn't know about."

"It sounds as if she did, but the question is why."

"Honestly, I think maybe because it made me easier to get along with, maybe more malleable or something." Kylie raised both hands. "She was all about making life easy for herself."

"I didn't like her before," Porter shared, "and you're making it even harder for me to like her now."

"Doesn't matter to me whether you like her or not," she declared. "Why would it matter to you?"

"It doesn't in a lot of ways," he conceded, "but she is your only living relative. So, if you wanted to have a relationship with her, I would like to at least be civil to her."

She stared at him as the implications of what he just said filtered through, but she couldn't be certain about exactly what he meant, so she wouldn't bring it up.

He smiled over his coffee cup. "I just love that about you," he admitted. "You're dying to ask questions, but you're absolutely not willing to get too involved or too invested in the answer. So you just stay quiet."

She frowned at him. "Now you're laughing at me."

"Never. I would never laugh at you. I might find a way to laugh *with* you though."

"I'm not sure I have very much to laugh about with anybody."

"Exactly. That's one of the reasons why I would never laugh at you. You have enough on your plate right now, and you're dealing with so much. You're being ultra critical about everything that you're doing, making it seem as if you can't do anything right, but I'm really proud of the way you're handling everything so far."

"I'm not handling anything," she argued. "I mean, listen

to that stupid recording from last night. It didn't sound like the one-sided conversation you were talking about earlier. It sounded like a completely off-the-wall nightmare."

"Have you had nightmares before?" he asked.

She shrugged. "Of course. Don't we all?" When he remained silent, she added, "I do have nightmares. I figured I would grow out of them, but I haven't so far."

"And I would expect nothing less," he said. "You're human. You may be deemed a sensitive too, like my sister. So working that casino crime scene would be more difficult for you to handle, yet you somehow worked that scene until your drawings were done. That may be partly because of the blocks."

She stared at him. "What do you mean?"

He hesitated and then replied, "I was just wondering if you were a precog as well."

"A precog," she repeated, shaking her head. "Is that supposed to mean something?"

"You see things in advance, and you might have even seen that casino shooting nightmare before last night."

"What?" she asked, leaning back. "No. Hell no."

"Hell no?" he repeated, with a smile. "Are you sure?"

"Of course. Obviously, if I'd known, I would have done something."

"Would you though?" he asked. "I think all these abilities of yours are blocked—locked up and blocked behind your psyche, compliments of your aunt. Whether right or wrong, she appears to have done one hell of a job trying to harness your gifts as well as your memories, and I think they're all in there. Her blocks maybe kept you from having even *more* nightmares."

She picked up her cup and sipped, as she contemplated

his words. She shook her head several times but wasn't exactly sure that he was 100 percent wrong. "I did have a pretty prophetic dream way back when," she shared. "And I don't remember where it's playing out, but it was another death of somebody close to me, and I vaguely remember my mother, things like that, other than with her. I'm not sure I remembered this correctly. I was so young," she explained, "but it's one of those little memories that just sticks with you."

He nodded. "So, if you ever said anything about your memories of your mother, and your aunt overheard you, how would she have handled it?"

"Not well, I suppose," she replied. "Absolutely no way she would have ever allowed me to say anything about it."

"If you told her directly, what would she have done?"

"Punish me for sure, and maybe that wasn't enough."

He nodded. "That could be why she started with the blocks."

"I don't know," she whispered, staring at him, "but that would mean all that time, all the time that I was with her, had been wasted."

He frowned. "I'm not sure *wasted* is the right word because, of course, she was just trying to manage whatever she was dealing with."

Kylie couldn't stay quiet. "We keep giving her excuses."

"She was raising a child who was injured and traumatized," he stated. "I'm not sure we can do anything but initially give her a pass, at least until we find out more."

Her lips curled at that, and then she shrugged. "I don't know. I feel as if everything is being rewritten, even as I sit here, and I just don't understand. I wish she would talk to me. I wish she would just tell me what the hell she was doing all those times."

"And maybe she just can't tell you. Maybe it's something that she's feeling bad about and doesn't feel as if she can share that with you."

"I think she would just deny it. Whatever it is, I think she would flat-out deny any involvement, and it would be a *too damn bad if you don't like it* response," she added.

"Did she ever attend any school events or do anything like that?"

She shook her head. "No, she went to parent-teacher meetings only if they demanded it. Otherwise she was as hands-off as possible."

"And if she was called in to the school?"

Kylie winced. "There was this one time, and I know she was extremely angry when she got home."

"Do you remember what it was about?"

"Not really. I supposedly said something to somebody, but I don't remember what." She frowned. "How come I can't remember any of this stuff?" Then she realized why. "She did put blocks in there, didn't she? No reason for me *not* to have remembered why she was so angry that one time, and she was horrifically angry."

"She probably put another major block in to confirm you couldn't ever do anything like that again."

She stared at him. "I don't think she gets a free pass for any of this shit," she snapped, as she bolted to her feet and paced the living room. "I mean, that's just disgusting. How dare she do something like that."

"And again we don't know the full story."

She stopped, headed to the living room window, and stared out at the early morning dawn rising in front of her. It was an absolutely stunning morning, yet it was hard for her to see the joy in any of it.

"I don't know," she murmured. "It just seems to me as if all this is so far-fetched, but now that I can piece together little bits and pieces of it, it feels right. And that just makes me so angry. I never really knew who I was, so I did my best to become who she wanted me to be. Which was somebody who caused her no trouble, gave her no guff, did all my schoolwork, helped in the house, and left as soon as she wanted me gone." Kylie was shaking now. "I never really had a chance to develop a personality or anything."

"You did, but you had to do it within the boundaries she allowed you."

"And who does that?" she asked, turning to stare at him. "Really, who does that?"

"Somebody who doesn't want to be bothered or doesn't know how to handle something," he suggested, walking toward her. "Again, I get it. You're feeling hard done by. I can see that Agatha's behavior really did hurt you. It really stifled something within you," he said, as he took Kylie's hand. "Agatha had gifts and should have been better able to handle you with yours. You deserved better. Just think how scary it would be for mothers without gifts to have a gifted child, probably not even realizing it."

Kylie looked at him and then slowly nodded. "I guess people who aren't aware of their abilities are probably doing this all the time, aren't they?"

"To a certain extent, yes. I suspect in your case, your aunt knew what she was doing or found out fairly quickly, then utilized it as a tool to get you to comply with whatever she needed from you. If she was afraid you would talk about people who would die soon, then keeping you quiet and keeping you off the school's radar and away from the neighbors would be Agatha's goal. If anybody heard you sharing your prophetic dreams, it could have gotten out to the world and back to her."

Kylie sagged in shock. "I didn't think of that."

"And that's why we try hard not to make a judgment call before we have the information. For all you know, this was literally only to keep you safe."

"Or to keep her safer."

"Yes, that's absolutely another possibility," he agreed. "But, in keeping herself safe, don't forget that she also kept you safe. And, without her, you would have been tossed into the foster care system, and who knows what would have happened to you there."

PORTER BROKE THE silence. "I suggest we get several changes of clothes from your place and plan to stay here for a few days, until we can see what your stalker guy will do."

"I also want to talk to my aunt again," Kylie told Porter.

"I'm okay with that too. Any answers we get will be good for both of us."

She rolled her eyes at that. "I get that you guys need to know more about this, but I'm much less concerned about what you find out than what is happening with me."

He smiled. "Believe it or not, we're all concerned about you too."

She laughed. "I doubt that. I'm not even sure why you are, much less anyone else. Regardless, my aunt owes me an explanation."

"She might not agree with that though," he cautioned.

"No, I'm pretty sure she won't. Yet I think it would help me a lot if I got answers. If she's in any way willing or can be bribed into providing answers, I think it would help me put all this behind me."

"Let's go now," he said. "She's probably been trying to escape the hospital today anyway."

She bolted to her feet. "It's not visiting hours."

"No, but you are family after all," he pointed out, "so you can go in right now."

She nodded. "Let's go, and you're right. No doubt she's planning on getting out and going into hiding today."

"If she hasn't left already," he pointed out.

Kylie replied, "Then no point in phoning the hospital because that'll just waste time, while we hang around and wait." And, with that, she picked up her jacket. "Let's go."

Surprised, he put down his empty coffee cup and asked, "Do you want to take your coffee in a thermos?"

"No. I want to go. I need to go now."

He got up and headed toward her, keys in hand. "That's good. Maybe we can get some answers."

It was a short trip to the hospital, and, as they walked in, Porter cautioned Kylie about even talking to anybody. "I'm not sure what the rules are at this hour, but we do need to see your aunt. So let's just keep our presence low-key, and hopefully we'll get in and out easily."

Kylie didn't say anything, just nodded. As they headed down the hallway, Kylie's footsteps got faster and faster.

"What's the rush?" he asked, easily keeping up, but wondering what was going on.

"Something's wrong," she muttered, as she broke into a run.

He bolted after her. As soon as they got to her aunt's room, Kylie dashed in first, and Porter noted the older woman on the floor, looking as if she was already gone. He headed back down the hallway to see if anyone else was out here. When he rejoined Kylie, he shook his head. "Nobody is out there."

"But there was someone," Kylie said. "It was him."

Porter didn't argue. "I'll go find the security guard." And, with that, he took off, calling the captain and sending the first nurse he saw back to help out Kylie with her aunt. The nurse frowned at him, and he all but bellowed, "Something is wrong with Agatha. We just walked in, and she's either dead or unconscious, on the floor."

The nurse took off, as the captain answered Porter's call, sounding sleepy, "What the hell is going on?"

"Kylie's aunt was just attacked in the hospital," he murmured. "I need access to the cameras."

"Hang on. You head to security, and I'll have it cleared by the time you get there."

It took a little bit longer than that, but not much, and soon Porter sat down with one of the security guards, looking at the most recent camera feeds on Agatha's floor. Almost immediately Porter tapped the screen. "That's him there."

They watched Hogan go into Agatha's room and then came right back out a few minutes later, smiling.

"Wow," the security guard muttered, "cold much?"

"A whole lot," Porter confirmed. "We've been after this guy for a few days now."

"And he just walks into the hospital?" the security guard asked, turning to look at Porter.

"Yeah, it seems as if anybody can do that," Porter quipped, staring at him. They watched as the killer headed straight to the stairs, and it took a minute to switch through the various cameras to see him coming out on the other side.

"That's him there." Porter was surprised to see Hogan still driving the same truck. "Get me that license plate, will you?" And as soon as he had it, he sent it on to the captain with a text. **This is the second time with the same vehicle for Hogan.**

The captain called him back, as Porter stepped out into the hallway. "It was definitely him though," Porter reiterated.

"What is out of pattern is that he kept the same vehicle. So, either he doesn't expect that he'll get caught, or it's a vehicle he knows he can use whenever he wants."

"Regardless, we need to get an APB out on that sucker."

"Will do," the captain muttered, "and what about the aunt?"

"I don't know. I'm on my way back up. For all I know, Hogan took care of Agatha finally."

"But why?"

"I don't know that either, and that's why we came here the first time, hoping to talk to her aunt. Agatha was as unfriendly as you can get. We returned early this morning, really hoping to catch her and to get some answers before she took off to hide. Honestly Kylie sensed the trouble as soon as we got into the hospital. She walked faster and faster, until she was running in the hallway, knowing something was wrong. When we got there, Agatha was on the floor and seemed unconscious at best."

"Why is it that I think this is a classic example of too little, too late?"

"I suspect so, yes," Porter replied. "And, if that's the case, I need access to her house."

"Yeah, consider it done," the captain replied in a gruff voice, just as Porter got back to Agatha's hospital room.

He stepped inside to see a certain amount of chaos happening around Agatha.

Kylie stood off to the side, chewing on her nails, as she watched the medical personnel attending to her aunt. She saw him enter and walked straight into his arms.

He locked them around her and held her close.

"It's too late," she muttered.

He nodded and could already see there was no hope, but the medical personnel didn't have the same vision that he had. As they continued to work on Agatha, Porter held Kylie close. When they finally called it, the nurse looked over and shook her head. He just nodded and didn't say anything. Kylie already knew it was too late, so there was no point in telling her that.

They waited until all the medical personnel had left them alone with Agatha. Kylie looked up at him finally and said, "I don't understand why."

"I know," he murmured, "and I hope to God that she left you a letter or something somewhere that gave an explanation of the craziness that was your life."

"Maybe, but I doubt it. This is just too damn horrifying. I don't understand why Hogan came back yet again to take her out."

"Because she got away," Porter offered. "Each time she has managed to get away."

"And was it her abilities that got her out of danger?" she murmured. "Or was it just some luck and some planning?"

"Probably all of that," he replied. "Do you want to say anything or to stay here with your aunt for a few minutes?"

She frowned at the body. "Not really. Everything I wanted to say needed to be done while she was alive. Now I just don't even know what to do."

"We'll have to deal with her body, and we'll have an autopsy anyway. It's obvious that something went wrong somewhere along the line."

"I know. So, let's get the autopsy done to nail this asshole. He has an awful lot of explaining to do."

"You're hoping that he'll explain, but I'm not sure you'll get any satisfaction out of that. I also have it cleared with the captain to go through your aunt's house."

She shuddered for a moment but nodded. "I guess we need to, don't we?"

"Yes, we do. She refused to say she had been attacked, which led to her ending up in the hospital to begin with."

"Once again afraid of being caught?" she asked.

He nodded. "I would suspect so, yes."

"Wow, that asshole's got a lot to answer for." She walked over to her aunt, seeing the pale fearful look on the woman's face, and shuddered. "She shouldn't have had to go to her death terrified like this," she murmured. "If only we were a few minutes earlier." He didn't say anything to that because the world was full of if-only situations. When she finally turned and looked at him, she announced, "I'm ready to leave."

He nodded and closed the door behind them. As they headed out of the hospital, he stopped at the front reception desk, showed the woman his badge, and said, "The coroner will be over to pick up the patient in room 418."

As they walked outside, Kylie stopped and took several deep breaths of fresh air.

"Are you okay?"

"No, I'm not okay," she snapped. "I don't understand any of this."

"I know," he murmured, "but that's okay."

Just as they were about to head out to the vehicle, a shout came from behind them. He turned to see the same nurse crying out for Kylie.

"She's alive! She's alive," she said, joy and excitement in her voice. "In 418, … the patient, she's breathing again."

He stopped and stared at her. "What?"

"Yes, your aunt is alive," she repeated, turning to Kylie.

Kylie was stunned, but she turned and headed back up to the room. For himself, Porter couldn't quite understand what the hell was going on. As he walked in, the doctors once again worked on Agatha, but this time she was obviously breathing, and they were taking tests and trying to sort out what just occurred.

When the doctor stepped back, he addressed them. "This does happen, though not very often. Every once in a while, sometimes the body just starts breathing again."

Kylie walked over and picked up Agatha's hand and held her close. "I'm so glad to see that you made it," she murmured. "We really don't want that asshole to win."

A shiver ran down her aunt's body.

Porter saw it himself, even from as far away as he was. He walked over, studying the woman whose pale features appeared to be completely unchanged. He looked back at the doctor. "Will she recover?"

"We don't know. Obviously we want her to wake up. At the moment she isn't conscious. So that would be a concern." He hesitated and then whispered, "Often in these cases they do survive, but I've seen just as many of them die within a few days."

"Right." Porter looked back at Kylie, who was murmuring to her aunt. "I'll let her know."

"Do that, but maybe Agatha will be one of the lucky

ones," the doctor said. "Yet I wouldn't count on it." And, with that, the doctor left.

The nurse fussed around, making Agatha as comfortable as possible, before the nurse told Kylie, "She's one of the lucky ones." And, with that, she turned and walked out.

Kylie shook her head. "What the hell was that all about?" she asked Porter.

"I don't know," he murmured, "but I sure want to." He sent a message out to Stefan but got no answer, so he waited and watched. "How long do you want to stay here?" he asked Kylie.

"I don't know. … I feel as if this is temporary, and I know that makes no sense, but I don't really know that she's in there."

He studied the energy around the woman and nodded. "Her energy is definitely faint, and I think, if she gets a chance to knock off, she'll take it."

Kylie spun to face him. "As if it's a choice?"

He winced. "In this case … I think it's an escape. I think she's done with whatever life she's been living and wants an end to it."

"I can't blame her for that," she murmured. "Her life hasn't been the easiest."

"I agree with you there. All I'm telling you is what I'm seeing."

"Which may or may not be the truth either," she noted pointedly.

"Absolutely, and I won't tell you it's right or wrong. I'm just telling you what I see."

She groaned. "I shouldn't be snapping at you. I'm just not sure what to do right now."

"You do whatever you feel is right," he suggested. "If you

want to stay, we can stay."

"I want to talk to her. I want her cognizant enough to answer questions."

The words filling the room were quiet, almost too quiet, but her aunt clearly stated, "I'm not answering any questions." Agatha slowly opened her eyes and stared up at Kylie. "And you, of all people, should know why."

Kylie stared at her. "I don't understand. Everybody keeps making remarks like that, but I just don't understand."

Her aunt closed her eyes, as if it were too much effort to keep them open. "That's because you don't want to remember."

"No, I probably don't. It seems as if everything in my childhood was horrific," Kylie muttered, staring at her aunt. "That still doesn't answer my questions."

"No, it doesn't. Sometimes there aren't any answers."

"You could help though."

"I could, but I won't," Agatha declared, her voice getting stronger as she opened her eyes and glared at her. "You had everything you could get from me years ago."

Kylie frowned at her aunt. "I was a child. You act as if I deliberately did something to you."

The woman hesitated and then shrugged. "In a way you did. You brought him to us every damn time. I never could figure out how or why, but you just kept bringing him to us. Only since you moved out have I felt any peace, and even then," she shared, tears trickling down the corner of her eye, "that didn't last long. I haven't figured out how you were doing it, just that it was coming from you every damn time."

Kylie stared at her, stunned.

"Do you know how many times we moved? How many times we ended up in horrific situations, all because of you?

Do you know how many times I wanted to deep-six you in the ocean? But I knew I couldn't, as much as I wanted to. God damn you, I just couldn't. I needed what you could do so much that I had to keep you alive long enough to do what I needed to do."

CHAPTER 16

EACH WORD FROM Agatha was like an excruciating blow to Kylie's heart, and she couldn't believe what her aunt was saying. "I don't understand," Kylie said. "I was a child. You shouldn't have held any of that against me."

"Sure, I shouldn't have," she muttered. "Maybe if it hadn't been so damn hard to function in this world, knowing that he was after us every damn minute, but that wasn't easy either."

"No, of course it wouldn't have been," Kylie agreed, "and yet you feel as if I'm the one who brought Hogan to us."

"You were. Absolutely you were. I gave you that pencil to hold things back and told you to always use it. I coded it into your damn brain, and every time I saw you with it, I would smile and think, *Okay, we're still good.* Then something would happen to all that coding, and I realized I needed you to just disappear from my life, once and for all. I thought that finally I could be at peace," she cried out softly.

"At peace from whom? From Hogan?"

"Yes, from the same killer who took your parents and your brothers, not that you ever cared."

"What do you mean, I never cared?" Kylie cried out. "How old was I? Four, five? I was a child. Of course I cared."

"Yeah, of course you cared, but you still had to play with

that stupid energy all the time. No matter how many times I told you to stop, especially the damn hopscotch. And yet that was so much better than everything else."

"What do you mean, so much better?" she asked. "I remember the hopscotch, and I remember playing with lots of people."

"Yeah, you played with lots of people all right, but every one of them was dead," she snapped. "Every one of them was dead, and how was I supposed to explain you to the world around me?"

"So why did you keep me?" she asked.

The aunt gave a broken laugh. "I didn't have a choice," she muttered. "I didn't have any damn choice. Otherwise I would have gotten rid of you in a heartbeat."

At that, her aunt fell silent.

KYLIE AND PORTER walked into the captain's office a little while later. Kylie remained silent since leaving the hospital.

The captain motioned to a chair. "Sit." She sat. The captain glared at her. "So, what the hell?"

"So, what the hell is right," she repeated to him. Now that she knew he was married to somebody who was also used to dabbling in this psychic stuff, Kylie felt much more at ease with him.

The captain looked over at Porter. "Answers?"

"Some, not enough," Porter said, and he repeated most of what had happened at the hospital.

"Agatha came back from the dead?" the captain asked, his eyes widening.

Kylie nodded. "And I don't know why."

"What do you mean?"

She raised both hands. "It feels as if she was supposed to tell me something and didn't."

"So, she's that scared of Hogan, even on her deathbed?"

"Seem to be, but I don't know for sure. She won't tell me those things," Kylie replied.

"The doctor did say these episodes happen, and the patients appear to be gone," Porter shared. "Then they suddenly come back, but they often pass away soon afterward."

"Which would make my aunt very happy," Kylie stated sadly. "She wants nothing to do with me at all."

"I'm not against that," Porter declared at her side. "Absolutely nothing she's shown me makes her somebody I would want to stay in touch with, much less have you endure her again. Agatha could have told you all kinds of things."

"Yes, but I'm not sure she's in any way capable of it."

"What is she trying to hide?" the captain asked.

"Herself," Kylie declared.

He looked at her. "Anything else?"

She stared at him, wordless, and then shrugged. "I don't know. I don't understand any of it, and it would do me an awful lot of good for her to talk to me, but I can't seem to force her to do that, so …"

The captain looked over at Porter. "Did you get a chance to talk to her?

He shook his head. "No, she was unconscious again fairly quickly after the conversation opened up with Kylie."

"Interesting." He shuffled the papers on his desk erratically, as if that would give him answers, and finally he looked over at her. "It sounds as if maybe you need to stay at the hospital, until you can get some answers."

"Sure, wouldn't that be nice. However, my aunt doesn't

want me there, so I'm not sure that will get me the answers anyway."

"Maybe not," the captain conceded, "so go to her house. See if you can come up with anything to question her about that'll give you something. Then go see her at the hospital and see if you can get any answers." He looked over at Porter. "What do you think?"

"I think that's a good idea. I was shocked when she came back to life, and I think, in a way, Agatha was too. There was that shock on her soul, as if I almost sensed her saying, *I escaped, I left. Nobody should have brought me back.*"

"It was definitely odd, very odd," Kylie confirmed. "One thing's for sure. She's not any friendlier after having died." Kylie had a wry look on her face, as if finding Agatha awake was an unexpected thing.

"So, was that her soul talking?" the captain asked cautiously.

She studied him, then shook her head. "I don't know. We hide so many things from ourselves, and Agatha hid everything, especially from me, apparently," she added, with a sad look over at Porter. "There was something about blocks, something about me talking to dead people all the time, so I don't know what Agatha was trying to say."

"Dead people?" he asked.

"Yeah, she mentioned my playing hopscotch, and all the people I played with were dead," she muttered. "I remember that too—not the dead people part—but I remember getting in trouble for it all the time. She mentioned she would keep everybody from finding out about me."

"So, she put those blocks in?" the captain asked.

"Your guess is as good as mine. She's definitely not sharing and doesn't want to open that door," Kylie explained, "which is just damn frustrating for me right now."

"Of course," he murmured, "but you got something out of her, and now you remember the hopscotch."

"Yes, and there was something else." She looked at the pencil in her hand. "She told me that she gave me this to me to help me keep things inside or whatever. I just don't know what that means to her."

"What would you have used instead?"

"Another pencil. Although I do love chalk," she shared, "but I don't know why I prefer chalk."

"Probably because of the hopscotch," the captain pointed out.

She looked at him and then nodded again. "You could be right." She stared over at Porter. "Maybe I need to go buy some chalk."

"I agree. We absolutely need to go buy some chalk for you," Porter declared.

"There is also the chance that whatever you draw with chalk might completely change everything," the captain noted.

Porter nodded. "You obviously have some a connection to dead people."

"Maybe you need to phone Stefan," the captain suggested, looking over at Porter. "Ask him."

"You're right, Captain." Porter now stared at the pencil she always used for sketching. "The thing is, I think you have turned and made that your own," he pointed out. "So, even if Agatha thought it would save her or would protect her, it appears to me that you created something that was geared more to help you than her. Or to help others. I would say that is a good thing."

Kylie sighed. "She never really talked a whole lot in the

hospital. I think there is more, a lot more, that she needs to say, or ought to anyway, but she probably isn't ready," she murmured.

"Which is why I think you need to go back."

She nodded. "I'm not against going back. Believe me that I want as many answers as I can get."

"So, give her an hour or two and then head back again," the captain said. "I wouldn't give her much longer because, if the doctors are correct, and this is not where she's planning on staying, if there is any way for her to change that circumstance, she is liable to do it as soon as she could."

Kylie frowned at that and nodded. "Porter, let's go to her house and check things out. Maybe we'll find some answers there."

"Did you ever look around her house, poke around at things? Any of them that you lived at?" Porter asked.

"Me, are you kidding? No matter where we lived, certain rooms were 100 percent blocked off," she stated, with a wry look in his direction. "I wasn't allowed anywhere. I was given a certain amount of space, and that was it. I wasn't welcome in her personal space."

"Jesus, I can't stand that woman," Porter muttered. "The more I hear, the more I dislike her." Turning, he looked at the captain and said, "We'll head there now and let you know how it goes."

As soon as they got back into the car, he asked Kylie, "Are you ready for this?"

"As ready as I'll ever be," she murmured, "which means not ready at all."

PORTER DROVE UP to the townhome and parked right in

front.

Kylie walked up to the door, quickly grabbed the key from under the mat, and stepped into a world that seemed so foreign and yet at the same time so familiar.

"Don't forget," she said, as she looked at him, "I never lived here with her. But, if I had, I would have been allowed into the kitchen, the dining room, my bedroom, the bathroom. That would have been about it," she muttered. "I was required to be in my space at all times."

He shook his head. "Does she have a home office?"

They headed there first and found almost nothing, except for a computer. He brought it up and a password was on it.

"I don't feel as if we should get into her computer, especially considering that she's still alive," Kylie pointed out.

He shrugged. "That's fine. Let's check out the rest of the house and see what's going on." They went upstairs to the bedroom, and Kylie paused and nodded. "She hasn't changed much. This is still pretty well the same bedroom as all of hers before."

He whistled as he entered. "This is a very esoteric bedroom, with all those protective markings." He pointed to the painting on the wall.

She looked at it and frowned. "I think I remember seeing those in some form every damn time I've ever been in her room."

"How often was that?"

"Not many. The few times I ever had to disturb her when she was in her bedroom brought such an outrageous response, I learned very quickly to not come in. But, as a child, you're curious, and a couple times I snuck into her room to see. She always knew though."

"Sure, she probably had hidden cameras or something going on. She's not the nicest or calmest person."

"No, she's not, but she managed to look after me."

He just smiled and kept on moving through the room. "She also doesn't seem to indulge much in the way of clothes. The closet is mostly empty, and it's a walk-in, with plenty of room."

"She did try to run, remember?"

"And she's got a suitcase packed," he noted, as he stared down at it on the bottom of the closet.

"We always did that," she blurted out, the memory coming up. And then she frowned, "Oh my God, that's right. We always kept a bag packed for emergencies and such."

"Interesting. So she was that afraid all the time?"

"Yes, we always had something ready to go," she murmured. "It must have been hard for her to go through life so terrified that she had absolutely no normalcy, no relationships, no friendships. I don't remember her ever having friends and certainly not a love interest. She would have blamed me anyway."

"In what way?" he asked.

"Just that I would have cramped her style. I do remember asking her if she'd ever been married, and she just laughed and said no, something about that time had come and gone—which didn't really surprise me, given her age. Now that I understand a little more about what was going on, I guess her responses were fairly easy to understand."

He dug further into the closet, and she noted, "You seem awfully fascinated by the closet."

"I am, not to mention it's a place where most people hide stuff."

"I don't know about her. She wouldn't have been most

people."

"That's true," he replied. "Still, answers have to be in here somewhere." As he moved farther into the closet, he pulled out a box from the far back corner.

"If you found a box, it won't be that one but would possibly be another box beside it, looking very innocuous. She always had these little tricks to hide things. I can't really remember what they were, but there was never any doubt that the obvious one was definitely not the prize."

And, sure enough, when he opened the first box, nothing was there. "Fascinating," he murmured.

She went into the closet next and then came back out again. "This one might have answers. I remember her getting really angry at me for opening it one time."

He took it from her, walked over to the bed, and laid it on top. "This would be something to look at anyway," he muttered to himself.

She stepped up beside him and added, "She always kept papers in here. I just don't know what the papers were. I was never given the freedom to find out."

"Not that we're necessarily allowed to be here doing this right now either, but, since something is going on, and the captain has okayed our visit, we are okay to go forward."

"But we're supposed to have a search warrant, aren't we?"

"He'll get one, if need be."

"But if nothing is here to warrant such a thing, that means we're doing this illegally, right?"

He smiled, "Yet you are her niece. Her only relative."

"Sure, but that doesn't give me the right to go prying into her things."

He faced her and said, "You need to ask yourself why

you don't want me to open this box."

She took a deep breath. "I really do want you to open that box, but I'm terrified of what's inside."

He popped open the box, just as a man spoke behind them.

"I have been looking for that sucker for a long time."

She slowly turned to see Keefe Hogan staring at them, a big smile on his face, a gun in his hand, and a feeling of relief in his expression. He looked at her and nodded. "I was hoping you would find it."

"You didn't kill her this time, you know."

His eyes lit up. "Really? Damn, she's worse than anybody I've ever known." He looked at her and then chuckled. "You do realize she's got this ability to appear dead, even to the point that you think for sure you wouldn't get a pulse. Then somehow she comes back." Kylie stared at him in shock, and he nodded. "I thought for sure she would have been 100 percent gone, but no. Once again, she came back from the dead. I'll just have to kill her again."

When Kylie gasped at that, he looked at her, then smiled. "If I told you the truth, you would want to kill her too."

She reared back at that, but he waved the gun at her. "You need to just calm down those reactions a little bit," he muttered, "because I don't mind fighting off the two of you."

Porter glared at Hogan. "What the hell do you want with this box anyway?"

"It's probably what I've been looking for the whole time," Hogan said. "I know you don't think a killer has any morals or ethics, and, to a certain extent, you're right, but this? … This is what sent me down that pathway."

"What pathway?" Kylie asked, her voice faint.

"The pathway of hell," he muttered. "The pathway of hiding for most of my life. The pathway that sent me to prison because of that bitch."

Kylie frowned.

"Oh, right, you don't know all about it." Hogan chuckled. "Some of us know a whole lot more." He waved his gun around at her again, getting Kylie's full attention. "You're the one who kept Agatha alive," he announced, with a smile, "and you didn't even know it."

Kylie blinked at him several times, her mind trying to grasp what he said. "I don't understand."

"Yeah, that was another thing Agatha didn't want to deal with. She never wanted to explain it to you. Then she got too scared and wanted to get rid of you," he shared, with half a laugh. "I kept as close as I could, but I didn't really intend to get too involved. Besides, I didn't intend on letting her live, and she knew it, which was why she kept you close and used you more as a radar system than anything." She blinked at him again, and he just smiled. "And, of course, none of this is making any sense to you."

"No, it isn't," she cried out. "How could that make sense to anyone?"

He chuckled. "I get it. You don't have a clue. I'm okay with that, but I'm sure you want answers. I guess I should allow Agatha to live long enough to confirm that you get those answers from her."

"Yeah, that would be nice," she said, staring at him in shock, "because I sure as hell don't have a clue what you're talking about. What do you mean, I kept her alive?"

"You have this little alert system that worked really well. Your mom didn't really understand apparently, but your aunt did, as Agatha had abilities of her own. You tried to stop your parents from going in the car that day. That is until Agatha decided to silence you."

"What are you talking about?" Kylie asked.

He laughed again, shaking his head. "I've always wondered if you had the same abilities as Agatha does." And, with that, he raised the gun, and he fired a shot, right in the center of Kylie's chest.

She felt the coldness sliding through her heart. She heard Porter's scream of shock and a second bullet being fired. She vaguely felt herself fall to the ground, wondering at the icy coldness in her system, and heard a voice calling out to her.

She wasn't sure who was calling or who was here. She felt a strange sensation of fullness, almost a weird awareness that life was about to change forever. Then in a distant part of her mind, she noted that Hogan walked over to the bed and picked up the box.

"Sorry about that, kiddo. No way I would let you stop me from finally getting the proof I needed. Whether your aunt lives or dies, I will confirm that people know what she did." He laughed more heartily this time. "It shouldn't really matter now because, after I was taken down that pathway, I never really got off of it. I was too angry, never giving up on the hope of revenge, and now you've finally given it to me." He raised the box, as if in a toast, and left.

And that was the last she knew, as she collapsed, unconscious.

AS BULLETS WENT, that second one had been deliberately placed to take out Porter. Only as he moved ever-so-slightly did he feel it snick at him and pass on by. He collapsed to the floor, expecting another bullet, which never came. He realized the gunman wasn't worried about Porter at all. In the back of his mind, he had to wonder how that worked. Yet all Porter was concerned about right now was to get to Kylie as soon as he could. She didn't understand what was going on either, but he had some idea that it would involve her aunt and this damn killer, who just seemed to float in and out of nowhere.

Porter heard something in the back of his mind, something about needing that connection, but then it was gone. After the door in his mind opened, Porter sent an SOS to the captain, then rolled over and shuffled to Kylie's side. He dropped down beside her, seeing the blood well up from her chest, and he whispered, "It's all right, honey. It's all right."

She blinked up at him several times and then whispered, "Goodbye."

He shook his head. "Nope, no goodbyes for you," he declared. "Haven't you figured out how your aunt got herself back alive again? From a weird energy defense system, and you have it too."

"What do you mean?"

"There was no reason for her to keep you all that time, if you didn't have something she could use. And that's what it was. Your ability to heal. Your ability to defend in a completely different way, just using energy," he explained. "So, although I see blood from your bullet wound, I don't see the amount of blood that there should be." He ran his hands over her quickly. "Your killer thinks that he managed to get rid of you, and chances are he's heading over to take out Agatha next."

Kylie just blinked up at him several times, and he smiled. "Keep blinking up at me, keep looking at me, keep questioning everything I'm saying," he suggested. "Give yourself time to recuperate because, right now, your energy is basically this mass of netting, and it went in with the bullet and even now is working that bullet back out again."

Sure enough, as he watched, a weird *plop* sounded, and the bullet hit the ground beside her. He grinned. "That is the best supernatural ability ever," he exclaimed. "I gather you didn't know anything about it."

Her hand went to her chest, as Kylie stared up at Porter in shock.

He nodded. "I've heard something about this, but I've never seen it, and this, sweetheart, is absolutely amazing."

She groaned, and a second bullet came out of her shoulder. "It feels as if they didn't even go in."

"They went in, but your energy did too. Think about the force behind a bullet. The energy just separates, allows the bullet to enter, yet at the same time you almost capture it with that same energy and work it back out again," he explained, fascinated. "A little bit of blood, not a whole lot, and a few minutes later, and you'll be just fine."

He laughed in delight, and then he frowned. "But we're definitely not telling anybody about this ability." He helped her to sit up. "Take it easy though. Take it easy, and don't move too quickly. I don't have a clue how fast that healing energy will work."

Stefan called into his head, *I'm not sure I just saw what I just saw.*

Porter laughed and replied out loud, "I saw it too. No wonder the aunt needed her."

Yes, but only as a protective system, and it wouldn't have helped her, at least I don't think so, if Agatha were alone. Then Stefan continued, now confused. *I'm not sure, but maybe, if*

Agatha was literally connected to Kylie, … maybe it would have made a difference. Jesus, just when you think you've come up against everything, you realize you haven't seen anything.

"I know," Porter agreed in absolute delight, "but considering Kylie just took two bullets, and she's now sitting up looking at me, it's like I'm the crazy one."

Hell, we're all crazy, Stefan noted in astonishment.

"And, if this is crazy, I'm more than happy to be here," Porter stated.

Stefan added, *Under normal circumstances, I would tell you to go see a doctor and get her checked out, but right now I don't think a doctor would even know what to do with her and would think you were crazy for bringing her in and for wasting their time.*

"Exactly," Porter said triumphantly. "I doubt Kylie's ever had a cold. I don't think she's ever had anything in her world that was physically wrong with her. … But you said if Kylie touched her aunt, then her aunt was bulletproof too?"

Maybe that is what brought the aunt back, to be near Kylie?

"Oh God, I don't know. Kylie was holding her aunt's hand for the longest time at the hospital, so, for all I know, that physical contact is possibly what let Agatha live." He looked down at Kylie. "How are you feeling?"

"Bizarre, but fine." She gave a whole-body shrug, almost as if the energy wafted back and forth, like an elastic band.

He grinned. "You are an absolute anomaly, and I am thrilled, and Stefan is here with us now as well."

She nodded. "I can hear him." She looked around the room, frowning. "That's got to get irritating though."

Stefan's voice filled the room. "Maybe, but that's a hell of an ability you have."

"And not one that we need anybody to know about," she

pointed out.

"No, I hear you there."

"But that is wild and useless if it's just related to me," she noted.

"I'm not sure it is just limited to you," Porter stated, "but we'll have to explore that afterward. Remember the *X-Men* movie? You would fit right in."

She snorted. "I so am not that." She walked over to the closet and stared inside.

"What's the matter?" he asked.

"I don't think Hogan got the right box," she replied, turning to look at Porter. "I think something else is in here."

"Where? Point me in the direction, and I'll dig in."

She frowned. "I think it's higher up. I feel as if it's quite high."

Immediately Stefan added, "Yes, it's much higher up. Whatever it is that you guys are after, a little door is up there, a hatch or something."

She nodded. "Yes, it's up there, whatever it is."

And, with that, Porter moved her aside. "Let me take a look." He kept glancing at her. "Are you sure you feel okay?"

"I feel fine," she replied in a wry tone. "I mean, I've just been shot twice, but, hey, don't worry about me," she muttered. "Apparently that's not an issue."

He grinned. "You can't imagine how thrilled I am that it's not an issue," he murmured. "The last thing I wanted was to have you taken out by a bullet."

"I don't think that'll happen at all," she murmured. "As a matter of fact, I'm not sure what this is all about, but I think it's time we go back and talk to Agatha."

"Not yet. Soon, just not yet."

"Why not?" she murmured, as he reached up into the

closet, trying to locate the hidden space.

"Because I think we need to sort this out first, and then go talk to your aunt."

"Did she use me as an antiaging talisman too?" she asked. "I always wondered how she stayed so young looking."

"Is she young?" he asked her. "I thought she was probably what? In her mid-forties, late-thirties, early-forties?"

"She's a lot older than that," she declared, staring at him. "But you're right. She looks very well preserved, doesn't she?"

"So then, maybe she was using some of your energy, along with the blocks, to help her stay young, and maybe it was part of her way of hiding. If she looked younger, and Hogan was always expecting an older woman, maybe she thought that would keep her safer."

Kylie frowned. "Didn't Hogan say something about proof? He did mention that he was looking for proof, right?"

"Yes, he was. Something about being on a path, sending him down a pathway."

Porter reached into the back of the closet, way up high, and sure enough found an attic hatchway there. He slid back the door and, using both hands, he swung himself up so he could take a look. Resting on his arms along the opening, he pulled out his phone, turned on the flashlight, and took a look around. It was empty, except for a very flat 9x13 inch box in front of him. He grabbed it and slid back down.

"And do we know if Hogan actually left?" she asked, frowning as she turned and looked around. "The last thing I want him to do is come back and find me alive. I did survive this time, but I don't know that I can do it every time."

"That's a good point. I suggest we get out of here with

the box, just in case."

She nodded, and, with the two of them moving as quickly as they could, they headed to his car, got in, and he headed down the road. She now clutched the box tightly in her hands. "Do you think it's safe to open?" she whispered.

At her wording he looked at her, almost as if she were a little girl, and he realized that once again the blocks were stopping her from being the person she needed to be at every step. The fact that she'd even been a fully functioning adult just blew him away.

He smiled, closed his fingers around her hand, and said, "We'll go somewhere safe, and then we'll open it. And, yes, it's definitely time to open up this thing."

She nodded and sank back into her seat.

Porter couldn't help but be worried that there would be some after effects from all this.

Kylie looked over at him. "I'm fine."

He frowned and nodded. "I hear you, but I just don't see how."

"I know," she murmured. "I feel as if there will always be that doubt."

"You've heard it before?"

"I think so." She looked puzzled at first. Then her face cleared. "At the hospital, after the car accident, they didn't understand why I was free from any injuries," she murmured. "I guess that's why, *huh*?"

"Maybe. And would Agatha have known that?"

"I don't know," she whispered, as she thought about it. "But I feel as if maybe she did." He found a coffee shop and pulled in and parked. She looked at him in surprise. "Are you sure you want to do this out in public?"

He nodded. "As much as it might be better in private, if

Hogan finds us here in a public place like this, it'll be a little harder on him."

"And is it harder on him?" she asked. "Is that who we're protecting?"

"I don't know, but this box is definitely something he is looking for."

"Right."

They got out, and thankfully the coffee shop was pretty empty. He took a seat at the very back and faced the entrance. She sat on the other side of the table.

She frowned. "I don't like having my back to the door."

He nodded. "Let's switch the chairs ever-so-slightly."

It was a little more awkward, but they finally had it so that both of them could see around the restaurant. When the waitress came over and frowned at them, he apologized. "Sorry, we've just been under some difficult times right now, and we need to both feel more comfortable."

She shrugged. "As long as you put the chairs back afterward. This area doesn't get a whole lot of use anyway, particularly when the weather isn't glorious. What can I get you?"

He looked over at Kylie. She said, "I just want coffee."

He ordered two coffees, and, when the waitress didn't appear to be very happy with that, he ordered a large sandwich for them to split. With her gone, he looked over at Kylie. She was still clutching the box in her hands but made no move to open it. He wasn't sure if he should nudge her in that direction or just let it wait. Finally he suggested that maybe she should take a look.

"Maybe." Yet she couldn't bring herself to put the box on the table. "This box could hold documents," she whispered.

"Yes, I would suspect so."

"So, it likely has information about my parents," she murmured.

"Yes," he agreed.

"I'm not sure I want to open it," she admitted.

He just waited. The waitress came back with coffee and said the sandwich would be coming soon. With cream in her coffee, Kylie picked up the cup and had a couple sips. Then she sat back again.

Porter noticed her fingers went right to her earring, and she massaged it.

He smiled. "That earring always makes you feel better, doesn't it?"

She shrugged. "I don't really know," she murmured. "It's something I tend to do when I'm stressed."

"Of course, and, if this place is something that's stressing you out, we can go somewhere else."

"No, it's not the location. It's the contents of the box."

"Of course." He just waited and let her have some time to settle in.

She let go of one heavy sigh and then a second one, and finally, with the third, she opened the box without warning and put the lid off to the side. Multiple file folders were inside. At the top was a file labeled *Keefe Hogan*. The next file was labeled *Ann Marie*, and at the bottom of the folders was a third one with Kylie's name on it.

She frowned as she looked at them. "I'm not sure what this is all about," she muttered. "Ann Marie is my mother's name."

He looked surprised at that. "You pick one, and I'll take one."

She handed him Hogan's folder, which Porter really was

hoping she would give to him. He opened it and found documented conversations, but it was also proof that he had been involved in the killings of Kylie's family. Porter frowned, wondering why Hogan would want this. It was proof that he had been involved, and that wasn't necessarily something he would want to keep. Surely he would want to destroy this. Yet Hogan felt this would somehow exonerate him.

Porter kept going through this batch of paperwork and saw emails back and forth between Agatha and Hogan, from many years ago. Porter frowned and pondered any relationship between the two of them. Then Porter brought up on his phone the digital file that he had on Kylie's parents' deaths and what he had known about the aunt's involvement in hunting down Hogan.

Did the police have it all wrong? Had Hogan and Agatha known each other prior to this? Or was this part of the trap she had set?

In a way that would make the most sense, but it also still didn't completely clarify this mess. As Porter sat here, his phone rang. He answered it quickly, and it was the captain.

"Progress?" he barked.

"Yes," Porter replied in a low tone. "We found something."

The captain dropped the tone of his voice too. "Good. What is it?"

"Not sure, and we are working on it. We're going through a box right now."

"Heads up. Agatha has disappeared. She checked herself out of the hospital, and nobody knows where she is. So, if you're at her house …"

"No, we're out now, at the coffeehouse on Fifth and

Main, but we did get the box from her house."

"That'll be fun," he muttered. "We didn't have a search warrant."

"I know, but then again, … her next of kin had ample worry that she wouldn't survive."

"And yet she came back to life just fine," the captain noted in a tone that clearly revealed he didn't like anything about this.

"I don't like it either," Porter replied. "We need to go through this box, and then we can give you more information."

"Hurry it up. I'm sending a few uniforms your way, just in case," he snapped, and, with that, he disconnected.

Kylie frowned at Porter, who shrugged. "The captain's looking for answers."

"Right, of course he is," she muttered.

He hesitated, then added, "Agatha has checked herself out of the hospital."

She gasped, and he saw the fear in her eyes. She looked down at the box and almost picked it up and smashed it against her chest, as if it were so important that she was afraid she would lose it.

He nodded. "I gather this is superimportant information."

"I'm reading my mother's will," she shared. "I don't really understand why it should be here, but considering my aunt was trying to help find her killer, … I guess it does make sense. The other document is a summary of details about how and when Agatha tried to find Hogan and then getting Hogan incarcerated," she murmured. "That's all I've read so far."

He asked, "May I?"

She hesitated, then handed over the folder. She did not ask for Hogan's folder. Instead she picked up her own.

Porter looked down at the few sheets in Ann Marie's file and read through the little that was here, but it struck him a moment later just how wrong one part of it was. When he heard a soft cry, he looked over at Kylie, staring down at the papers with tears in her eyes. "What's the matter?" he whispered.

She stared at him in shock. "You probably need to read this. I don't think I can read anymore." And she handed him the file, her hand shaking so badly that the papers trembled in the air. "And now I feel as if she's here," she whispered, looking around in a panic. "If Agatha's not here yet, she's on her way."

"The only way she would know that is if she can track you."

Her hand went to her earring and twisted it nervously. "I don't know about that, but she's always had this uncanny ability to find me whenever she wanted to."

"Take off the earring," Porter ordered.

She frowned at him, then took a moment for the comprehension to click in, and she pulled the stud from her ear and dropped it on the table, staring at it in shock. "Agatha told me that it was from my mother."

"And maybe it was, and just because Agatha said that doesn't mean that it wasn't from your mother," he replied. "It just means that maybe Agatha found a way to utilize it, to keep track of you. And by telling you it was from your mother, you kept it close."

"Yeah, of course I did." She stared at him. "It's the only thing I have of hers." She tapped the file Agatha had hidden away that he currently had in his hand. "Did you read it?"

"No, I'm trying to," he said, with a note of humor. "Give me a minute."

She sat here, staring at him, her eyes beady and hard, as she watched him read through every page. When he came to the end, he slowly closed the folder, his mind completely overwhelmed.

"Did you see everything Agatha did to try and find my mother's killer?" she asked.

"Yes," he confirmed, wondering if Kylie really understood what was in this file.

"I don't understand why you're looking at me like that," Kylie noted. "It's heartbreaking enough for me, but I didn't think it would affect you quite so badly."

"It's not that it didn't affect me," he began. "It's the fact that I don't think you understood exactly what it said."

She stared at him, then at the file. "Maybe you better tell me."

"It's everything that she did to find Hogan, yes."

Just then a woman spoke up. "Now I know where that file went."

Porter saw Agatha in full outrage beside them. She was vibrating with fury.

"How dare you come into my house and steal from me?" she snapped, her voice growing louder and louder. She stared down at her niece with such venom that Porter pulled Kylie's chair closer to him. So much hatred filled Agatha's gaze. "I always knew you would be trouble," she snapped at Kylie.

"Trouble?" Kylie repeated, staring at her. "I was never trouble. I went out of my way to *not* cause trouble."

Agatha laughed. "You were trouble right from the beginning. You just didn't realize what kind of trouble you were causing everybody. Even if you had understood, I don't think you would have changed one bit." Agatha tried to snatch the box, but Kylie hung on to it.

For that, Porter had to give Kylie full props.

"Give me my box," Agatha yelled. "This is private and personal and has nothing to do with you."

"It has everything to do with me, considering you have files with my name on one and my mother's name on another," Kylie snapped.

Porter was happy to see Kylie reacting defiantly against her aunt, but something was almost painful about it, as if Kylie was just finally waking up to the fact that an issue existed.

"As if you didn't cause me enough trouble all these years." Agatha glared at her.

"I don't know what you're talking about," Kylie declared. "I spent a lifetime doing my best to cause you no trouble. As much as I appreciate the fact that you raised me and didn't dump me into the foster care system, sometimes I wonder if I would have been better off elsewhere."

Her aunt gave a hard laugh. "Yeah, you probably would have been, but I couldn't allow that."

"I don't get it," Kylie murmured. "Why? What the devil did you even want to hang on to me for?" Kylie asked. "I don't know what foster care would have been like, but I know that life with you was not easy."

"Life isn't supposed to be easy," Agatha spat, with a wave of her hand. "You take what you need, what you want. However, nothing is out there that others can't take back."

It was such a harsh philosophy that even Porter had to stare at her in surprise. She was so bitter and so angry over everything. "I don't understand your mindset," Porter stated. "You had choices. You didn't have to take Kylie in. You could have handed her off to the authorities. Somebody would have adopted her."

"Maybe, but she was too damn dangerous. So I couldn't let her go. Anybody could have utilized her abilities."

At that, Kylie stiffened. "You wouldn't ever let me use my abilities."

"Of course not." Agatha frowned at Kylie. "Everything I did was to keep you safe, you, … you ungrateful little wretch," she snapped. "And look at you. You broke into my house, and you steal from me."

Porter watched the shame appear very quickly in Kylie's expression. "That's enough of that, Agatha," Porter announced. "You do realize you almost died, and that these records would have been something Kylie would have gone through anyway."

"No," Agatha declared. "I would have left nothing to her. She took everything of mine already all these years ago. I wouldn't give her one more penny."

He saw the hurt in Kylie's eyes, but she stiffened and replied, "I don't care. I don't need anything from you."

"Not now, but you sure did before, and I couldn't be rid of you fast enough," Agatha muttered, as she glared at Kylie. "Now give me my damn box."

Porter picked up the empty box and handed it to her. "Here. Have it, but you're not getting the contents of it until I have a chance to go through these folders."

Agatha pinned him with a skewered look, almost as if to wound him.

And he did feel some pain. She was incredibly powerful, and he realized suddenly that they were up against something else. "Why are you so adamant about us giving these over to you?" he asked, sensing something was incredibly wrong about all this.

"One, it's mine. Two, it's personal. Three, I'm hardly dead. How dare you go on the assumption that I would die anyway," she stated, glaring at him. Then she caught sight of Kylie's earring on the table. Agatha's mouth twisted. "And of course you would ditch everything I worked so hard for, wouldn't you?"

Agatha's fury was building, and Porter felt it in his bones.

"Your poor mother, how the hell she thought that the sun rose and set with you, I don't know."

Bewildered, Kylie picked up the earring and went to put it back in her ear, but Porter stopped her. "Don't. Just wait."

Her aunt spun and glared at him. "Men," she snapped. "Interfering pieces of shit, that's all you are," she roared. At this point her outrage was causing a scene at the restaurant.

"Is that what you want?" he asked Agatha. "Everybody to hear and to see you? You've spent a lifetime in the shadows. Surely you have a reason for that, things that you don't really want everybody to know about you now."

She muted her tone, but her fury was almost out of control. "I gave her that earring when her mother died. It was her mother's, and look at you. How very quickly all she wants to do is get rid of everything that mattered to her, and all because *you* told her so."

Porter watched a growing sense of something happening here that Kylie didn't understand.

Kylie replied, "I don't understand your reaction, Aunt Agatha. Why are you so angry? If I do nothing else but take off this earring to clean it, it's still not removing the memory of my mother."

"Of course not." Agatha gave a harsh laugh. "I worked

hard for you to understand how important it was for you to keep that earring in your ear. But he says one thing, and you ditch it just like that." Agatha shook her head. "I shouldn't have expected more from you. You're so much like your mother that it's unbelievable."

At that, Kylie glared at her. "Once again, you're insulting my mother."

"Your mother was pathetic. She would have done anything for your father and look where that ended up. She's dead."

"And so is he," Kylie pointed out. "I don't know what the hell your problem is right now."

"I'm angry," Agatha snapped. "And I want my things. I'm not leaving here without it, and believe me that I will call the cops—and not this sorry excuse for one. I'll confirm this becomes a massive issue." At that, she glared down at the files, seeing that some of them were already opened. "You just had to snoop, didn't you?" Agatha asked Kylie.

Kylie explained stiffly, "We were trying to figure out what was going on and how to stop Hogan from coming after you again. As you always told me, *We were doing it for your own good.*"

"Right." Agatha sneered. "As if you could do anything. You just don't understand who and what *he* is. I do, and I've spent a lifetime avoiding people like him. Yet, the first chance you get, what do you find?" Now Agatha sent a sneer to Porter. "Just another piece-of-shit man."

"Wow." Porter studied Agatha. "It's not just me then. Apparently you hate all men."

"No, I don't hate any man," she corrected. "I despise them. They're weak, and, when they don't like things that turn out differently than they expected, they turn around and want payback."

"Oh, is that what Hogan was for you? You found him, helped the police put his sorry ass in prison, and then, when he escapes, wanting revenge, you can't seem to understand or expect that from him? Is that it?"

Agatha laughed in such a chilly tone that people about to enter the dining area of the restaurant turned and walked away. Nobody wanted anything to do with this tirade of anger and fury. Agatha glared at Porter. "I'll take my files now. They're mine."

"Maybe, but I also think some of them belong in a criminal file," Porter declared, sending a wry smile in her direction. "I've read two of them, but I haven't read the last one yet. So you're not taking that one."

"Oh, I can assure you that I am," Agatha stated, as she went to snatch Kylie's file out from under her nose.

A harsh voice spoke behind them all. "Well, … now, now, not so soon. We have a whole reunion gathered here. Isn't that sweet?"

Agatha froze and turned to look at the man who had just joined them. The fiery expression on her face evaporated, and she suddenly looked terrified.

CHAPTER 17

KYLIE STARED AT the man who had killed her family.

Keefe Hogan gave them a hard cold smile, as he stared at Kylie's aunt. "I've been looking for you again," Hogan shared. "You have this amazing ability to survive everything I try to do to you. Just like Kylie here. Even this guy survived."

Agatha stiffened and took a step back from Hogan but a step toward Kylie.

Kylie immediately knew something more was going on here than she had thought. She glanced over at Porter, who gave an ever-so-slight shake of his head. She frowned at that, not sure what she was supposed to do in the midst of all this. Hogan didn't appear to have his weapon on him this time, but Kylie didn't trust him.

Hogan smiled at her. "Isn't that nice. … You and your aunt are so cozy. Have you told them the truth yet?" he asked Agatha.

Agatha just stared at him, half afraid and half furious, almost sputtering in place. "What are you doing here?" she snapped. "Haven't you tormented me enough?"

"Oh, I don't think so," he stated. "Not nearly enough, not until the whole world knows." He chuckled. "Then, and maybe only then, I'll be happy."

"You'll just go back to prison," she stated. "How come

that doesn't matter to you?"

"I didn't do anything." He laughed. "If I did, I probably should go to jail. However, I don't have any intention of doing so. It's not really the place for me." He smirked at Agatha. "You, on the other hand, would do very, very well there."

She glared at him. "That won't happen."

"You might be surprised." Hogan sent a hard look in her direction, before turning to Porter. "And you're still alive too. That's fascinating. But it's really this lovely lady who I'm most interested in at the moment." And he turned his gaze to Kylie.

Kylie stared at him. "You seem to know an awful lot more about me than I know about myself," she stated. "Maybe you can fill me in."

His gaze widened in delight, and then he nodded. "Not a bad idea because I know for a fact that Agatha will deny everything."

"Of course I'll deny everything," Agatha confirmed. "She would be a fool to listen to you and your lies."

"A fool?" Hogan repeated. "How many times have you called Kylie that and so much more in her life? So maybe she would understand that's how you are and would listen to me anyway."

Agatha moistened her lips, while Kylie stared from one to the other. "I understand this has something to do with my family," Kylie began. "And regardless of what the outcome of all this is, could I please have the truth?"

Hogan nodded. "I think she deserves to know. Don't you, Agatha?"

Agatha shook her head. "No, I don't. She doesn't and won't understand." Agatha returned her ever-watchful gaze to Hogan.

He smiled. "And you, Agatha, don't you look well for your age? Of course not quite as well as you used to look."

"I'm getting older," she snapped. "That's to be expected."

"Yes, yes, it is. It's sad though, isn't it? That whole *fountain of youth* thing can only go on for so long. It was working wonderfully, but then somehow, somewhere along the line, you lost it."

"I did one decent thing in my life," she muttered, "and I let it go."

"Yeah, but not quite, did you? You waited just long enough until you had the skill to do what you needed to do but from a distance." When Agatha stared at Hogan in shock, he nodded. "I admit it took me quite a while to figure it out, but I had some time on my hands in prison. But poor Kylie? … She has no clue."

Kylie spoke up. "No, I really don't, and I would appreciate it if one of you would explain."

Agatha snapped, "I won't explain, and you can't listen to anything that comes out of his mouth."

"Maybe," Kylie conceded, "but somebody needs to tell me what's going on."

"Why?" her aunt asked in a mocking tone. "You won't believe us anyway."

"Maybe I will," Kylie stated. "Maybe it isn't all that bad."

"No, it's way worse," Porter declared. "That's why Agatha's hemming and hawing, still trying to protect herself."

"You!" Agatha said, with a sneer. "You don't know anything."

"Maybe not," Porter replied. "Maybe I'm completely

wrong, but somehow I don't think so." He looked back at Hogan and asked, "Right?"

Hogan laughed. "I think it's hilarious, but—"

"I just want a damn answer," Kylie stated forcefully. "Surely after all this, somebody owes me that much."

"Nobody owes you shit," Agatha spat, with a sneer. "I sure as hell don't owe you anything."

Kylie stared at her and nodded stiffly. "Fine, you don't owe me anything, but I still want to know."

"That's nice." She glanced down at the box in front of her and added, "I might tell you if you give me my papers back."

Kylie reached for them, but Porter slammed his hand atop them. "Oh no," he told Agatha. "You're not getting those papers."

At that, Hogan laughed and laughed. "Look at that, Agatha. You suddenly don't seem to have that same pull you used to have."

She glared at him. "This is all your fault."

"Really? And why is that?"

"If you hadn't gone after my sister, none of this would have happened."

"Oh, kinda like, if you hadn't helped the police, then I wouldn't have been incarcerated. Is that it?"

"Yes," she snapped.

Hogan turned and looked at Kylie. "And do you believe that?"

"I don't know what I'm supposed to believe at this point," she shared. "I still don't understand why you would have killed my mother."

"Oh, that's an easy one to answer, you clueless little bird." Hogan beamed as he pointed at her aunt and added,

"Because Agatha hired me to do so."

NOW THAT MADE the most sense yet. Porter slid his hand to his gun, sliding it ever-so-slightly free of its holster. It was still in a position where he couldn't quite grab it, if he needed to. Still, he did manage to get his phone out and place it on the table, hoping he could transmit something to someone. The captain did say he had two officers coming here, but Porter had yet to see them.

He'd already sent a telepathic message to Stefan, who had checked in and then disappeared. Porter wasn't sure what that meant, but, hey, he could only hope that something good would come out of this. In the meantime, he watched Kylie's world come tumbling down, as she stared in horror at her aunt.

Her aunt waved her hand. "You can't listen to a word he says. What absolute and complete BS. She was my sister, and I helped the police find Hogan and put him away."

"Yeah, you did," Hogan agreed, "but why do you think I'm back? Because you broke our agreement. We had a letter of agreed terms. Yet you cheated and lied to me and then lied to everybody else. I did prison time because of you, you bitch, and you got off scot-free. How fair is that?"

She snorted. "I don't understand what you possibly think you deserved after killing my sister," Agatha replied in a strangled tone. "You're nothing but a mercenary, and I highly doubt anybody paid you. I think you did that one for free."

"And why would I?" he asked, staring at her, a smile playing at the corner of his lips. "You were the one using me for your own ends."

"*Of course I was,*" Agatha quipped, with an eye roll and heavy sarcasm in her tone. "As if anybody will believe that."

Porter checked to confirm his phone was recording, and, with that, he sat back, wary, his foot rubbing against Kylie's. She glanced at him, shrinking in her seat, the growing fear inside her, as the truth slowly worked its way through her psyche. Agatha hiring Hogan to kill Ann Marie felt more likely to Porter than anything else he'd heard so far, and it also explained why Hogan had come back after Agatha.

"But of course you were using me, sweetheart," he said, with a gentle smile. "Do you think I don't remember what it was like to have an older lover, only to realize afterward how manipulative you were? I owe you for completely changing my life. I wanted to be a doctor, remember?"

"A doctor," she snorted. "A doctor who kills people, right?"

He shook his head. "My life was going great until I met you, and then ... wow."

Agatha gave him a mocking smile. "You think anyone would believe I slept with you?"

"I don't know what others will believe, but you remember the truth. I didn't have a chance to find all the proof, but I certainly know that our relationship was true because I was there," Hogan replied. "I realize that most of these people look at me now and say, *Oh, that's so gross.*"

At that, Agatha's face pinched.

Hogan nodded, then continued. "Of course you were looking way the hell better than you do now. You were what? Twenty years older than I am? Still, that didn't seem to bother you one bit at the time. You had a young buck in your bed, and that was just fine, wasn't it? We had some good times, didn't we, sweetheart? But then you couldn't stand the fact that your sister had this lovely little lady here," he shared, as he pointed at Kylie.

"I don't understand." Kylie frowned, looking at her aunt. "Why would you care?"

"Because Agatha can't have children," Hogan stated succinctly. "Even with someone as virile as myself," he added, with a tone of mockery, "Agatha couldn't have any. More than that, your mother knew about your abilities. She wouldn't let up about it, and apparently it was just a little too much because Agatha had planned on having her own little witches running around, and yet that never happened."

"That's ridiculous. If she wanted children, I'm sure she could have gotten some help and had some," Kylie noted, "particularly with the energy you're talking about."

"Maybe, but her sister didn't think so, and it remained a bone of contention between the two of them. You know how sisters are," he said, with a hard smile at Kylie, "and Agatha just couldn't stand it."

"So, you hired Hogan to kill my mother?" Kylie asked Agatha in shock. "And my brothers, my father? What did any of them do to you?" she asked, staring at her aunt in horror. "There was no reason to hurt anybody. How do you justify that?"

Agatha sneered. "What do you know?" she asked. "You've been causing all kinds of chaos and trouble since the day you were born. I didn't want to look after you. Hogan was supposed to deal with all of you."

At that, Kylie stared at her aunt in shock. "Oh my God. You did it. You really did arrange for my mother and my father and my two baby brothers to be killed?"

"Yes, I did," Agatha snapped. "So there, now you know. Not that it'll do either of you any good. I have no intention of going to prison, and I'm also not the one who did the deed. Hogan was. Even, … even after I called and told him to forget it."

"That's a lie. You never called to tell me to forget it," Hogan declared, with that dangerous smile lighting up his face. "And it's been a twisted scenario ever since. I don't even know how the hell I got conned into doing your bidding, but my life went into a hellish loop. I'm still not sure you didn't somehow use your abilities against me to compel me to do it because I can't see that I would have done it any other way. I was doing well and on track for a great career, until I got involved with you. I just know I owe you for the complete destruction of my life."

Hogan sighed. "My family couldn't handle the horror of it all. My dad went to his grave, knowing what I had become but never understanding why or how. I tried to explain it to him one time, and he just sat there, shaking his head, as if nothing made sense. And, to him, it didn't make sense. He was a good God-fearing man, who'd raised his family right," he shared. For the first time, palpable pain filled Hogan's words.

"But somehow, after I met you, *dear Agatha*, I made all kinds of decisions that nobody could understand, and afterward neither could I," he explained. "Once I went down that path, there didn't seem to be anything else for me. I lost everything, so there wasn't much to be done but to keep going ahead with my newfound profession. Did I have to? No, but I was angry at the world and really angry at you. I found you a couple times," he stated, with a smile, "but I wasn't quite ready to knock you off. I wanted you to suffer. I wanted you to feel what I felt every day. But you kept finding ways to get away from me," he said, with a mock smile. "I wasn't even sure how that worked, but regardless, before I die, I will make you pay for everything you did to me."

Agatha sneered at him. "You're deluded," she muttered. "I would never have had anything to do with you, no way."

Immediately Porter opened the file on Hogan in front of him and flipped to a picture. The picture was one he now recognized quite easily. He lifted it, so that Hogan could see it as well.

Hogan's face turned to fury and then satisfaction, as he nodded. "And yet you kept a picture of us." And, indeed, the photograph was of a man and a woman, still curled up in bed and in each other's arms. "I remember taking that," he murmured.

"I got angry with you for it too." Agatha stared at it. "God, that seems so long ago."

"It was a long time ago," Hogan confirmed. "If I had the chance to go back there again, I would completely change those decisions and choices," he said to her. "But not you, I bet. You would probably repeat the same life."

"I would have made one change," she noted, with a negligent toss of her hair. "I would have made sure you couldn't come back, and I probably would have ditched this one earlier." Agatha pointed at Kylie. "She's been such a pain. Raising her—God, what a trial. It's a good thing I never did get pregnant. Having raised this brat, I don't think I could have had kids and not killed them," she stated. "What a waste of space and energy."

"I think if it had been your own child, you might have been fine," Porter suggested. "But Kylie represented everything that was wrong in your world. She represented everything that you coveted. It was your guilt staring back at you, and you just couldn't see past it."

"Oh, that's bullshit," Agatha declared in a no-nonsense manner.

"Is it?" Porter asked, a note of humor in his tone. "You didn't kill Kylie all those years ago, and you certainly could have."

"She had her uses, not that they're of any value now," Agatha spat, as she glared at the earring on the table.

"Was it even my mother's earring?" Kylie asked.

"It was, and I used it on her all the time too. Whenever she pissed me off, I got my revenge one way or another. Remember all the sick days she had? That was usually me dropping her energy down, so she felt as if she needed to go to bed. She spent most of that second pregnancy in bed and couldn't even look after you. I thought that was great."

Kylie shook her head. "So that was you pulling my energy from me and why I was so tired lately. You did it to my mother, and now you are doing it to me."

Agatha gave a half-mocking laugh. "I couldn't quite bring myself to kill her though. She was my sister, after all. However, then, … then she had the twins. Two healthy boys. That was just way too much. Such a slap in the face."

"Jesus," Porter muttered, staring at Agatha. "So, somebody in your family is blessed, and you can't be happy for her? Instead you turn around and destroy it all?"

Agatha sneered at him. "You're one to talk."

He frowned at her. "Can't say I've ever done anything like you have."

"Everybody does what they need to do to make their own lives happen," Agatha declared in a hard tone. "Don't make it sound as if I'm some abnormality because I'm not. You are all just like me, every one of you. It's just that not everybody gets caught."

"And what are you here and now, if not caught?" Porter asked, staring at her. "Right now, Hogan's looking for retribution. Your niece now knows exactly what you've done, and you are the same pathetic woman you've always been."

"So what? Kylie doesn't know everything. She only knows about her pathetic little family."

"Isn't that enough horror?" Kylie asked, staring at her aunt.

"Not likely," Agatha replied. "Thanks for the hospital visit though."

At that, Kylie stared at her, nodding now. "It really was me bringing you back to life, wasn't it?"

"Oh, it absolutely was you," Agatha agreed. "Very kind of you. I wasn't quite able to pull that one back. It's a little harder when you're older, and energy gets that much harder to work with."

"It's not supposed to get harder," Kylie stated, staring at her aunt. "It's supposed to get easier."

Porter nodded. "Only if you're coming from the heart. When you're manipulating and hurting others, certain things do inhibit your abilities as you grow older. Not enough, not nearly enough to stop people from being assholes," he explained. "But, in some cases, particularly when Agatha surrounded herself with so much negativity, I can see it being harder for her to do what she was trying to do. For decades though, Agatha utilized your energy instead," he told Kylie.

She frowned at Porter, and he nodded. "That's what makes sense, and it's why you were so weak as a child. It's why you struggled with your schooling sometimes, and why sometimes you thought something was wrong with you. But, as it turns out, all that was your aunt, this monster who kept you around, as if some personal generator."

Kylie stared at him in shock.

Agatha gave a hoarse bark of laughter. "That's not a bad description." She glanced at Porter. "So now what?"

Porter shook his head. "You really are a complete bitch, aren't you?"

Agatha shrugged. "I don't think so. I don't think anything is wrong with me at all. I simply did what I needed to do, and that's all anybody ever does," she snapped. "So, stop with your BS holier-than-thou attitude. Having loyalties, morals, and ethics come with problems. The world would be a whole lot easier place if we could avoid all of it."

Kylie stared at her. "And my mother, did she know about you?"

At that, Agatha stiffened. "I don't know whether she knew or not. … I'll worry about that when I cross over." She shrugged. "I'll face that when I get there."

"You absolutely will," Porter declared, staring at Agatha. "As somebody who talks to dead people, I put out the call to talk to your sister a couple times. I always got a muddled response and never really had a clear signal."

"Good, maybe she's just as stupid over there as she was here," Agatha replied, staring at him. "If you can talk to dead people, you should be talking to all of Hogan's victims."

At that, Hogan turned to Porter. "Can you really talk to dead people?"

"Yes, but that doesn't mean that dead people can always talk to me. It depends on how they died, where they're at, and their life over there. Speaking of which, did you have a son many years ago?"

"Not that I know of." Hogan swallowed nervously. "Will they be waiting for me over there?"

"Yes," Kylie replied. "Don't worry. All your victims will be waiting for you. And your son too."

"Ah, shit." Hogan looked around the emptiest part of the restaurant.

Kylie followed his gaze to the cops standing at the entrance, just far enough back that they couldn't hear, but all of them with their weapons drawn. She nodded. "Now, this is an interesting place to be," she murmured. She figured that Porter had already seen them. He was just trying to figure out how to get everybody here out alive, or at least some of them. She wanted to be included in that, but she wasn't at all sure that was what anybody else had planned. She looked at her aunt. "You're obviously ready to go, but you don't have to take anybody else with you."

She laughed. "Oh no, Hogan and I need to go together," she said comfortably. "Nothing for him is here." She turned and looked at him. "Right?"

He stared at her, his jaw working. "That would be a hell of an ending on my part, wouldn't it?"

"It's where we started though, love," she replied, her tone softening. "It's really the only answer right now. Unless you want to spend the next forty years of your life in prison? They might even give you the death penalty, but I'm not sure."

He swallowed, staring at her in shock.

Agatha continued. "It would always come down to this, and you knew that. It's precisely what we put in our pact so long ago."

He closed his eyes and nodded. "I wondered if you even remembered that."

"Oh, I remember," Agatha said, "I just wasn't quite ready for it."

"And yet you denied me a relationship all these years."

"I felt you should have gone off and had your own life, without somebody as old as I am," Agatha revealed. "I realize now it's an energy we couldn't walk away from, a shared energy that entwined us forever. It isn't something we'll separate from. It's just us right now."

"And your sister," Porter noted. "Ann Marie's here right now. She says you haven't told Kylie something."

Agatha stiffened and glared at Porter. "You're just trying to make trouble."

"You're already at the end of this anyway," he pointed out. "So why play games? Why not just tell the whole truth?"

"What truth?"

"The truth about why you really wanted Kylie. It's not just that you were jealous because your sister had a daughter, or that she could have kids and you didn't. It was also about something completely different."

Even Hogan looked at her in surprise. Agatha glared at Porter. "You don't know anything about it."

"No, but it is something your sister wants you to explain to Kylie."

"That's too damn bad. I don't give a shit what Ann Marie wants. She's dead and gone. Her time is done. That's not anything I have to listen to now."

"Maybe not," Porter conceded, "but she'll be there, waiting for you."

"So what?" Agatha stated boldly, but it was obvious that the thought bothered her. Agatha shrugged. "What do I care? I won't be there in the next little bit anyway." She turned to Kylie. "You don't remember anything, do you?"

"No. Should I?"

"That just means the blocks worked better than I

thought," she murmured, "and that's good." Then she shrugged and sighed. "What the hell. You want the truth, Kylie? Well, here goes. … You were still alive when I came up behind you. Hogan took out the car but ended up having to finish off almost everyone. The babies died immediately, your father not quite. I was there and stopped Hogan from killing you, but you were already trying to help your mother stay alive. I couldn't let that happen, so I separated the two of you. Even then Ann Marie was already fighting hard to stay alive, so I took her out," Agatha said simply. "Hogan killed the rest of your family, but I killed Ann Marie."

"How …" Kylie was too shocked to get the words out. "Why?"

"That's what happens. Siblings are like that." Agatha gave a laugh and a careless wave of her hand.

At that, Hogan sighed. "I'm really glad you finally confessed. I've been waiting a lifetime to hear it."

"You were responsible for killing the family," Agatha pointed out.

"Yes, because you hired me to do so."

"I barely paid you anything for it," she clarified, "so it was hardly *being hired*. Don't you think?"

"Maybe," he insisted, "but you urged me to do it."

"That's all old hat now," Agatha replied. "Besides, what we had was special. Yet, after that, it all went to pot."

"I know, and you turned on me like a rattler."

"Self-preservation," Agatha muttered. "That's all it was, once I realized the cops were looking at me oddly. At least I thought they were. Maybe they weren't. Who even knows," she said brokenly. "I was just so terrified, and I blamed you. Then you were gone, so I could spin whatever tale I needed to spin to get them to believe me," Agatha added. "I've always been good at that."

Glaring at her, Hogan said, "You fed me to the lions, disappeared with Kylie, then used her the whole time to prop up your failing abilities."

Agatha seethed with anger as Hogan continued on.

"You just couldn't resist keeping Kylie close and making her do what you needed her to do, even though Kylie had no idea. All those blocks you put in her mind to make her amiable and to keep her toeing *your* line. Just so you could have your living generator beside you."

"A living generator, to regenerate me. Antiaging and healing energy all at once." Agatha laughed. "I love that."

"It's a seriously ugly way to describe it," Porter said. "You took Kylie's whole childhood to figure out how to use it from a distance, only to finally cut her free."

"And not a moment too soon," Agatha declared. "I was so damn sick of having her around. I couldn't stand it. I hated her."

Porter shook his head. "You didn't hate her. You hated what she represented. Your own deceit, your own guilt, your own murderous intent." Porter stood up. Immediately Hogan pointed the gun in his direction. Porter shrugged. "Go ahead and shoot me, but shouldn't you be shooting Agatha? Wasn't that the pact you two lovebirds made so long ago? Besides, with all that love between you," Porter said in a mocking tone, "don't you want to have your one final shot to share the afterlife together?"

"Final shot, *huh*?"

"Think about it. You both go together. ... You would both be together."

His eyes opened wide, and he asked, "Really?" He looked over at Agatha and, without warning, drove a bullet into Agatha's brain. She collapsed without a sound onto the floor.

A muffled scream came from Kylie, as Porter wrapped his arms around her. She stared at Agatha, her hand over her mouth, the next scream frozen inside her, and he nodded. "And now what?" Porter asked Hogan. "Don't you think Kylie's suffered enough?"

"Yes, she has. I've felt bad for her all these years, after I figured out what Agatha was doing. No way I could talk to Kylie. Not after Agatha had sicced everybody on me, had turned me into a felon, destined to be a fugitive for the rest of my life. I did prison time and got myself the hell out and disappeared, and I just hated Agatha for all of it."

"Except you didn't."

"No, of course not," Hogan admitted. "You can't hate the one person you really, truly love. We were the same in so many ways, and that I could understand. It took a while, but I finally realized what Agatha was doing and why. Though I didn't like it, I knew why she was doing it," he explained. "You've got to admire Agatha's resourcefulness on some level. She's a hell of a bitch, but"—he looked over at her dead body—"she was my bitch."

And, with that, Hogan smiled and added, "Now, Porter, you have something very precious beside you. Make good use of your gifts and don't go down the pathway I did." Without warning he jammed the gun against his head and fired.

As Kylie cried out, Porter wrapped her up close and held her, turning her head aside so all she saw was the nearby wall. The police stormed in from the sidelines, where they'd been waiting. Porter rocked her back and forth, as he whispered, "It's okay. It's over now."

She trembled in his arms and nodded. "Good God, what a murderous family."

"But not your family," Porter stated.

She looked over at him. "What do you mean?"

"Agatha was adopted. Your mother was not her sister by blood," he explained. "So, when I made the comment to Hogan about you being family, … he was confused about what that meant. However, to your mother, Hogan and Agatha were family because Ann Marie accepted your aunt Agatha as a blood relative. However, Agatha herself never felt as if she really belonged. That must have stung, since she coveted what you had, your gifts and your loving parents, with two baby brothers added to the mix."

"Good God. So many years and so much death between them," she murmured. She wrapped her arms tighter around Porter and held him close.

The captain was suddenly there in front of them.

Porter looked over at his boss. "It's been a hell of a ride, but I need to take her out of here."

"You do that," the captain said. "And maybe when this is all over, and you've had a chance to recover"—he turned to Kylie—"my dear wife would like to meet you."

Kylie smiled up at him. "I would like to meet her too," she said warmly. "Other people in this craziness who do what I do would at least have had some idea of what Agatha was doing to me," Kylie admitted. "But I don't even know what I can do, much less what Agatha could do. So anyone who has a clue would be very welcome to share that with me."

The captain laughed. "When you're feeling better, we'll make it happen. In the meantime, you need to get out of here."

"I'm taking her back to my place," Porter shared, "and we'll set up a time frame with Stefan to see about dealing with the blocks that need to be taken care of."

The captain shook his head. "I don't even want to know what that is, but you go do whatever you need to do."

Porter sighed. "This is one hell of a mess, but we'll work our way through it."

Kylie added, "More is in this paperwork that we got from Agatha's house. Lists of Hogan's other victims are here. Agatha apparently kept track of Hogan all these years and had compiled all these cases that she thought Hogan had been involved in," Kylie shared. "I guess we still need to go through all these papers ourselves." She looked to Porter.

"Not right now though," Porter said. "We can deal with that later. Most of it is details about your family life. You know most of it now, so anything else you need to know can wait a little while longer."

"Sure," she whispered, "but it's horrific, isn't it?"

"It absolutely is, but you'll be okay," Porter replied, "because now you're on the other side of it."

She smiled and whispered, "Let's get out of here."

CHAPTER 18

A WEEK LATER Kylie sat on her living room couch and whispered to Porter, standing behind her, "They can start working."

Immediately Kylie heard Dr. Maddy and Stefan, speaking telepathically to her. This was the third day in a row, as they worked away at the blocks that had been installed in her head, blocks proving to be difficult to remove. But they had made great progress yesterday, and Kylie knew that today would be the end of it. Almost immediately with that thought, the ice encasing her memories seemingly shattered all around her, and suddenly she was free. She burst out laughing in joy at the sensation.

Dr. Maddy's voice in Kylie's head was warm and gentle. *Now that's what we like to see. You're free, my dear.*

Kylie opened her eyes and stared at Porter, who stood in front of her now, a big grin on his face, as she murmured, "It's finally over."

"I can tell," he said, with a nod of approval. "Besides, your mom is here. She's been watching everything."

Kylie smiled up at him. "I really want to get to know her."

"And you can," he pointed out, "but she needs to leave soon."

Kylie's heart fell, as she nodded. "But can I have her

with me just for a little while?"

"Just for a little while," he replied. "You'll have a few days, and then we'll send her where she needs to go. She has other family members to look after."

"My brothers?"

"Your brothers," he agreed, with a bright smile, "but it's okay. She stayed to confirm you were okay, and it's been hard on her all these years."

Kylie couldn't even think about what her mother had been through, watching all this happen over all these years. Kylie wasn't seeing dead people yet, as she had as a child, but she hoped that ability would return soon. "I'm glad that I've had this moment with her at least," she whispered, "so thank you for that."

Porter nodded. "It's a healing time for both of you."

She stood up, and he opened his arms, and she walked straight into them. She'd spent a lot of time in his arms, but at his insistence had waited to take the next step until all these blocks were gone. Making sure that she was who she wanted to be and understood who she really was on the inside, before making big decisions and taking the course of her life in a direction that she might regret later. She looked up at Porter, smiled, and said, "No regrets."

He chuckled. "I'm glad to hear that." He picked her up in his arms, with her laughing and squealing, then carried her into the bedroom, where he dropped her on the bed.

She looked up at him in surprise and then whispered, "Is anybody here?"

He shook his head. "No, everybody's gone. I am so glad everyone appreciates privacy enough to give it to me as well."

"I'm glad to hear that too," she murmured, as she stood up and quickly stripped down to the skin.

He smiled at her and whistled. "You've gained some weight. Looking good."

She chuckled. "Not exactly the response I was expecting."

He rolled his eyes. "I just want you healthy, and that's all I care about." With that, he stripped down and joined her on the bed, then rolled over and pulled her into his arms. "How do you feel?"

"Lightheaded, almost euphoric, and yet, in a funny way, … like myself. Like myself in a way that I'm not sure I've ever experienced."

"That would be your soul feeling more like it should now," Porter explained, nuzzling her neck, "and it's important to remember that our souls survive. Our bodies just come and go."

She chuckled. "I'm all for being in this body right now," she murmured, "particularly since I know the captain is expecting us back at the office tomorrow."

"Yes, we do have jobs," Porter agreed, working his lips alongside her neck and up to her ear, his warm breath making her toes curl. "Somehow we forgot about that in all of this mess, but thankfully he gave us some unofficial leave time." Porter laughed. "But we must find a way back to the office sooner or later."

"We will," she murmured, "but tomorrow. Everything is tomorrow." And, with that, she slid her heel up the back of his thigh, her hands sliding down his back to explore his hard muscles and his rounded butt cheeks. She smiled. "We waited a while for this."

"Too damn long," he muttered, yet chuckling, "but it was more important that it was your decision and not based on other people playing around in your head."

"Nobody will play around in my head anymore. I had a lot of trouble even letting Dr. Maddy and Stefan in there to get the blocks down."

Porter nodded. "Which is why it was so hard to get the blocks out. You were fighting it, but now you have freedom. … You did great."

She smiled and kissed him. "Good. Now how about we stop wasting time?" She wrapped her arms around him and pulled him down and kissed him thoroughly.

He gave a murmured groan and settled deeper into her arms, his lips meeting hers, his tongue playing in a light-hearted way that she had yet to even explore with him. And before she realized it, her body was hot and sweaty, as she arched under his ministrations, while he soothed and stroked her to a higher and higher level.

She shuddered in his arms, so close to the edge, when she murmured, "Why are you teasing me?"

He chuckled. "Because you're so beautiful in your passion. Nothing is more beautiful than seeing a woman enjoying herself and her body at this very moment," he said, "and you are truly beautiful."

She rolled over ever-so-slightly and pulled him closer. "Prove it."

And, with that, he lowered his head once again, his tongue driving deeper into hers in a pulsing movement imitating what was to come, as he settled deeper into her thighs. Then he drove home. She shifted, adjusting to the weight and the size of him. He soon lifted his hips and drove again and again and again and again. When she finally came apart in his arms, he waited, brought her back up to the edge again and flung her over once more, this time joining her.

She lay completely relaxed beneath him, as she recovered

slowly. He held her close and then slowly slid to the side, pulling her with him.

"It's a good thing we aren't working today," she murmured. "We'll need the rest of today to get this out of our system."

"I'm hoping we don't ever get this out of our system," he murmured, as he lay back, groaning.

"I wasn't thinking *completely* out of our system, but you're right," she agreed. "I just want to spend enough time with you that I don't feel so rushed all the time. However, I suspect, for the next few times," she murmured, "it'll have that same urgency. It feels as if you've always been there at the edge of my world, just not quite in my world."

"To a certain extent I have been," he replied. "I'm the reason you got this job, yet I saw you a long time ago. However, you never really saw me."

She smiled. "The good news is, you were smart enough to look out for me and to keep me close."

"The bad news is," he clarified, "you almost got hurt in the process."

She shook her head and tapped him on the nose. "You don't get to claim any guilt over this mess," she murmured. "Besides, … we survived."

He nodded. "Any thought about what you want to do with your gift?"

"God, no. I haven't even really got a clue of exactly what this gift entails. I'm not sure how effective it is, and I don't want it to be something that turns sour over time."

"You should talk to Stefan about that."

She laughed. "And I will, one day, but right now? It's all too new. It's all too weird. I'll just keep drawing crime scenes, as I did before."

"*Hmm*, but now I bet it may come with a twist."

"Absolutely there will be a new twist," she declared, with an eye roll. "The twist being that I'll probably see the energy and recognize what I'm seeing rather than hiding from it," she murmured.

"And that's a good thing too," he noted, "because, with this gift, you always want to be honest."

"Got it," she murmured, as she shifted onto her elbows, leaned over, and gave him a big grin. "Ready to go again?"

His eyes widened, then he pulled her down and whispered, "With you, sweetheart? Always."

This concludes Book 26 of Psychic Visions: Coveted.

Read a sneak peek Endgame: Psychic Visions, Book 27

Endgame: Psychic Visions (Book #27)

Tandy's every instinct told her to jump in and to take over the care of her two half siblings. They were twins, born to her mother later in life. Tandy hadn't been in a position to help her older siblings, a guilt that still ate at her. These twins, however, had special needs, and she wasn't sure she was up for the challenge. Nonverbal, they appeared to live in an alternate world, one she didn't know how to reach.

Keller worked alongside Grant in the FBI and was considering how his own growing psychic skills could be better utilized, when he was asked to help on a case that had very unusual elements. These were elements that Stefan and Dr. Maddy hadn't seen before—and that was saying something.

Not until he meets Tandy does Keller realize how unusual and potentially sinister this case truly is ...

STEFAN PICKED UP the phone, his tone warm and cheerful. "Dr. Maddy, it's always good to hear from you."

Her tone on the other end was stark and devoid of all humor. "We'll see how you feel when you hear what I'm calling about."

Immediately his good mood fled, and he nodded. "It's so often that way between us, isn't it?"

"It shouldn't be, though," she grumbled, "and I wouldn't be calling about this if I had any solution."

"Which means you don't, so speak up. What's going on?" he asked.

"Twins, boys, five years old, nonverbal, both synesthetes."

"Seriously?" Stefan asked in astonishment. "Nonverbal? How do you know that they're synesthetes?"

"Well, I wouldn't, except for what appears to be an older sister, who brought them in to me as a special request. Honestly, she's been emailing and calling me for quite a while, looking for some assistance," she explained. "Normally I wouldn't take on anything like this, but this case? … As soon as she said they were both synesthetes and both nonverbal, it really piqued my interest."

"Naturally," Stefan confirmed. "So, what did you find?"

"Well, it's more about what I didn't find," she shared, "and it makes no sense, but, according to the older sister—"

"How much older is this sister?" he asked, immediately interrupting.

"Quite a bit from looking at her, but I don't really know. I would say, early thirties, as a rough guess."

"And they're siblings? That's an awful lot of years between them.”

“According to the sister, the mother was a drug addict and took drugs quite freely throughout the pregnancies. This sister was the result of a teenage pregnancy, and then her mother lost several children in between, including a couple lost to the foster care system. This older sister spent time with her grandmother to avoid foster care, but the grandmother couldn't handle all the younger ones, and there was a lot of back-and-forth between all the children and the mother, the grandmother, and foster care.

“Once this elder sister was old enough to be out on her own, she worked hard to improve her circumstances and to build something better, trying to move on from such a chaotic childhood. Meanwhile, her mother kept making poor decisions and, at some point, became pregnant with these twins.

“This older sister had gone into early childhood development and, after her mother died of a drug overdose, ended up caring for these siblings, who were almost five at that point in time. So I think she's only had them for a few months. Her mother didn't tell her about any of the developmental issues, and this sister had been away from the family house long enough that the kids were strangers to her, and she didn't know what she was even looking at.

“She found a letter from her mother, explaining something about the twins, even adding that the mother herself also had the same abilities but never managed to learn or to make sense out of anything she saw in the world. Drugs provided a far easier way to handle it, so that's what she did. Of course the older sister is quite pissed, but she's also very worried about how best to care for these children.”

"Well, that's wonderful of her," Stefan stated. "A lot of people wouldn't take on children like that."

"No, but I think she's in a quandary and not at all sure what she's supposed to do to help them."

"What is it you're supposed to do?" Stefan asked, letting the humor back into his tone. "People ask all kinds of things, but we don't always have answers."

"No, no, we don't," Dr. Maddy agreed, "though I did sit down and do a full physical on the twins."

"And?"

"Physically I would say that they're fairly healthy," she shared. "I'm not sure of the reason they are nonverbal. I didn't see anything suggesting they had any kind of health condition that prompted that type of response. However ..."

"Ah," Stefan noted, "here comes the famous *however*."

She groaned. "I definitely feel there's an issue between them that is not of this plane."

Stefan let that sink in, as the silence deepened between them. "And did you get any idea of just what is wrong on the other plane?"

"No," she admitted, "and I guess that is why I'm so stumped and kind of upset because I can't see what is happening."

"So, you want me to take a look?" he suggested.

"I know you're busy, but I was wondering if that was ... possible."

"Are they in our children's hospital?"

"No, that's the other thing. I have found no medical condition that requires hospitalization for these two boys. Just because they're nonverbal doesn't mean they can't lead full, healthy, happy functioning lives."

"No, of course not," he murmured. "So, they're at home?"

"I have them here at Maddy's floor temporarily," she said and then took a deep breath. "And I mean *temporarily*. It's certainly not a place for them, if that's not where they need to be, and, of course, all the beds here are at a premium."

"Of course," he agreed. "So I presume you had somebody moved out in time for them to come in."

"Yes," she said, "and the twins absolutely love being here, but it's not where they belong. I think the sister is relieved that we're at least looking at this, but she wants answers that I'm not sure we have."

"Of course not, and answers of this nature are never easy to give anybody anyway. Do you have any idea if she has abilities?"

"Oh," Dr. Maddy said, "I didn't even think to ask her that, and I don't think she would consider any of this in the realm of abilities. She doesn't know quite what *synesthetes* or *synesthesia* means, though she did look up the terms. So she has a basic clinical understanding, but doesn't really understand what form the twins have. The mother said something about colors."

"Absolutely nothing wrong with that," Stefan declared, with a note of humor, "and in many ways that just enhances their daily existence."

"And potentially," Dr. Maddy murmured, "that's why they want to stay where they are."

"That's also an interesting theory," he muttered. "I can take a look at them this afternoon, if you are okay with that."

"I would really like that," she said warmly, "particularly … No, I'm not going to give you any heads-up. You let me know what you find."

"Is this something you haven't seen before?"

"Honestly," she replied, "I'm pretty sure it's something you haven't seen before either."

Find Book 27 here!

To find out more visit Dale Mayer's website.

https://geni.us/DMSEndgame

Simon Says... Hide: Kate Morgan (Book #1)

Welcome to a new thriller series from *USA Today* Best-Selling Author Dale Mayer. Set in Vancouver, BC, the team of Detective Kate Morgan and Simon St. Laurant, an unwilling psychic, marries all the elements of Dale's work that you've come to love, plus so much more.

Detective Kate Morgan, newly promoted to the Vancouver PD Homicide Department, stands for the victims in her world. She was once a victim herself, just as her mother had been a victim, and then her brother—an unsolved missing child's case—was yet another victim. She can't stand those who take advantage of others, and the worst ones are those who prey on the hopes of desperate people to line their own pockets.

So, when she finds a connection between more than a half-dozen cold cases to a current case, where a child's life hangs in the balance, Kate would make a deal with the devil himself to find the culprit and to save the child.

Simon St. Laurant's grandmother had the Sight and had warned him that, once he used it, he could never walk away. Until now, her caution had made it easy to avoid that first step. But, when nightmares of his own past are triggered, Simon can't stand back and watch child after child be abused. Not without offering his help to those chasing the monsters.

Even if it means dealing with the cranky and critical Detective Kate Morgan …

Find Simon Says… Hide here!
To find out more visit Dale Mayer's website.
https://geni.us/DMSSHideUniversal

Author's Note

Thank you for reading Coveted: Psychic Visions, Book 26! If you enjoyed the book, please take a moment and leave a short review.

Dear reader,

I love to hear from readers, and you can contact me at my website: www.dalemayer.com or at my Facebook author page. To be informed of new releases and special offers, sign up for my newsletter or follow me on BookBub. And if you are interested in joining Dale Mayer's Reader Group, here is the Facebook sign up page.
http://geni.us/DaleMayerFBGroup

Cheers,
Dale Mayer

About the Author

Dale Mayer is a *USA Today* best-selling author, best known for her SEALs military romances, her Psychic Visions series, and her Lovely Lethal Garden cozy series. Her contemporary romances are raw and full of passion and emotion (Broken But … Mending, Hathaway House series). Her thrillers will keep you guessing (Kate Morgan, By Death series), and her romantic comedies will keep you giggling (*It's a Dog's Life*, a stand-alone novella; and the Broken Protocols series, starring Charming Marvin, the cat).

Dale honors the stories that come to her—and some of them are crazy, break all the rules and cross multiple genres!

To go with her fiction, she also writes nonfiction in many different fields, with books available on résumé writing, companion gardening, and the US mortgage system. All her books are available in print and ebook format.

Connect with Dale Mayer Online

Dale's Website – www.dalemayer.com
Twitter – @DaleMayer
Facebook Page – geni.us/DaleMayerFBFanPage
Facebook Group – geni.us/DaleMayerFBGroup
BookBub – geni.us/DaleMayerBookbub
Instagram – geni.us/DaleMayerInstagram
Goodreads – geni.us/DaleMayerGoodreads
Newsletter – geni.us/DaleNews